I0700060

THE GREAT QUIET

A Novel

Bekkah Frisch

Bombus Books, LLC

Fulton, NY: 2023

Bombus Books, LLC
P.O. Box 343
Fulton, NY 13069

Library of Congress Cataloging-in-Publication Data

Names: Frisch, Bekkah, 1992— author.
Title: The Great Quiet: A Novel / Bekkah Frisch.
Fulton, NY: Bombus Books, LLC, 2023.
Library of Congress Control Number: 2023903654
ISBN 979-8-9877421-0-5 (trade paper) | ISBN 979-8-9877421-1-2 (ebook)

CONTENTS

Prologue

The morning air is filled with birdsong and the sound of waves crashing against the island's shores. This time of year, Huahine is at its best in the morning—birds flying in groups to fish out at sea, the scent of her father's prized tiare and frangipani bushes tickling her nose. The two species only bloom together for a few short weeks, but it's one of Ari's favorite seasons.

The quiet, unpaved streets let her imagine the entire island is still sleeping. It's just her and the birds as the sun breaks over the horizon. She sips a steaming mug of coffee, satisfied with the solitude and the heady perfume of her morning.

But her and the birds aren't alone for long. The world's simple magic is broken by a low, industrialized whine. She struggles to tune out the sharp cries of the koleas hiding in the coconut trees so she can make sense of the sound. The whirr of a plane, struggling to gain altitude. She walks out of the house, not bothering with the tattered flip flops on the covered veranda. Dewy grass crumples under her feet, a few plucky blades sticking up between her toes. A breeze stirs. She licks her chapped lips and tastes the salty ocean air.

The noise, meanwhile, gets louder until it's deafening. The wind is tainted with fumes by the time the plane comes into view.

Trees crack as the aircraft slips dangerously low. Fire consumes the cockpit, and she catches sight of him—hands beating flames away from his body, face twisted in agony.

She screams, but it doesn't matter. The wreckage is coming for her.

Her only escape is bolting upright in the dark of night, sweat beading on her forehead and his name flying off her lips.

Chapter 1

"Councilman, over here!" Reporters shout questions at Manu from all sides of the one-room meeting house. "How are you adapting to being a councilman and a single parent?" From another corner of the room: "Why become a politician now, when you are already so busy as a pilot?"

He's only been an elected official for two hours and already, his head aches from so many new responsibilities. The enterprising journalist from the Tahiti Gazette keeps pestering him for a quote, but he can barely breathe in the overstuffed room, much less give her or any of the other reporters a thoughtful answer.

What he needs is a few minutes alone. His old friend Robert—long a member of the Territorial Assembly— had convinced him to swap his piloting gig for an open spot on Huahine's municipal council. It's a decision Manu's regretting already. Instead of looking down in silent awe on the island and the beautiful waters of the Pacific from 2,000 meters in the air, he's being elbowed by strangers, many of whom are wearing starched button-downs that are stained with sweat.

A quick excuse gets him out of the meeting house. Knowing he only has a few minutes, Manu speed-walks out of town and up the winding road that follows the island's only inland lake. Solitude envelopes him with the lake in front and a thick forest behind.

It's a relief to be alone and he drinks in the muggy afternoon air. Manu perches his slim yet sturdy frame on a boulder facing the water. The spot boasts a perfect view of the airport across the way, though he knows there are no scheduled flights to watch. He loosens his tie, glad he'd thought to leave the suit jacket behind in his old green jalopy.

With a sigh, he stares at that point where sky blends into water, past the lake and the airfield, where the ocean opens up beyond the island's shores.

His mind wanders back to the day when smoke could be seen all across the island. The fire on the edge of the runway might be long gone, but he'll never forget.

. . .

Arietta isn't surprised to see her father take off alone. It's been just the two of them for several years now, and they have both gotten used to the relative quiet. After he disappears, she grabs yet another cup of punch and starts yet another conversation with yet another council member's daughter. The heavy scent of fresh-cut flowers and the glaring sun have her feeling a bit dizzy, but this girl—Marie, she said?— doesn't notice. Not wanting to draw attention to herself, Ari leans nonchalantly against a Greek-style column. The pose might be necessary, but it still makes her feel like the newest, youngest member of the Brat Pack. Won't get detention for skipping school this time though.

After a few more minutes of listening to the girl complain about her mother, she spots her father returning. "Oh hey—gotta go!" She quickly makes her way to his side, glad to get away.

Her father doesn't acknowledge her because he's busy making an announcement into one of the many cameras focused on his smiling face. "I'm creating a new department for public safety. This measure is long overdue to ensure that all of our residents—and visitors—have a first-class travel experience. Thank you." He shakes the reporter's hand after they've finished shooting the clip.

Ari can't remember his name right now, but her father's friend—the one who managed to get him into politics—looks none too pleased with what's happening. She's leaning against her father's back for balance, which is the only reason she's able to hear him hiss into her father's right ear. "What are you doing? You were just supposed to pick up the social cohesion department now that Pierre's retired."

"But Robert, you said the department practically runs itself. I thought I was supposed to create a new department."

"For heaven's sake, no, you were just supposed to be our party planner," Robert says, wiping his clammy forehead with a kerchief. Ari scoots to her father's left side, knowing that if the man spots her, the conversation will die until she's out of earshot. "Then again," he says, "this will sound great in the papers."

"It will also be good for our people," Manu replies.

"Of course, of course, you're right. We can make this work even though it could get expensive. From now on, don't say anything to the press unless we've had a chance to talk it over first, okay?"

"Of course," Manu responds. "I'm sorry. I'm not used to how politics works."

"Aha, and that's why we love you!" He gives Manu a hearty hug until a few digital cameras flash.

By the time Ari and her father arrive at home, she's exhausted. She might have been allowed to skip high school to be a part of her father's *tamaaraa*, but it has still been a long day of smiling and wearing her nice dress and keeping a fresh flower in her free-flowing dark brown hair.

First things first. She drops her sandals on the veranda and changes into the comfiest T-shirt and cargo pants she owns, flower tucked into a side pocket for the pleasant aroma. Papa heads for the outdoor shower, so she grabs the worn Walkman she keeps in a chest under her window and returns to the veranda. She slips on the headphones, but the tape stops when she presses play. She must've forgotten to rewind it the last time she'd listened to it.

"Damn," she says under her breath, fingers automatically finding the right button.

Days like today make her miss her mother. Mama would have been so proud of all that Papa is doing. To some, it might seem that he entered politics almost randomly, but Mama would have understood. Papa is a man of action whose biggest passion has always been helping people get what they need most, whether that's working to end dangerous nuclear testing in the islands or providing safe transport between them. It was only a matter of time before someone saw that and convinced him to run for a seat on the council.

She sits on the cool wood floor and presses play on the tape. Mama's warm and soothing voice fills her ears with an old bedtime story about animals working together after a rainstorm. She used to spin tales with all sorts of twists and turns for her at bedtime, stories about family, teamwork, and friendship. Papa tried to do it too, for a little while, but his stories were stilted and the endings never made any sense. Ari was thankful when he stopped trying.

Whenever she needs a story now, she listens to Mama's tape. Her brother Henri's voice pops up once or twice in the background too—something that used to irritate her to no end but has become its own kind of comfort. The story may not be one that surprises her any longer, but she is forever grateful to have it.

"Ari, you must remember that no matter what decisions you have to make, it takes courage to know the way. Just as important as courage, you need to be able to trust your own team—your family, friends, and even kind strangers can help you be brave on the darkest of days. Never forget that, my daughter."

The Walkman clicks off. Ari stays almost perfectly still, not bothering to restart the tape or remove her headphones. Without them, she wouldn't be able to remember the melody of Mama's words or the cadence of her storytelling. As it stands, she struggles to remember Henri's laugh, and he's been gone less than half the time that Mama has. She wonders what he would have thought of Papa entering politics.

Outside the veranda, locusts hum in the late afternoon sun. She can hear the shower turn off. A few minutes later, Papa's slow, steady footsteps approach. After slipping off the headphones, she sets the Walkman down carefully.

"Did you have a nice time at the feast?" she asks her father.

"My flower, I am feeling invigorated and ready to make our island a better place." He stifles a yawn.

"Do you plan to start with naptime?"

"Aahh, I've raised a jokester!" He laughs and wraps her in a bear hug.

Her voice is muffled against his fuzzy cotton robe as she says, "The celebration today was very nice for a man who smothers his daughter."

"Smothered only with love," he says, relaxing his grip and looking down on her with affection.

"Yeah, right," Ari responds with a quick roll of her eyes.

"The town did put on some very lovely festivities. Did you have fun?" he asks.

"Yeah, but I'm glad we're home now. All that stuff tired me out."

"Are you feeling okay?" His eyes take on a hint of concern.

"Yes, Papa, I'm fine. Just a long day."

"Mmhmm." Papa doesn't sound convinced. After all, parties normally invigorate her.

"Where did you go before making your announcement?" Her voice brightens as she tries to change the subject.

He smiles softly. "Just a short walk to clear my head. I would have brought you along, but you looked like you were having a great conversation with one of the girls."

"Spare me—those girls were complaining about stuff like travelling or big families. I just don't get it."

"Oh, Riri..." He chuckles.

That was Mama's nickname for her. Manu rarely ever calls her that anymore. It's too painful. It feels strange and yet wonderful to hear it again.

They embrace for a moment longer before Ari sits in her father's rocking chair. "So, anyway, what are you gonna do with the public safety thingy?"

"My grandfather always said that a wise leader listens before acting, so I'm going to bring the *matahiapo* and the council members together for a meeting. I want to have them all here for dinner tomorrow night, and then we can work on it together. Because we're starting from scratch, it could take us some time to agree on how to proceed."

"The elders will be here? Are the Osferaiis going to come?"

"Yes, but they won't be bringing any food—you know that's my responsibility. Should I make crepes?"

Ari looks down in disappointment. "Nobody's crepes beat theirs. You going to be talking politics all night?"

A nod.

"Can I go to Natua's after school then? Please?"

Manu tucks a stray strand of hair behind her ear. "Only if *Tantie* Raina says it's okay, and you help her get the top coconuts from her trees."

"Fine." She huffs. "I don't see why Natua can't do it— he'll never get over his fear if he doesn't just face it."

"Well, you've got to pitch in somehow if you expect to eat dinner over there. Make sure you also ask if you should bring anything."

"Thanks, Papa, I will." Ari meanders inside to grab the phone, leaving Manu on the veranda. He sinks into his rocker, exhaling slowly.

The chair makes Manu feel closer to his father. The man has been gone for almost two decades now—a heart attack while Manu was serving in the French Air Force. They wouldn't let Manu come home to bury him.

For years, his father's spirit haunted his dreams and startled him awake each morning, but the rocker has always been a source of great comfort. His father had crafted the chair from the trunk of an ancient coconut tree especially for Manu's birth. He was the last of their seven children, a happy surprise.

He sits, pondering what advice his father would have given him about politics and his oddly exhausted teenage daughter. He drifts off to sleep while the locust hums fade into cricket chirps, no closer to the answers as the mild winter twilight transitions into night.

○ ○ ○

The bell rings, signaling the end of school. Ari heads outside and leans against a boulder by the edge of the dirt path that separates the school from the rest of the village. She's chitchatted with most of her classmates and twirled a lock of hair around her finger four times before realizing Natua is sitting in the tree across the way, picking at his nails and waiting for her.

A laugh springs up from her belly and she calls out to him. In one smooth motion, he hops down and heads her way, wavy dark hair sliding over dancing eyes. "Where have you been?" he asks with fake exasperation, hands thrown comically in the air.

"Oh, stop that, Natua." She slaps his arm lightly, a smile teasing the edge of her lips.

"I was up there forever! Don't you ever look around?"

Ari groans and pushes herself off of the rock. "I told you I'd be waiting by the path. Why couldn't you just walk up and tell me when you were ready to go?" She wipes imaginary dirt off the back of her shorts.

"It's more fun this way. Oh, and by the way, you don't have to grab the coconuts—our old groundskeeper Afaitu stopped by last night, and he got them down for us."

"Cool. We should go paddle boarding sometime soon—maybe tonight since the coconuts are taken care of? I haven't gone in forever, and Joe's place always does half-price rentals in the afternoon."

"I don't know about tonight—it'll be dark by the time we get way over there." Natua turns to give a group of his buddies high-fives. A few of them are carrying fishing poles.

Ari watches enviously as the guys head towards the water. "Ugh, fine. What do you wanna do then? Go fishing?" She jerks her head towards the retreating group.

"Nah, my pole's busted. We could practice the dance together at my house."

"You're so good at it, you hardly need to practice." She scuffs her sneaker against the dusty ground. "You'll just spend the time laughing at me."

Natua giggles. "But you have to practice to get better! Besides, we're supposed to do it together."

"I can do it by myself, and I will," she replies stubbornly. "We can practice together once I figure out my part a little more."

"You keep putting off practicing, and that day will never come."

"Natua, you say that like I never do the routine! I'm working on it. Twice a week with Papa and Nona Alii. They're good teachers because they don't laugh at me."

"If we don't do it together, you'll never get better at it."

"We do it together every week during our lessons. Besides, it's your fault I don't wanna practice with you the rest of the time anyway. You and your teasing." She crosses her arms in feigned anger, but she can't entirely tame her smile.

"Can't help it," he responds with a shrug. "Your attempts at dancing are funny. A little sad, but funny."

"Are you trying to inspire me to never dance again? Because it's working."

"Okay, that was the last of the teasing, promise, as long as you practice today." He gestures towards the path that will take them inland.

"Natua, can't you let it go?" She takes another glance over Natua's shoulder at the dancing waves cheerfully winking at her in the late afternoon sun.

"Come on, it'll be more fun if we start doing the whole routine side by side more often."

She shakes her head and sighs. "I don't wanna hear a single laugh, not now and certainly not later."

Natua grins as they walk down the path. "I'll do what I can."

"Fiiiiiineeee. But first, I have to stop at the post office—Papa asked me to grab the mail."

"Your dad lets you do that?" Natua turns to her in surprise as they wait to cross the road.

"Uh... yeah?" She huffs. "Not much of a privilege. You know how much crap he's started getting now that he's part of the council? Everyone wants to send us junk."

"Mama doesn't let me check ours. She wears the key around her neck most of the time."

Ari laughs. "She should talk to my dad then. Get him to take care of our overflowing box himself."

After Ari stuffs the mail in her backpack, they continue on in jovial silence under the palm trees lining the sidewalk, their shadows casually overlapping and drifting apart. "Quit bumping into me, would you? Not being able to dance is one thing, but can't you at least walk straight?"

"I would but you're in my way." She digs playfully into his side with her elbow. "By the way, how do you think you did on that science test?"

The two continue chatting as they make their way to the northeastern edge of town, then use a twisted footpath to cut through a wooded area with the confidence that only comes from lifelong familiarity.

A few minutes later, they emerge on a well-groomed lawn shaded by several ancient rain trees. A cluster of fruit trees—including the troublesome coconut—backs up to a pension that can accommodate up to twelve vacationing couples. Natua's mother has been the sole proprietor of the hotel since her parents retired almost a decade before.

There have been few guests roaming its halls these days, even though peak tourism season has technically already started. Both mother and son have downplayed the trend, saying only that bookings usually pick up towards the end of winter.

Ari notices that this is the third week in a row the place seems deserted. But Natua doesn't mention it and she has a dance to practice, so she brushes it off. *The Rainas will be fine. They always are.*

The nice part about the pension being empty is that Tantie Raina will let them hang out wherever they want. "Courtyard or lawn?" Natua asks.

"Lawn."

"Worried about falling?" A smirk flirts with the edges of his lips.

"I thought you said you weren't going to laugh at me."

"I'm not laughing." Natua puts up his hands in mock defensiveness. "I'm just wondering why the lawn. Mama has the fountain going."

"Well, you didn't tell me that. Maybe we can dip our feet in after," Ari says in a conspiratorial whisper.

"Don't let her see you if you do. You know how Mama is with that fountain."

They make their way to the front of the pension, the temperature a few degrees hotter in the sunny courtyard. Natua heads inside the shed to track down the ancient boom box and the right cassette tape. Ari had long ago given up asking Natua if they could use the sound system that his mom Angela sets up whenever there are guests in the pension. She only plays boring background music with harps and birds chirping, but she's incredibly protective over it.

Instead of worrying about the speakers, Ari heads straight over to the semicircular courtyard and splashes some fountain water on the smooth cobblestones with her hands. Guests invariably comment on how tropical and bohemian it looks, so Natua's mom is paranoid about anyone mentioning that the stones and most of the other building supplies were shipped over from England back in the '70s. A few plain benches made by local craftsmen dot the edges of the courtyard underneath fruit-bearing starfruit trees. Angela planted the trees under advice from a board member with the tourism association, who claimed that they "smell like paradise." She always says they just smell like starfruit (and taste like shit), and Ari wonders why she went along with the tourism board if she hates starfruit so much.

The crown jewel of the courtyard is undoubtedly the hand-carved stone fountain. Water springs from the hands of a voluptuous woman who could just as easily pass for a Greek goddess as a Polynesian maiden, what with the olive leaf laurel across her brow and flowing dress draped carelessly across her bosom. Natua's mom is always complaining about the scandalous statue that the tourism board had forced on her parents. The board said it would give the pension a reputation. Whether that's a good thing or not is another question but, in the end, they didn't argue with the tourism board either. And so, the maiden's dress rests outrageously low, a strap casually sitting at her elbow.

Natua and Ari don't care about the maiden or her stone robes no matter how often Angela gripes about it; they simply work through the dance routine that Manu, Nona Alii, and Pop Tama are teaching them. The dance is an ancient one that tells the history of their people, before the French or English arrived and started outlawing their way of life. Many dances from that time are lost, but this one's survived, so it's vital they learn it well.

Ari's grateful this routine doesn't include any touching between the dancers. A perk of having her dad and grandparents teach the dances, she supposes. Natua makes enough fun of her when they're simply dancing next to each other. She tries to tell herself that's the only reason it'd be embarrassing to get up close and personal. In her distraction, she almost misses her cue.

Even though he's not leading her, Natua still catches her every mistake. "You're not supposed to move your hips so harshly—this part calls for the *varu* movement, where your hips go in figure eights. Why do you keep doing the *afata* instead?" Natua attempts to demonstrate the smoother movement the dance calls for. "Well, you know what I mean," he says.

"Sorry, I just can't concentrate today," Ari replies, already breathing hard.

"You okay?"

"Yeah, I'm fine. I keep copying your part on accident, so it's like I've done the dance two or three times already." She hopes he won't notice the lie. *Why does my stomach cramp up so fast every time I do this damn dance? I must be more out of shape than I thought.*

Natua rolls his eyes and giggles. "This is why we have to practice together—so you learn to concentrate on your own part. Again?"

She nods, still trying to catch her breath. "All right, start the music."

The pair run through the routine twice more before Ari heads for one of the benches. "I gotta sit down, Natua. I'm bushed."

"No problem. Want something to drink? We've got some cold tea in the fridge."

"I don't want to be any trouble," Ari says instinctively.

"It's fine—I'm going to get some for myself anyway."

"Okay, grab me a glass then."

After Natua leaves, she lays down across the bench, head hanging low off of the edge. She decides that maybe sneaking a quick dip of her feet in the fountain will wake her up. But when she stands, her vision goes black and her head pounds. She falls back on the bench heavily and her eyesight returns almost immediately. *What the hell?*

Natua returns with two glasses of iced tea, and Ari's fingers are trembling when she takes the glass. He doesn't say anything about it, though he has to notice. Instead, he takes a seat beside her and sneaks glances her way while pretending to stare at the fountain.

After several long swigs of tea, Ari turns to him and says, "Thanks for not laughing at me today."

"No problem. It's not much fun when you get mad about it, anyway."

She laughs. "Saying things like that does not score you any points."

"I'm not trying to score any points, Ari, jeez. You're practically my sister."

"I didn't mean *those* kinds of points."

"I only want those kinds of points with Paulette. Or maybe Marie—I'm not fussy."

"Gross, Natua. I don't want to hear about your weird fantasies."

"Hey, it's not weird! Most the guys in our class have a crush on Paulette."

"That bitch." Ari huffs through her nose. "The rest of us like some attention now and again too!" Natua starts to speak, but she cuts him off. "Not from you."

"Well good, because ew. You owe me, though—without my help, your dance moves would look like the tourists'." In one smooth motion, he stands, puts his hands under his armpits, and swings his elbows around. "Squawk! Squawk! Squawk!"

"Okay, okay, I get it. At least I'm getting better." Her smile comes as easily as the banter. "No thanks to the dance partner who keeps laughing at me."

"I didn't laugh this time!"

"Right. What does squawking like a chicken count as?"

. . .

Back at Manu's house, the council members and *matahiapo* are just arriving. The first council member to arrive is a lifelong politician named George. "Good evening, Manu," the man says.

"Hello, my friend. How was the walk over?"

"Quite refreshing. I haven't gotten rained on in the middle of a walk once this week!"

"Careful what you wish for!" Manu replies. "I saw rain in the forecast for the weekend. Would you care for a drink—perhaps some wine or kava?"

"Some kava sounds wonderful. Thank you." George leaves his shoes on the veranda and follows Manu into the house.

The man takes a sip of the glass Manu offers and sighs appreciatively. "This is the best kava I've had in ages." When he sets his glass down on the palm tree counter, a bit of the earthy-brown liquid spills over the edges of the full glass. "I don't want to be indelicate, but there is a small matter the council needs to consult with you about. We've been planning a celebration between Huahine and her sister city in New Caledonia for months now, and it is far too late to change any of the dates. I don't know what arrangements you may have with the airport, but if you are doing the Sunday schedule, you will need to ask for several dates off."

Manu draws his brows together. "What do you mean if I'm doing the Sunday schedule?"

"Well, I don't know the specifics of your piloting job, but it has been voiced among a few of us that your position may create some time conflicts. I felt it less than tactful to bring it up in front of everyone, but of course the issue needs to be resolved as soon as possible."

"You think I'm still at the airport?"

"Of course, you understand your job as councilman must—what's that now?"

"I quit last week. You mean I didn't have to?"

"Heavens, no! You don't expect you'll stay on the council forever, do you?"

Ignoring the perhaps unintended slight, Manu asks, "So I can go back, as long as it's a restricted schedule?"

"It couldn't hurt anyone—you wouldn't want them to replace you permanently during your time in politics."

Instantly, Manu's mind is on other things. He had saved quite the sum of money to complement the council member's salary, which he knew would be a pay cut from his full-time piloting position. After all, there were only two other pilots in the place, and one hadn't flown as more than co-pilot in weeks when Manu had announced he was leaving. But having both jobs!

The mere possibilities are enough to keep him distracted all night, as the elders and council members—including the mayor—clash on how to focus this department he's created. He half-hears the disagreements, which center on whether they should model the department after other departments on Huahine or after a safety department from another island. Instead of fleshing out his plan and bridging the gap between the elders and the politicians, he's dreaming of all the things he can do with the little nest egg he's built up. *I should give back to the community, especially now that I hold public office. Maybe I'll sponsor a child for the* Saga Tahiti. *I always wanted Henri to learn traditional wayfinding.* But that doesn't feel like enough.

He's thankful when the council members and elders leave, and that Ari comes in and goes straight to bed. He needs time to think. And he needs to call Frank down at the airport, first thing tomorrow morning. Hopefully it isn't too late.

· · ·

At dinner the next evening, Ari sets the table for two—her mother's parents, Nona Alii and Pop Tama, have been practicing a new dance routine for the *Heiva* festival with a troupe of friends, so father and daughter have been dining alone on Fridays.

Tonight, Manu made *i'a ota*—her favorite seafood dish. Ari always piles on the coconut cream so high that he jokes her fish will drown in it. She even convinced him to start doubling the cream recipe for her. She's still *mmm'ing* and *hmm'ing* when he asks how she feels about expanding their family.

Her stomach falls. "Who is she?"

"No, no, I could never replace your mother. She was the light of my life." His eyes glisten over the loss.

"What then?" Her words sound sharper than she'd intended.

Papa sets his silverware neatly next to the plate like he always does when he's finished eating. "Your mother and I dreamed of having a large family, with many children to comfort us in our old age. God had different plans for us, but that doesn't mean we can't have the kind of big family we always wanted." He reaches up to scratch his neck, and Ari's entire body tenses in anticipation.

"How would you feel about me adopting Natua?"

"What?"

"You have no brothers. He has no father and his mother is sickly."

"*Tantie* Raina isn't that sick. And I do too have a brother." Her cheeks burn with anger.

Papa sighs. "That isn't the same, Ari. It isn't good to be alone. Besides, we have to think about Natua too, and his future."

"I'm not alone—we have each other, and Nona Alii and Pop Tama and Aunt Wendy and Uncle Kai and Aunt Poe and Aunt Alepina and Uncle Caleb and Aunt Ani and Nona Reia."

He waits until she stops to take a breath. "Riri, it's important to have siblings." His voice is heavy. "Living ones."

"Don't call me that." She bites her lip and stares at the smeared coconut cream on her plate.

"Is it because you want him to become my son in another way?" A brief twinkle appears in his eyes.

"No!" She recoils like the very table has offended her. "God, you're so embarrassing!"

He chuckles lightly. "Fine. If it's not that, then what's the problem?"

"I already told you. I don't want a new brother. Besides, since when am I not enough for you?"

"Oh honey," he replies, tone softening. "You know it's nothing like that. I just want to help him. Not much will even change. Natua still has a mother he needs to take care of, so he will continue to live with her."

"Then why adopt him at all?"

"Because he needs a father, and I can help. Besides, it would be good for us and the Rainas to have more family to count on." Papa stands and picks up his empty plate, as if it's as simple as that. "Are you done?"

Chapter 2

Ari stops the cassette and rewinds it. She stares off into space, foot swinging beneath her perch in what she privately calls her thinking tree. She shifts a bit on the branch, sap sticking to cotton shorts.

Underneath her mother's words and the familiar story of the worm who ends up a team player, in the fuzzy background, Henri's voice is barely audible.

"Are you there? Yes, of course we will..." He must have been on the phone. Maybe the words were part of an attempt to set up a fishing day with his buddies, or maybe he was trying to convince someone's dad to let him borrow a boat, since the Fonua family boat was notoriously unreliable. Once, it had quit when Papa had taken the boat too far out of the lagoon. He'd had to get out of the boat to swim and push the little dinghy out of the currents by Motu Mahare.

But that was before. Even Henri had been a baby then.

She presses play on the tape and grabs an orange she had balanced on a nearby branch. "This is a story of great courage and hope..." Even worms and no-no flies stick together better than her family. She turns up the tape's volume to the loudest setting in an attempt to drown out the rest of her thoughts.

"Are you there? Yes, of course we will..."

I'm here, and I'll never forget you. No matter what.

She's been in the tree for hours now, straining to catch the only bits of Henri's voice that still exist. It's the least she can do to show his spirit that she isn't letting go, isn't trying to fill the empty place he left with any old fatherless boy. She loves Natua like a brother, but no one could ever actually replace Henri in the Fonua family—no matter what her father thinks.

That's when she feels a tap on her knee. She looks down and scowls, but he doesn't leave, just tilts his head at her quizzically and starts talking to her. Reluctantly, she pauses the tape and pushes her headphones back until they rest around her neck. "What's up, Natua?"

"Do you still want to go paddle boarding? Mama gave me enough money to rent two boards for the afternoon if we go to Joe's place."

"No. Why are you even here?" Ari snaps at him. He knows she only ever comes out here, so far inland and away from the village, when she really wants to be alone. How did he even find her spot? She's always careful to conceal it because Papa wouldn't want her to hike up the steep, occasionally dangerous Traversière—much less alone, much less with headphones on.

"Uh, hello... you were the one who wanted to go! You don't even have to ask your dad for money to cover the rental!"

"Natua, seriously, how did you even find me? Did you follow me or something?"

"Come on, don't ruin this chance to have an awesome day," he pleads.

"It's already ruined," she replies.

"It's beautiful today—what do you mean?"

"Don't play dumb with me." She shakes the last quarter of her orange at him.

The confusion in his voice is genuine. "I don't know what you're talking about."

"Wait, don't you know?"

"Know what?"

"My dad wants to adopt you."

"That's a day ruiner?" His nonchalance catches Ari by surprise. "I like your dad. He's always been really nice about teaching me the dances of our people, and he helps me with my homework when I have trouble."

"But only half of your heritage is on this island," she says pointedly. "What about your *real* dad?"

"I'll find him someday."

"Don't you think he'd be upset to know you just up and replaced him with someone else?"

"I hope he would be happy I've been taken care of."

"What about your mom?" she baits him. "Wouldn't she be upset by this—like maybe it means she isn't doing enough?"

"My mom does more than enough." His tone turns defensive.

She shrugs, sensing the chink in his armor. "Well, if my dad wants to adopt you, don't you think he's saying that without saying it? And if you're good with him adopting you, that you're agreeing with him?"

He sets his hand on his hip, but he's standing at eye level with Ari's dirt-brushed toes so his attempt at annoyance comes off a bit comically.

"My mother is very much alive and present and she does everything that needs to be done." His voice takes on a harsh edge and he stamps his foot into the ground. "Whether he adopts me or not has nothing to do with that."

"You might think so, but the rest of the island won't see it that way. Besides, I've got a brother already. And that doesn't matter much to Papa right now either."

"Right, but your brother's..." Ari glares at him. "Oh, never mind. Dammit, now I don't want to go paddle boarding either. You really think everyone else will take the adoption as my mom not doing enough?"

"Why else go through with it? If my dad thought your mom was doing a great job, he wouldn't need to step in and help, now would he?" Her annoyance fades into guilt over manipulating him, and she offers him the last of her orange. *How can Papa act as though*

Henri never existed? As though he can just be replaced and forgotten about?

Natua declines the fruit and instead interrupts her train of thought. "Anything good on the tape? Maybe some old school Italian rap?"

"No, nothing like that. Can you just leave me alone? I need time to think."

"Fine. Apparently, I do too." He starts to turn away, but then he looks back. "Wait, so, does he want me to come live with you and stuff?"

"No. Your dad living on the other side of the world might not make a difference to him, but he realizes you have to stay with your mom at the pension."

"Oh, that's good. I don't want to live with someone who thinks my mom isn't good enough anyway." He begins walking down the hill but turns again after a few steps. "What made him decide adopting me was a good idea, anyway?"

"He says you need a dad. Except that you already have one."

"Yeah, that doesn't make any sense."

"I tried telling him that, and he just wanted to know if we were seeing each other."

"You're kidding me."

"Nope."

"Huh." Natua turns around and begins walking away, but then he stops, hesitates. "Doesn't he—"

"Just go, Natua. Please." Her voice is weary as she leans against the trunk of the old banyan tree.

"Wait, but—"

"We can talk about this another time, promise, but not today. Today I need to think."

"All right. See you later then."

Ari pulls her headphones back on and blasts the tape at full volume. She's already rewinding it for another play by the time he disappears into the woods that lead back to the island's notorious inland road.

. . .

As Natua heads down the tiny path, he nearly gets lost a dozen times. He's paying more attention to his thoughts than the way out because apparently Ari's dad thinks Mama is doing a bad job.

How dare he, Natua thinks as he stumbles through a thicket he definitely didn't go through earlier. *Mama runs the entire pension by herself and she's a good mom on top of it all too.* He has to stop twice to backtrack, even though he's walked this path hundreds of times.

One day a year or two ago, when it was still getting dark early, he'd followed Ari here from school. His plan was to make noises in the woods on her way home and creep her out. To his surprise, she took a detour, climbed up a tree and started to cry. That day, he crept back to the Traversière and went home in secret shame, but since then he's always come back to that place to be alone.

The isolated path cuts away from the Traversière before the inland road becomes impassable, but it's far enough outside of town that no one comes in the area unless they're on a hiking trip. The few scattered houses out this way are far from here, so the road is essentially abandoned. It's a good place to hide out with your thoughts.

But with Ari unwilling to have him around, he heads towards home. *No sense going paddle boarding when you don't even want to see people.* He finally finds the Traversière and stumbles down the steep dirt road until he reaches the gravel marking the edge of town.

He winds his way through the streets as quick as he can, trying to avoid running into anyone he knows. After what seems like an eternity, he reaches the trails that lead to the pension. He takes up residence in one of the few suitable climbing trees and thanks his lucky stars that the pension's empty and there are no stray vacationers to disturb him.

Really, how could Mr. Fonua think like that? I'm not hungry, I'm still in school, and I get a new pair of shoes every year. I'm better off than plenty of other kids in the village. Just because my dad's not around doesn't mean I need anyone's pity.

He sits and stews for a good hour or two before heading into the pension. "Hi Mama," he says as he walks in from the courtyard.

"What's wrong?" She stops dusting to look him over carefully. Her long dark hair is splashed with silver, and the premature wrinkles in her face are lined with dirt.

"Nothing."

"Something's wrong. You never come back from paddle boarding this early." There's no arguing with her tone.

"Mama, can you tell me about my father?"

She drops the rag on one of the tiny, pub-style tables in the hallway where they are standing. "What do you want to know?"

"What's he like?"

"Well, I haven't seen him in, oh, fifteen years, so I'm not sure what he's like now." Natua doesn't try to hide his disappointment at this answer, and she continues, "But when he was here, he was wonderful. We met while he was on holiday—he came to be a part of the Hawaiki Nui. The day before the race, though, he sprained his wrist and he couldn't lift an oar, much less steer a canoe."

She's told the story a thousand times, but still his eyes hunger for more.

"He'd been preparing for the race for years, but he didn't let his injury bring down his spirits. I took him on a private tour of Fare that day to get his mind off of things. I know they say love takes time, but in the space of an afternoon we both found it."

"So why didn't he stay?" He shrugs his bony shoulders lightly, as if it would've been that easy.

"His whole life was in Spain—his family, his career, his house. He was visiting on a tourist visa, so there was no future for him here. And you know the pension doesn't bring in enough to support another adult."

"I still don't see why you couldn't make it work." His voice takes on a stubborn note.

"It was complicated—you'll understand when you're older. Things don't always work out the way we want them to," his mother says dismissively.

He sighs but doesn't move away.

"Is there any particular reason he's on your mind today?"

"He's my father. Isn't he allowed to be on my mind?"

"Ignacio, what has gotten you so on edge? You know you can talk to me." She's always called him by his full name—she's the only one who doesn't use his nickname. He used to like that, but right now it's grating on his nerves.

"I don't really want to talk about it."

"Fine. How was paddle boarding then?"

"I didn't go."

"And why not? You've been after me to let you and that Fonua girl go all week!" She looks up at him and asks drily, "Did she ditch you?"

"Kinda."

"I told you to find better friends, didn't I? You should spend more time with your classmate Wan. He's such a studious young man."

Natua rolls his eyes. "He's failing biology because it doesn't matter to his so-called 'life plan.' He's only doing extra credit stuff so his parents don't ground him over his grades. And anyway, how does being studious make someone a good friend?"

"Whatever. How about that sweet girl you did your French project with—Etienne, isn't it?"

"Mama, stop trying to replace Ari." Natua keeps his eyes on his feet as he slips off his sneakers. The tile floor feels cool against his toes through his threadbare socks.

"I only want what's best for you. Neither of them would have bailed on you at the last minute."

"Ari didn't bail on me last minute either. I didn't ask her until today and, besides, she had a good reason to say no."

"Try me." Mama wipes the dust from her cheek.

"You really want to know? Her dad thinks you don't do a good enough job on your own. He wants to adopt me because you're a bad mom."

"Mr. Fonua? I don't think so."

"He's a council member now, so he thinks he can do whatever he wants without even asking you or me what we think."

"Don't be ridiculous."

"He asked Ari if she was okay with it just last night and told her exactly that."

Her grey eyes narrow. "You really need to quit being in the school plays, you know that? You're getting incredibly melodramatic."

"Why would I exaggerate something like that?" He snorts. "It's the truth—you can ask Ari yourself."

"Well I don't understand why she would be so upset to have our families tied together. Unless, of course, you two have had your share of afternoons together, if you know what I mean." She winks at him and grins.

"Adults—you're all the same!" His face gets hot with anger. "That's exactly what Ari's dad said!"

"If it's not because she likes you, then why is she so upset about it, hmm?"

"I don't really know," Natua admits. "I hadn't thought about it that way. Maybe she thinks I'm not good enough to be a part of her family or something."

"If anything, it's the other way around," his mother replies. "Though I do wonder why she's so upset about the idea of joining our families. It all sounds like a bunch of hog wash to me. Whether he's a member of the council or not and whether I like his politics or not, Mr. Fonua has always been a reasonable man and none of that seems reasonable to me. Why would he even bother judging how I parent?"

"I don't know. She didn't say, but she did say that he thinks I need a father."

"Hmph." She picks up the rag again. "And that girl needs a mother, but I don't go around acting all high and mighty about it. Don't worry about what Mr. Fonua is or isn't thinking."

"But—"

"No buts." She shakes the rag at him. "Now listen, I need to finish cleaning up in here—we have some honeymooners checking in on Monday. Can you go out and pick the ripe breadfruit and papayas?"

"Sure." He turns towards the kitchen to grab a bowl.

"And son?" She waits until his head turns and their eyes meet. "If you ever feel like what I've given you is not enough, you can tell me. I do everything I can for you. You know that, right?"

"Of course I do, Mama," he replies, turning around. "But it's not the same as having a father."

"I know," she says, her voice low. "Do you want Mr. Fonua to adopt you?"

"No!" He makes a face. "I already have a father—one who *doesn't* think badly of you. I just need to find him."

She clears her throat. "I don't know, Ignacio. Finding him won't be easy."

"We have internet and I know his name. I can do it."

"It's not just that, my son. It's been so many years, and he left before I even found out you were on the way..." she trails off, her voice gentle. "I don't know how he and whatever family he has now would react, knowing he has a Ma'ohi son."

"Why do you always assume he'll hate me? If he ever loved you, then he'll do right by me. I just have to find him."

Before his mother can respond, he turns and heads into the expansive kitchen. He wishes he could have dinner with both of his parents just once but instead, he's being offered a new father he doesn't particularly need or want. He grabs a metal bowl and heads out to the garden, longing for a day he hopes desperately will come.

. . .

Manu isn't surprised that Ari's run off with her Walkman. He tried talking to her over breakfast, but she barely looked at him. *Teenagers. Everything is always the end of the world with them.*

Even though it's a Saturday, he heads down to the town hall. His dedication to the job may seem surprising to naysayers, but he isn't there to organize the safety department or pore over last year's budget. He's there to see just how much paperwork is involved in formally adopting someone with an absentee father and a sickly mother.

He's trying to determine whether it would be better to go through the formal process or simply let the adoption be a verbal agreement between himself and Natua's mother, Angela, because he wants to be well-informed before he asks Angela and Natua for their permission. Given her precarious health and how close the kids are, he's not worried about getting their approval. Instead, he focuses on sorting through the details of the process so they won't have to.

Angela does all she can for the boy, but she's been limited for many years due to her health. Manu worries about the consequences for the boy if something happens to her—he's sure Angela does too. Both Natua and Ari will turn 14 in the coming months, and that's not old enough to handle life alone. Manu imagines the boy dropping out of school, like so many other islanders do, to spend his life catering to tourists.

He flips past Ari's doubts like he flips past irrelevant papers in his new office. She's just afraid of having another brother pass away too young. Manu chokes up at the mere thought of Henri, and he's thankful he's alone as he searches for a box of tissues. Her hesitation is understandable, but he'll get through to her. All that's left to do is have a few delicate discussions with Angela and Natua and figure out the best way to go about it.

The more he reads, the less he cares for the legal process involved. As long as Angela backs him up when it comes to parental rights—and mentions something about it in her will—Manu can't see any reason why he would go through the expense and long waiting periods. The entire thing is daunting and, truthfully, appears almost entirely worthless. He can start calling the boy his son and taking responsibility for him tomorrow and no one in the islands would question his right to do so. All he and Angela have to do is hold a big tamaaraa to celebrate the occasion with their families and neighbors and put it in writing somewhere. To get that official piece of paper, though, he must move mountains. *I wish I was in charge of making rules about adoptions so I could make it easier. At least Natua and Angela can agree informally to an arrangement— those poor kids in orphanages have no option but this insult to humanity.*

He ends up staying at the office far longer than he'd intended, drafting a more streamlined version of the adoption policy with fewer reasons for delays. It might not be his job, but he can't help but feel for kids who thought they would be going home and then ended up the victim of a process that "falls through" on a regular basis. He wonders briefly who he can send his plan to, then starts daydreaming and looking out of the window.

When he notices sunset staining the lagoon orange and pink, he cleans up his desk, files the papers, and gets ready to go. He and Ari are heading over to Alii and

Tama's for dinner tonight, and they still have to pick up something for dessert. He hops into his car and drives back to the house to pick her up and ask her what kind of sweet she's in the mood for.

His body hums with energy as he drives, his decision so obvious now. He will ask Angela if he can adopt Natua informally, and with his nest egg, he'll throw a party worth remembering to celebrate it. He'll call Angela tomorrow to discuss it with her and get her agreement on it—he's certainly not asking to take her son from her, and he's sure she will appreciate knowing her son's future is protected should anything happen to her.

Back home, he calls into the house, "Ari! We've got to head over to Nona's and Pop's for dinner." No answer. "Ari, let's go!" He kicks off his sandals and walks inside, wondering how loud that tape player can get. All of the lights are off, and her bedroom is empty. He opens the chest under her window and feels around in its shadowy depths—the Walkman is still gone.

He heads back outside with a sigh to check for her in the empty backyard. He cups his hands around his mouth and yells. "Ari! We've got to go!"

She couldn't be far—maybe she'd left a note and he hadn't noticed it in the gloom already settling in the house. His strides are quick as he heads back in and flicks on a light, but the note board next to the refrigerator is empty except for the memo he'd left himself this morning. *Dinner at Nona Alii's and Pop Tama's at 19:00. Bring dessert.* They're going to be late if Ari doesn't show up soon, so he decides to give Alii and Tama a call. Maybe she'd walked over there earlier to talk through her feelings about adopting Natua and lost track of time, knowing they were eating dinner there anyway.

"Alii? Yes, it's Manu. How are you? ... Listen, is Ari with you by any chance? ... you know how she is, always wandering off somewhere... Well, we're going to be a bit late. She must have forgotten we were having dinner with you tonight... Yeah, 20:00 should be fine. Thanks, Alii... Yes, we'll still bring dessert. See you soon."

He takes another look around the house and makes an extra pass through the yard, but Ari is still nowhere to be found. He looks up the Rainas' phone number and gives the pension a call.

"Hello, Angela, it's Manu—is Ari over at your house by any chance? She seems to have forgotten about our dinner arrangements... Would you put him on the phone then?... Natua, how are you? ... Your mom tells me you've seen Ari today—can you tell me where she is?"

. . .

Upon hearing that Ari still isn't home, Natua hesitates. Should he tell Mr. Fonua about the thinking tree? Ari will be very angry with him—again—if she's just avoiding her father like Natua suspects, but she didn't say anything about being upset with her grandparents. She and Nona Alii have always been very close, especially after Mrs. Fonua passed away, and it seems odd that she would take out her anger with Manu on them.

"Yeah, I saw her in the village around lunchtime. If she's not home, I don't know where she could be." Feeling guilty about the lie but still miffed with Mr. Fonua, Natua decides he will just go out to check the Traversière and the tree himself. Twilight is setting in, but she could easily get home before night falls completely. She's probably almost home anyway. "I'll let her know you're looking for her if I see her." He hangs up, worried about her walking back all alone through the narrow path and down the Traversière in the rain that's starting to fall. "Mama, I'm going to head outside for a bit."

"Don't go too far," Angela replies, a cigarette drooping between her skinny fingers. "I don't want to have to go calling all the neighbors when *you* don't come home."

"Of course I won't, Mama." He slips into the backyard and strikes out on the wooded trail leading inland.

. . .

Manu hangs up the phone and takes another hopeful glance outside, but all that's visible are the no-no flies and mosquitoes crowding the light at the bottom of the veranda steps. He looks up to see how bright the moon is tonight, but the sky is covered with thick clouds and it starts to sprinkle. He'd almost forgotten it was supposed to rain tonight—she'd certainly rush home any minute now and they could get on their way to Alii and Tama's for dinner.

As the minutes pass and the isolated drops turn into a deluge, his emotions shift from irritation to worry. Where in the world is she? He decides to give the Rainas another call. When Angela answers the phone, she asks if Natua is with him. "When he took off, did he say where he was going or anything else about where Ari might be?"

"No," she replies, exhaling heavily into the phone. "I'd told him not to go too far, but you know how kids are."

"Especially boys," Manu replies. "They can get themselves into real trouble if you're not careful."

"You mean like Ari has?" Angela asks pointedly.

"Right," Manu mumbles, too focused on finding Ari to care if he's offended Natua's mother or if she's just as stressed as he is. "Anyway, if we don't hear from either of them in the next—say ten minutes—I'm going to head out there to look for them both. This is very unlike Ari, and I'm a little unnerved."

"Well, Ignacio never acts this way on his own either." She sounds annoyed, but Manu writes off her tone as stress. "But teenagers are unpredictable, aren't they?"

Manu is caught off-guard hearing Natua's full name. "Yeah," he says. "He's a good kid, but very adventurous, that's for sure. Anyway, give me a call if either of them shows up at your house, and I'll do the same. Hopefully, I'll talk to you soon."

He hangs up the phone and heads outside, where he paces around the covered veranda. "Ari!" he calls into the night. There's no answer.

Minutes crawl by as the darkness deepens. Night-time noises he hasn't paid attention to in years are making him jumpy—a tree branch cracking, tupa crabs digging through sandy soil, waves whipping the nearby shore. When he heads inside to call Angela back, the phone is already ringing.

"Hello, Angela? Have you found them?"

"No," comes the voice, along with the pounding of rain in the background. "They're still not with you?"

"No. I'm going to give my in-laws another call and get in touch with a few neighbors. If nobody's seen them, I'll head out and see if they've gotten caught in the village or something like that. Neither of them has a cell phone, so they probably just can't get in touch."

"Keep me posted." Angela's voice sounds strained. "I'm going to check the trails behind the house—I'll buzz your cell if I find anything."

"Thanks." He presses the end call button and immediately dials Alii.

An hour later, when neither of the kids have shown up and additional friends and relatives have been asked to keep an eye out, Manu's starting to feel genuinely worried. Angela found no signs of them on the trails behind the pension. When Tama arrives to keep watch at the house, Manu grabs his keys from the hook next to the door and rushes into the night.

The first place he goes is where Natua claimed to see Ari last—the village. He parks the car and walks up and down the alleys between shops, then checks down by the shore. The streets are empty aside from a few smokers spilling out of Chez Maitai, and Manu is soaked to the bone by the time he's checked their favorite hang-out spots. So, he heads into all the ritzy restaurants and dive bars, looking for Ari's thick mop of hair and Natua's lanky figure. Time after time, he relaxes and heads up to someone, only to realize he's mistaken.

So, he asks around, telling drunken neighbors and strangers alike what his daughter was wearing when she left that morning.

. . .

Natua slips and stumbles his way back to the thinking tree. He can barely see anything, even with the flashlight, thanks to all of the rain. Ari's probably stuck at the tree waiting out the storm.

Finally, he reaches the clearing. At first, he doesn't see her, but a flash of lightning illuminates her crumpled figure at the base of the old banyan tree.

"Hey, you okay?" he yells over the din of the storm. No answer. There's blood on her forehead.

"Oh, this is bad, this is bad, this is bad," Natua moans. He's starting to give into panic when he realizes she's still breathing, and he's the only one who can help. "Don't mind me, just getting you out of the rain as much as I can," he tells her as he lifts her shoulders and pulls her closer to the tree. *Now what?* "Gotta get help. Ari needs help."

He takes off down the path once again, leaves and twigs digging into the sides of his face. When he emerges back onto the deserted road, he bolts towards town.

"Hey! Hey! Help me!" he yells when he sees an older classmate on the streets, struggling to stay dry.

"Some rain, eh?" the teenager replies, a hand shielding his eyes from the deluge. "Come on, let's get inside."

"No! My friend needs help, she's hurt."

Picking up on the desperation in Natua's voice, he puts a hand on Natua's muddy shoulder. "Calm down man. What can I do?"

"I need to get in touch with her dad, but I don't have a cell phone. Can you call him?"

"Sure." He pats his pockets, then lets out a groan. "Ugh, forgot it *again*. Take me to her, I can help."

"It's too far—her grandparents live nearby, across from the tourist shop in the bright green house. Please, go to them for help. They'll know what to do. I don't want to leave her alone, so I've gotta head back."

"I'm on it."

"By the way, tell them Natua sent you!" he yells as he runs back into the forest.

. . .

Another hour goes by, and Manu's about to give up when his cell phone rings. The caller ID says it's Alii. "You've found them?" he asks hopefully.

"Well, sort of. A young man by the name of—what did you say your name was?—by the name of Tehai just came in. He says Natua found him by the Traversière on the edge of town and asked for help."

His voice drops. "What do you mean 'help'? And why would they be over there?"

"I don't know, honey, but he says Ari is hurt."

"Did he see her?"

"No—Natua told him."

"Well, did he say what happened?"

Alii confers with the boy. "No, just asked him to come here. Said Natua was frantic."

"Great," Manu says sarcastically. "I'll call 15 for an ambulance and meet you over there."

"We're on our way in a second. I'm grabbing a couple of blankets and fresh clothes—those kids have got to be soaked."

Manu sprints up the street to the car. He's shaking and fumbles with his keys. They fall into a puddle with a soft *plish*, and he lets out a few choice words. He finally manages to get into the car and stomps on the gas. The jalopy fishtails a bit as he speeds towards the Traversière, fingers already punching out the emergency number.

He arrives before Alii and parks haphazardly on the gravel roadside. "Natua! Ari! Natua! Ari!" Intermittent flashes of lightning illuminate the sky but do little for the heavily forested road. He runs back to the car and turns the lights on, hoping to spot the kids or at least traces of where they've gone. "Natua—can you hear me?"

Alii pulls up with Tehai. "You're sure this is the right spot?" she asks as she climbs out of the car. "Where did he go?"

Tehai hops out and walks on the right side of the road, already slipping up the muddy incline. "He was going in this direction, but he didn't stay on the road very long. He went off to the right up ahead, by the bend."

"Tehai, would you come with me?" Manu asks him. "We'll need an extra set of hands to bring Ari out if she can't walk on her own. Alii, would you stay with the cars and keep an eye out for the ambulance?" He tosses her the cell phone. "And please, call Angela. Let her know Natua is all right."

"I'm on it." She gives Tehai a flashlight before heading to her pickup.

Manu sprints up the steep roadway, Tehai falling behind as the shadows close in around them. "Natua! Holler if you can hear me!"

There is no answer but Tehai. "Sir, don't go any farther on the road! Hold on, and I'll show you the way."

Manu plunges off the road and straight into a thick tangle of brush. "Dammit! Where am I going?"

"Hold on—I'll show you." Tehai catches up, breathing hard. He shines the light on Manu and then moves the flashlight's beam several meters to the right, illuminating a narrow footpath. "Down there!"

"Give me that thing, wouldja?" Tehai hands over the flashlight. Manu barrels through the opening and continues calling the kids' names.

Tehai follows closely behind and speaks up after a moment. "Hey, why don't we listen for a minute in case we can hear them?"

"Right." Manu realizes his fears are getting the best of him. He holds up his hand and they both stop, out of breath as they listen to the rain falling among the trees.

Faintly, they hear a young voice calling back. "Over here!"

"This way!" Manu takes off towards the voice. "We're coming, kids!"

They forge their way through the night, twigs slapping their faces as the path gets narrower and wilder. "Whoah!" Tehai yells.

"What happened, did you find them?" Manu half-turns.

"No, no, just going too fast for me."

"Well, keep up!" Manu yells. "We have to find them as soon as we can."

"We also need to pay attention or we could run right past them."

Instead of replying, Manu calls their names again as he rushes forward.

Natua responds, this time much closer. "We're over here, in the clearing!"

"What clearing?" Manu asks under his breath. The path curves sharply to the right, almost disappearing, and then a half-flooded meadow comes into view.

Manu sweeps the light back and forth and calls Natua's name again.

"Right here, Mr. Fonua!" Manu sees his muddied arm waving. The kids are obscured by a small rise. A banyan tree on top of the hill is tossing in the wind. "She's bleeding—I think she hit her head."

"Let me see!" Manu runs over, mud sucking on his sandals and splashing his pants. Ari is unconscious, blood and rain mixing on her forehead. There's a flooded hole that looks like it was dug by a tupa crab at the base of the tree and a large rock sitting a few centimeters from his daughter's head. He takes a deep breath to calm himself and look for other injuries, being particularly cautious as he checks for back and neck trauma. "We should be able to move her," he says before turning to Natua. "Do you have any idea how long she's been out here?"

Natua shakes his head. "She's been here all day, but when I saw her around lunchtime, she was fine."

"Then why the hell did you tell me she was in the village? Do you know how much time I wasted?"

"I'm sorry, sir. I didn't think—"

"Of course you didn't. Now, guide us back to the Traversière so we can get her to the doctor. Tehai, will you help me carry her?" Manu strips off his shirt and wraps her head to stem the bleeding. Between the rain, mud, and darkness, it's impossible to tell if she's still losing blood.

Tehai says, "I'll get her legs."

"Be careful." Now that he's found Ari and assessed the situation, Manu's composure has returned. "On three."

When they finally emerge onto the Traversière, they nearly collide with a medic who parked a van next to the path, lights flashing in the darkness.

"Lay her on the stretcher," he instructs. Behind him, a paramedic preps equipment. Manu takes Ari from Tehai and lays her down gently. She's filthy, and the vehicle's interior lights make her look more washed out than he'd expected. Manu doesn't let himself linger, but forces himself out of the way so they can work.

"Thank you, Tehai, for all of your help tonight." He shakes the boy's hand. "I don't know what we would have done without you."

Tehai bows his head in respect. "I know if someone I cared about was out here hurt, I would want all the help I could get."

"You're a good man. Mrs. Ania will give you a ride home if you need it, and we would love to have you over for dinner when this is all over."

"Of course, sir. I hope she pulls through okay."

"Thank you." Manu decides the handshake isn't enough and pulls the boy in for a hug. They are both completely soaked, and he realizes the boy is shivering. "There are some extra blankets and dry clothes in the truck. Why don't you head down there and get dried up a bit?"

"Yessir." He turns and nearly bumps into Alii.

"You go ahead and grab what you need—the truck is unlocked. I'll be there in a minute to drive you home." She turns to Manu, voice thick with anxiety. "How is she?"

"Not sure yet," Manu replies, "but it looks like she's lost a lot of blood. I think she's been out for a while."

Natua is edging towards the back of the van to check on his friend when his mother arrives. "Ignacio! Thank God you're all right." She bumps into Manu and the medic standing guard behind the van as she takes him into her arms.

"I know we're all relieved to have found the kids," the medic says, "but can you folks back up and give us some space to work?"

"Of course!" Angela replies. "We need to get you home."

"What about Ari?"

"We will check in tomorrow. Alii, thank you for keeping in touch with me tonight! If you or Manu need anything, don't hesitate to call." The two women embrace, and then Angela and Natua disappear into the night. As they head down the road, Manu hears Angela ask, "Why in the world did you head off alone like that up here? You know how dangerous this area can get at night. And in the rain, too!"

Manu and Alii link arms, both waiting anxiously to hear the paramedic's assessment. After what seems like an eternity, the medic gets out of the truck and says, "She most likely has a concussion, but she's bleeding much more than we would expect from her gash. You're lucky you found her when you did—she needs a hospital and fast."

"But getting a helicopter or even a boat at this time of night to get to Ra'iatea will take time," Manu says.

"I know. While we're waiting, we'll head to the clinic so we can stabilize her and stitch this wound."

"Can I ride with her in the back?"

"Of course."

Manu jumps in the back of the rig. "Then let's go. Alii, can you arrange for someone to pick up the car?"

The sun is rising before they get a room at the hospital on the neighboring island of Ra'iatea. The admitting doctor arranges for an emergency blood transfusion, as well as an array of tests to check for internal injuries.

Manu waits in Ari's room for her return, foot tapping incessantly. Although his nerves have calmed, he fixates on the fact that she hasn't woken up aside from a few incoherent mumblings in the night. The doctor keeps telling him not to panic, that they can't know anything for sure until they've given her the transfusion and done more tests. But it's a head wound, and who's to say how long she was out there?

He's bracing himself for the worst—again. The last time he was here, he lost his wife. Amaru was in and out of consciousness after miscarrying their youngest, a boy named Oscar. She'd gone into labor twelve weeks too early, and they couldn't get to the hospital in time to stop the contractions.

She was in the recovery room after delivering the stillborn. Manu sat in the chair next to the bed, pushing hair out of her sweat-streaked face. "I'm so sorry, Amy," he said with tears in his eyes.

"I'm sorry too," she replied. Shortly after that, she became delirious and passed out. He grabbed her hands and was surprised to find they were cold to the touch.

He shouted for the nurse, and they discovered massive amounts of hemorrhaging which caused her to go into shock. Before the afternoon was over, Manu had lost his newest child and his wife. He couldn't bear to lose Ari before her time too.

He stands and heads to the nurse's station, where a matronly woman is rapidly checking charts and rigging a new IV bag.

"Hi, can I help you?" Her tone is polite but terse.

"I need an update on my daughter. She was supposed to be back from a blood transfusion 30 minutes ago, and no one's told me where she is or how she's doing."

The nurse sighs and heads to the station's sole computer. "What's the last name?"

"The last name's Fonua, F-O-N-U-A. Arietta."

She types it in quickly and waits for the screen to load. "She's been transferred to the ICU ward," she says. "Head down the hall and take a left past those double doors. She's in room 4 on the right side of the hallway, just past the nurse's station."

"Thank you so much," Manu replies before turning and heading down the hallway. By the time it registers that someone should have taken the time to tell him that and explain why the move was necessary, the nurse back in the general ward has already replaced one patient's IV bag and administered a dose of antibiotics to another.

When he reaches the room, Ari is alone and appears to be stirring. Instinctively, he takes her right hand and sits next to the bed, mindful of the IV drip going in her left. "Ari, it's Papa. I'm here, honey." She murmurs and turns her head towards him, but her eyes remain closed. "It's okay, Ari, it's okay." He slumps in his chair. "It's okay, it's okay."

He says it more for his benefit than hers.

.   .   .

Manu awakens from a short nap to the sound of pen scratching against paper as a doctor checks the various monitors Ari is connected to. His daughter still appears to be out cold. The doctor introduces herself as Elodie and determines that Manu is, indeed, Ari's parental guardian before continuing her note-taking. Her manner is reassured. In her light brown hands—with age spots betraying life experience that the rest of her body denies and nails worn smooth from scrubbing—Manu knows Ari will be well cared for.

Finally, he brings himself to ask, "Is she going to be all right?"

"As far as the head wound goes, yes, she's out of the woods."

"As far as the head wound goes? Is there something else going on?"

"We were giving her an X-ray to determine if there were any other injuries due to the suspected fall, and the results were not quite what we'd expected."

"Oh god, is it her back?"

"No. We found evidence of a bone lesion on the right side of her pelvic bone. Typically, this is not the type of injury sustained in a fall."

"What? Where did it come from? What even is that?"

"A lesion is just a term for an abnormality in the bone. Children and young adults who are still growing are at the highest risk to get them, but we will need to investigate it further to understand what's causing it.

"We've scheduled Ari for a full-body MRI and a more comprehensive panel of blood tests to help us figure out what's going on and check for any other lesions. I don't want to scare you, but you need to prepare yourself. Some of the things we'll be testing for include benign bone tumors, bone infections, inflammation in the bone, and certain types of cancer."

"You think my baby has cancer?" He feels the blood draining from his face.

The doctor's clinical tone softens. "We don't know anything yet, sir—it could be something as simple as an overgrown cyst that needs to be removed. You can help me start to figure that out though."

"How?"

"Can you tell me a bit about Ari's activity levels? Have you noticed any changes in her behavior or lifestyle in the last few months or so?"

"She's been tiring out very easily in the last few weeks." Manu looks up as he thinks. "She'll come home and go straight to bed after having dinner. My in-laws and I have been teaching her and one of her pals a historical dance, and lately she's the first one out of breath. But up until then, she'd always been the most energetic kid in the neighborhood." He pauses.

"Tired every single day or just once in a while?"

"It's been almost every day this month," Manu replies.

Meanwhile, the doctor is taking prodigious notes. "This is really helpful information," she says. "Has she been sick or had a lot of infections recently?"

"I don't think so. I wrote it all off as her being a teenager, that maybe she had become a woman and that changed her." He feels his cheeks warming.

"Has your wife talked with her about that at all?"

Manu fingers his wedding ring. "My wife died six years ago."

The doctor tilts her head sympathetically. "I'm sorry to hear that, sir. Unfortunately, though, I don't think that normal body development is at the root of the symptoms you're describing. Other than that, have you noticed anything unusual?"

Manu thinks hard for a moment before speaking. "It's hard to say—most of it seemed to be girl stuff. Taking longer to get ready for school in the morning, some stomach aches, taking more bathroom breaks than normal. They're the kind of life changes that mothers talk to daughters about, not fathers."

The doctor finishes her note-taking and nods as if that is exactly what she expected to hear. "It must be difficult," she says in a quiet tone. "I can't imagine trying to parent my boys without my husband. But she's in good hands, and we will help you both figure out what is going on as soon as we can."

"Thank you." The knot in his stomach is loosening now that the doctor hasn't blamed him for his embarrassment, for not knowing how to ask the questions he intuitively knew had to be asked.

As she breezes out the door, he stops her. "How long will those tests take?"

She turns. "We'll start getting results back in the next three hours or so. She's scheduled to have an MRI done on Wednesday, and that should be the last test we're waiting on. Depending on the results of this first batch of blood work, we may need to run another, more extensive panel."

"How long will she need to stay here?"

"Once she wakes up, we'll move her out of the ICU, but we'd like her to stay under observation at least another day or two. If she's too weak to travel to and from your home island, it may be advisable for her to stay in Ra'iatea until the MRI is conducted on

Wednesday. We could arrange for a hotel room if you'd like."

"For now, we'll just wait and see. Thank you, Dr. Elodie."

"You're welcome, Mr. Fonua."

With that, he is alone, and he weeps.

Chapter 3

"Mama?" Natua calls. No answer. "Mama?"

Angela had been quite worked up last night after he'd run off to find Ari, passed out and bleeding off the Traversière. "I don't know whether to be proud of you or pissed," she'd said. "You did a reckless thing, Ignacio, when you should have just told me what was going on."

"I'm sorry, Mama." He must have apologized a thousand times, but it never seemed to be enough.

"I thought I was going to lose you too." Her eyes filled with tears as she spoke. "I can't even stomach the thought!"

When they finally arrived home, he was adequately shamed and went straight to bed without thinking about how quick and shallow her breathing had become.

He strides through the pension now, checking the kitchen and all of the empty rooms that normally remind him of other problems. A few minutes later, he comes to the last room in the pension—Mama's bedroom.

The door is closed, and he knocks tentatively. No answer.

"Mama, are you in there? I wanted to apologize. Would you like me to make you some breakfast?"

He's about to walk away and check for her on the back lawn when he hears her labored breathing.

"Are you all right Mama?" he calls. He's unwilling to burst in on his mother in her bedroom but he's starting to feel something is amiss. "Can you please answer me so I know you're okay?"

He's met with silence. He thinks back to the night before and curses himself for not paying more mind to his mother's fragile health. He should've talked to her before running off to find Ari, if only to protect her from the stress he'd caused.

"I'm opening the door." He announces himself loud enough that he's thankful the pension is reliably empty.

It takes a moment before he can make out anything in the darkness beyond the strip of light from the door. Angela's used blackout curtains for years in an attempt to maintain some form of privacy from the prying eyes of curious guests who just want to know "how a *real* Tahitian lives." Never mind that Tahitians live on Tahiti, and this is Huahine.

He doesn't need to see much to realize something's wrong. His mother isn't in bed—she's on the floor, chest rising and falling so quickly that his first thought is that she's having a seizure.

Natua rushes to her side. "Can you hear me?"

Angela turns her head towards him but the effort is too much and her muscles go slack.

"I'm calling an ambulance. Stay with me, Mama. Please, please, stay with me."

· · ·

Ari's on the runway when he starts the engine.

"Henri, stop!" she yells.

He pauses for a moment but doesn't acknowledge her.

"No, please wait! Something's wrong!" She waves her arms, but he ignores her.

The plane shudders into motion. She has to duck to avoid the wing as he taxies into position on the small runway. Seconds tick down to the point of no return.

"You have to stop! Henri!" Tears spring to her eyes.

She smells the fuel leak, sees the sparks near the

cockpit. But Henri doesn't stop. He's still on the plane, and he's out of time.

• • •

It's the second time Natua's needed an ambulance for someone he loves in the last 24 hours. When the paramedics arrive, he hurries them to his mother, who is still breathing hard but has recovered enough to sit upright.

They fit an oxygen mask over her face and pepper Natua with questions.

"How long has she been like this? Does she have health conditions? What medications does she take?"

He answers the questions to the best of his ability and points the medical professionals towards her bedside table, where she keeps her prescriptions in a drawer. Natua is thankful they lay off after they catch sight of the way his fingers are shaking.

After what seems like an eternity, his mother's voice breaks through the rhythmic noises of the oxygen tank. "Get those damn peeping toms out of my bedroom." Her voice may be muffled by the noise, but her anger is perfectly clear. The paramedic looks up from his spot a meter or two away, where he's checking the types and dosages of her medicines.

"Mama, relax. They're here to help."

"Get them out," she repeats. She pauses to catch her breath, then continues, "I'm not going to Ra'iatea. I'll call my doctor tomorrow."

"Are you sure that's a good idea? You scared me."

She nods. "You're one to talk—" she pauses to take a breath, "—about scaring people. I'll be fine."

The paramedic walks over and squats down next to Angela. "Ma'am, we do need to be sure you're all right. We'll give you a few more minutes of oxygen, and then we'll observe for a bit after we remove it. If you still feel comfortable staying home after ten minutes of breathing on your own, we'll leave without you—otherwise, you'll need to go to the hospital. Will that suit you?"

She exhales, and it's hard to tell if it's a sigh or labored respiration. "You're not going to accept anything else, are you?"

The man shakes his head. "I can't leave you here if you need a hospital."

The minutes pass without further incident, and finally the ambulance pulls away from the pension. Angela is back in bed with one of Natua's sloppily made egg-and-cheese crepes for breakfast.

After she reassures him for the hundredth time that she's feeling much better now, *so leave me alone dammit,* he walks outside and plunks in the cool grass under the largest of the rain trees on the back lawn. His head is pounding and heart still racing. *What if Mama isn't okay next time?*

. . .

Ari awakens in a cold sweat, still half in the world of her nightmare. "Henri, you have to stop!"

After a moment, she is aware of the beeps and hums of hospital machinery and Papa, leaning against the doorframe and closing his eyes. "Ari…" He trails off. When he opens his eyes, they're shimmering with sadness. "It's far too late for that."

Fully awake now, Ari averts her eyes to avoid her father's pained expression. How selfish of her to make Papa relive that, as if she hasn't already done enough. "I'm sorry Papa. I just—" she sniffs and realizes she's been crying—"I was having a terrible dream."

She turns, only to realize with a sharp pang that her hand is attached to an IV drip, and there are sensors on her chest and is that gauze on her head? "What am I doing in the hospital?"

He takes a seat next to the bed. "Honey, you had an accident. What's the last thing you remember?"

"I... I don't know."

Manu leans down to hug his daughter. "It's okay. We don't have to talk yet."

The embrace might tug on one of the sensors attached to her chest, but she doesn't care. She loses herself in the warmth of it.

"What day is it today?" she asks when they break apart.

"It's Monday," he says. "And you've managed to skip school twice in two weeks."

"Right," she says, unsure of what he's talking about but willing to play along. Hopefully, she'll be able to put the pieces together soon. "Well, skipping school makes me starving. Is there anything to eat here?"

"I'll have to go get something, but what sounds good?"

"Mmm, I could really go for some ice cream."

"I'll see what I can do," Manu says. Ari notices his smile is painted too bright on his face, like he's holding something back. Maybe being in this hospital again is bothering him.

Ten minutes later, he returns with ice chips and a nurse. "Sorry hon, they won't let me give you ice cream just yet," he says apologetically.

The nurse, a Ma'ohi woman with a cool brown complexion, steps into the room with a clipboard. "Hi, Arietta? My name is Rosine. I'm here to help figure out just how much you've forgotten thanks to that nasty bump you've got on your head."

"Okay."

Rosine sits down in the chair next to the bed and uncaps her pen. "Can you tell me what you ate for dinner last night?"

She thinks hard, and then says, "Mahi-mahi and yams."

"And what day of the week was that?"

"Sunday."

"Great! Is there anything exciting happening in your life soon?"

Ari nods. "There's a celebration for Papa winning a seat on the municipal council on Friday..." She groans and turns to her father, agitated. "Wait, is that what you meant by skipping school twice in two weeks? Did I forget your *tamaaraa?*"

Manu starts to speak, but the nurse holds up a finger to quiet him. "Don't make a fuss about what you've forgotten. We see a lot of cases like this, and most of what you've forgotten should come back to you in a day or so. It's just good to be aware of how far back your memory loss goes."

Rosine rearranges herself in the chair. Ari doesn't see the woman taking any notes, and she wonders if the nurse is just doing this to get rid of Papa's jitters. There's a bump on her head, sure, but he's been looking at her like it's the end of the world.

"You're a very lucky family, and I don't want you to lose sight of that," Rosine says. "Things could have been much, much worse. Now Dad." She turns to face him. "How many days back was your Sunday dinner with mahi-mahi?"

"It was last Sunday, so 7 days ago," he replies.

She jots down some notes on her chart. Ari is able to read the words *father* and *calm* before the nurse tilts her clipboard. "Now, I don't want either of you to stress about when those memories will come back. You're probably going to get things back in bits and pieces over the next few days, my dear, but focusing on it won't accomplish anything. Your body needs time to heal, and everyone's body heals at its own pace, so don't try to rush anything."

Ari nods. "Fine. When can I go home?"

"Not just yet—we need to keep you under observation for a day or two, but then we hope to get you on your way." With that, the nurse bids her goodbyes and moves on to the next room, where they can hear her muffled chatter through the wall.

"What happened, Papa?"

"I'm not sure. You were by yourself somewhere off the Traversière, and you didn't come home for dinner. Natua found you, covered in mud and bleeding from your head."

"Ouch." Ari wonders what sent her to her thinking tree instead of wondering what would've happened if Natua wasn't always following her around.

"I don't know what you were doing out there, but please don't go there alone ever again. It's dangerous, especially when it rains."

"Apparently," Ari says, feeling troubled about something. She wouldn't have gone to her thinking tree without it. "Wait, so where's my Walkman?"

"Natua rescued it for you. Nona Alii has it."

"Was the tape inside okay?"

Her father looks at his hands. "I'm not sure, Ari. Everything was so muddy, and I haven't left your side since that night. We'll have to hear from Nona to be sure."

Her eyes mist over. "I can't lose that tape, Papa. It's the only recording of Mama's voice—and Henri's—that I have."

He tilts his head, as if wondering how she knew she had her Walkman and that particular tape. There's no need for him to know how often she sneaks away to the thinking tree.

Reassuringly, he says, "I know, Riri, I know. We'll have to wait and see—we can't afford to worry about that right now. I need you to focus on getting better first."

She shakes her head and puts on a brave face. "How about giving me a spoon for these ice chips then?"

. . .

A few hours later, Angela is dressed and sitting in their dining area while Natua puts a simple lunch on the table.

"Thank goodness you taught me how to cook for the tourists," he says with a nervous laugh.

"You call this cooking?" She gestures to her plate. "You warmed up shrimp and leftover veggies."

Natua shrugs. "It's better than nothing, isn't it?"

She murmurs in response, and the pair eat in silence.

After Natua scrapes the last of the veggies off his plate, he takes a long drink of water and then catches his mother's eyes. She gazes back at him.

"Thank you for your quick thinking today," she says. "You're a good son."

He shakes his head, unconvinced. "I shouldn't have run off like that last night—you obviously can't handle stress like you used to."

"Now Ignacio," she starts with a sigh.

"No, Mama, let me talk." He fusses with his napkin, stalling even as he knows they can't avoid having this conversation. "What's going to happen to me if..." he chokes up.

"My son, my son..." She pats his hand awkwardly. "Nothing is going to happen to me. Besides, you know you'll go live with your Uncle Alain in Pape'ete if something does. Everything would be fine."

"Seriously Mama? You and Uncle Alain haven't spoken in years! I couldn't bear to leave everything and everyone I know on top of losing you." He can't meet her eyes as he confesses, "I'm scared."

"That's why I'm not planning on going anywhere." The determination in her words is undercut by a violent cough into her napkin.

He shifts in his chair. "I'm not sure that your plans are enough."

"Would you rather have Mr. Fonua adopt you then? He blames you for the trouble his own daughter gets herself into."

"What are you talking about?"

"Last night he called me again, after you ran off. Said you could be trouble if I didn't take care, like Arietta wasn't the one who ran off like a little fool."

"Wow." Natua is momentarily silenced by anger. "And I was the one who found her!"

"I know."

"So obviously I don't want *him* to take care of me."

"And I don't either. But let's imagine for a minute he hadn't said anything bad about either of us. Would you be okay with him taking care of you if—"

"Don't say it," he interrupts. "If it weren't for that, then I guess it'd be fine. He's always been so nice, I thought. But he did say that stuff and who knows how long he's secretly been thinking it?"

"You're right. Forget it." She pulls a finger through her graying hair. "He does have something of a point about me though. Look at me. I'm not even 50 yet, but I look like an old woman. I live like an old woman. And old women are not good parents. They're good grandparents."

"Mama, don't say that."

"It's already said."

"What other options do we have though?"

"I don't know," she admits. "You were always close to Afaitu."

"Mama, he doesn't have a job. You had to let him go, remember?" Natua knew it had broken Angela's heart to lay off the loyal groundskeeper after so many years and he hates to bring it up now.

"Right," she says quietly.

"Besides, he already has six kids. Don't you think that's enough?"

Angela shrugs. "In a crowd like that, what's one more?"

"When you aren't working, I'll bet it's a lot."

They obviously aren't going to solve this today, so she changes the subject. "Let's get this mess cleaned up. Grab me my pack of cigarettes from the table in the hallway?"

"You're really going to smoke right now?"

"I do everything I can for you, Ignacio. Let me have this one indulgence."

He sighs and walks away, muttering under his breath so Mama can't hear. "So much for your plans to stick around."

. . .

Doctor Elodie returns to Ari's room with a somber look on her face. She's carrying a sturdy clipboard and medical supplies arranged on a metal tray. When she comes in, she closes the door behind her and sets the tray down on the bedside table. On it are a needle and several tubes, already labeled: "Arietta H. Fonua. Née 25.06.1996."

Ari and Manu look up from the card game they'd been playing to pass the time. Manu's throat tightens in anticipation of the worst.

"Arietta, I'm not sure if you are aware of this, but we were checking for signs of other injuries from your fall, and we found some oddities on the right side of your pelvic region."

"Oddities? Did I break a bone or something?"

"Not exactly. You have what appears to be a bone lesion that formed over time on your pelvic bone, and we have been running tests to determine what could be causing it."

Manu squeezes his daughter's hand, trying to comfort her on a bad day he's sure will only get worse from here.

"We ran a full blood panel on you before your transfusion—and we've got some results back that I need to share with you now that you are awake and on the mend from your fall." She takes a breath and flips to a new page on her clipboard. "We've found evidence you may have a disease called myeloma."

"What's that?"

"Most people haven't heard of it because it's a relatively rare form of blood cancer."

Manu's cards slip through his fingers to land on the tired tile floor.

"What?" Ari asks.

The doctor continues. "Don't be scared of the word 'cancer.' This is a disease that many people live with for years and years, and it can go into remission with proper treatment."

"Wait, if it's a blood cancer, then why is it affecting her bones?" Manu asks. He's briefly hopeful that the doctor is reading from the wrong chart, that she's got the wrong room, that there's another Fonua in this hospital somewhere that can take this bad news away from them.

Elodie replies gently, "The disease typically affects the blood plasma created in your bone marrow, and it causes the wrong types of antibodies to be created in the blood. With too many antibodies your body doesn't need, and not enough of the right antibodies, your bones are unable to function properly. The disease has also caused Arietta to become severely anemic, which we will treat with a simple iron supplement."

His momentary hope deflated, Manu asks, "Are you sure about this? She's only a child."

"Unfortunately, yes, we've double checked all of our results. While your daughter is unusually young to have this disease, it's not impossible."

"How did she get something like that?"

"Like many other cancers and health problems, myeloma can be caused by a number of biological, genetic, and even environmental factors, such as radiation exposure." The doctor turns to Ari. "Have you spent a lot of time around any radioactive areas in the islands?"

"I don't think so. I mean, come on, most of that stuff is over a thousand kilometers away."

Manu clears his throat. "What about exposure while she was in the womb? Would that matter?"

"It's possible—there are very few studies on this disease, especially in someone so young, which makes it hard to say. Why, did you and your wife protest the nuclear testing?"

"We spent a few weeks in Mururoa and Pape'ete with our son, Henri. We, uh, we wanted to show him how to stand up for something you believe in. I never thought that it could lead to something like this."

"As I said, myeloma—like most other forms of cancer—has numerous risk factors so it's nearly impossible to pinpoint a single reason it developed. That's just a screening question I'm required to ask all new cancer patients." Manu winces at hearing Ari described as a cancer patient. The doctor continues, "What's most important to us is how we are going to treat it."

"What are we going to do?" Ari's voice sounds small and Manu puts a reassuring hand on her knee.

"First, we are going to need to do some additional testing to determine what stage the disease is in. If we've caught it early enough, monitoring may be all that's necessary. We are also going to give you some medication to strengthen your bones so you don't fracture your pelvis, and an iron supplement to—"

"And what if the myeloma is at a later stage?" Manu interjects.

"We would consider drug therapy and possibly a stem cell transplant from Arietta's own healthy blood cells to the area that contains the myeloma cells. Radiation or chemotherapy are some additional options. It all depends on how the other tests come back, so we have to wait a few hours to know. I've put your name high on our priority list for an MRI, so your appointment may move up if we have any last-minute cancellations."

"Wait, so you treat a condition that's caused by radiation with more radiation? How does that make sense?"

She turns to Manu. "It's simply one of the ironies of life."

He grunts, dissatisfied that his only daughter's life could be changed forever by irony. The doctor, however, has already moved on.

"Like I said before, we don't know if prenatal radiation exposure caused this, as there isn't enough known about the risk factors for such an early onset of myeloma."

She sets aside her clipboard and pulls on a fresh pair of gloves from a box on her tray. "I know you both must be full of questions. This is a lot to digest at once. So, I'm going to collect some blood for our next round of tests, and you can take a moment to process everything I've said and ask me any questions you think of."

She stands and places a tourniquet around Ari's arm, tying a quick knot around her tense muscles. As she wipes down the inside of Ari's elbow with an alcohol pad, the doctor says, "You don't need to worry— you'll only feel a quick pinch."

"I've never had my blood drawn before," Ari replies.

"Now that's not true." The doctor inserts the needle. "Where do you think we got the blood we tested before?"

Ari grimaces and stays very still as the blood flows into the tube, trying not to gag. "But I wasn't awake for that."

Elodie nods then changes tack. "Let me guess... you're in ninth grade."

"You usually work with younger patients, don't you?"

"What makes you say that?" She taps Ari's tightly clenched fist. "Relax your fist please."

Her fingers uncurl. "We both know that my birthday is written on both of those tubes."

Manu shakes his head. Even a cancer diagnosis can't throw off his daughter's wit.

The corners of the doctor's eyes crinkle from her smile as she swaps out the full tube for an empty one. "Fine, then, smarty pants. What's your favorite subject?"

"I like history," she says, "but Tahitian's my favorite."

"Mmm, lucky you. Maybe you didn't learn this in history class, but when I was in school, they didn't teach us Tahitian."

"Why not?" Ari looks at Manu instead of the needle in her arm, and he shrugs at her.

Dr. Elodie replies, "It was illegal."

"Weird," Ari says with a chuckle.

The doctor wears a patronizing smile that Manu recognizes. It's an expression that says *you have no idea how much things have changed* and *I'm glad you don't have to know* all at the same time. Seconds later, she removes the needle and bandages the site.

"See? Not so bad. Now, I'm also going to need you to give me a urine sample, so I'm going to leave a collection cup in the bathroom. You can push the call button for the nurse when it's ready to be picked up. Before I go, do you have any questions that I can answer for you?"

"Not yet," Manu says. Ari shakes her head weakly.

"Okay. Let us know when you do, and we'll do our best to keep you informed."

"Now what?" Ari asks her father after the doctor leaves. There's a lost look in her eyes and it's breaking Manu's heart.

He picks up his cards. "Play another round?"

• • •

By the time the afternoon is over, Ari's and Manu's fears have been somewhat calmed. Ari's MRI appointment is moved up and, on inspection, no other lesions are found. Several doctors agree the cancer is stage one, and so Ari is sent home after receiving an IV treatment to bolster her bones and iron supplements for the anemia.

While Dr. Elodie has strictly forbidden high-impact activities like dancing and she highly suggested Ari use a wheelchair, it isn't yet necessary for Ari to go on any harsh drugs or undergo radiation to treat the cancer. For that, both father and daughter are thankful.

Her first day back at the house, Nona Alii and Pop Tama arrive with freshly made *i'a ota* and piles of extra coconut cream. "Mmmmm." Ari eats in heaping mouthfuls. "I've missed this. Can I get some more?"

As Nona reaches for the dish, Ari looks down at the lumps of left-over cream on her plate. *Riri, it's important to have siblings.* She shakes her head back and forth, a sense of foreboding building in her gut.

"Are you okay?" Nona pauses, the fish-laden spoon dangling over the ceramic serving dish.

"Papa," Ari looks up, her dark eyes distressed. "When was the last time we ate this?"

He puts his fork down neatly next to his plate. "Actually, it was the night before your accident."

At this, her memories come rushing back—the fight, the angry day at the thinking tree, the short words she'd flung at Natua, the sudden onset of nightfall and rain.

"Sorry, Nona, I've just lost my appetite. I think I need to lie down."

Nona exchanges glances with Manu and Pop, serving spoon held perfectly still.

"Here darling, let me help you to your room," Pop says. "You can use my walking cane."

As the pair shuffle off together, Nona drops the spoon back into the dish and sits, hands folded in an arch over her plate.

"What was that all about?"

"I think she just remembered our dinner on Friday night, but nothing that happened should have bothered her in the first place."

"She obviously disagrees."

He leans forward, speaking low. "I've been thinking about the good I can do in the community, and I want to help care for Angela's boy—you remember him from that night, I'm sure. His mother is unwell and his father long gone, so he and Angela need to know who will step up and be there for him if her health gets worse or, God forbid, something happens to her."

"And Ari doesn't approve of this plan, I take it?"

"No, but I haven't gone through with anything yet— I haven't even talked to the boy's mother yet. I wanted Ari's take on things first."

"Are you still going to go through with it?"

"I don't know. I'm hoping I can get through to her and change her mind about it. They're such close friends, and I'm pretty sure Angela's estranged from her only sibling. He moved to Pape'ete years ago—the boy doesn't even know him."

"I see. Does Ari have feelings of a non-brotherly kind for this boy?"

Manu shakes his head, still in doubt himself. "I asked her that, and she acted like it was the most horrifying thing I ever could've suggested."

"She's a young girl—you can't just say these things outright like that and expect an outright answer. You're her father, not some chum from school she tells her secrets to."

"But I'm only asking because it's relevant!"

Nona unfolds her hands. "Well, you've seen them together. Does she act as though she likes him?"

"I don't know," Manu says. "They flirt, but I don't get the impression there's really anything to it."

"Do you know of any other reasons she could be against it? Maybe something she said that could clue you in?"

"She said she didn't need a new brother."

"Hmm." Nona purses her lips. "What an odd thing to say."

"I know. I think she's afraid of adopting him because of what happened with Henri and her mother."

"Could be. Lashing out because she's scared, maybe."

"That would make sense. I've always believed in heaven, Alii, but no loss ever hit me as hard as Henri's. You're not supposed to outlive your children—and Ari was far too young to experience that kind of grief."

"I know, trust me. I know." She stands and places a hand on his back. Neither one speaks for a minute. Manu considers all the loved ones they've had to say goodbye to far too young.

"When she's feeling a little better—if you want me to—I'll talk to her," Nona promises. "Give her some time. Her whole world just flipped faster than a canoe in a cyclone."

Chapter 4

Over the next few days schoolmates, relatives, and friends flood the Fonuas' home with their food and their sympathies. "We're so relieved they found you and that you're okay," Aunt Wendy says when she brings Ari a cup of hot tea. It's as if everyone has implicitly decided to focus on the accident with the concussion and ignore the very real myeloma diagnosis that followed on its heels.

Ari puts on a brave face and attempts polite conversation, but she spends most of her time in bed avoiding the extended visits and each well-wisher's exhausting good cheer. Part of her withdrawal comes from the Walkman, which Nona Alii left behind after their dinner earlier that week. The tape wasn't harmed, but the player is cracked and she doesn't have the strength to hold it together as it plays. So, she stares at the ceiling and runs through the story in her mind, mouthing the words as she imagines every lilt in Mama's voice.

She doesn't have to deal with the visitors for very long at least. Papa keeps hovering and obsessing over whether she needs more water or help getting up. But company keeps him distracted. The town council has only given him a few days to stay at home because he's so new, and Ari's counting the hours until he's forced to leave her alone. Not like his worrying is going to change anything.

By Friday, the flow of guests slows to a trickle and her father is driving her up the wall. He won't even let her close her bedroom door. After school lets out, Natua stops by. She can smell the crepes he's brought, doubtless from one of the *roulottes* by the dock. The screen door creaks when he walks in. "Hi, Mr. Fonua," he greets her father.

"Good afternoon, Natua."

Ari wonders why the two sound so reserved, then it hits her. She'd convinced Natua that the adoption was her dad's way of insulting his mom. Maybe they'd come to blows while she was out of commission.

"Ari's in her room," her father adds.

"Thanks. I brought some crepes—do you want one?"

"Maybe later. Good luck getting Ari to eat—she hasn't even left her room yet today. And trust me, I've tried everything."

Ari sighs and mentally addresses her father. *At least in here, you aren't staring at my every move while pretending to work on your political crap.*

When Natua comes through her open door, he seems surprised to find her under a blanket so late in the day. Suddenly, she wishes she'd changed her clothes or had Papa open a window. She knows the room smells like it belongs to an invalid, and she's briefly embarrassed.

"Hi." Natua holds the crepes up in front of his nose. "Brought you something."

"Thanks, but I'm not hungry." She turns onto her side. Let him hang onto the sweet-smelling treats.

"I've got your top three favorite kinds," Natua adds. Ari sighs and pulls herself up in bed, her back against the wall.

"You got chocolate hazelnut in there somewhere?"

"Yep." He sounds proud, and he holds out one of the paper-wrapped crepes expectantly.

She accepts and takes a small bite. "Mm. Thank you."

Natua sets the other crepes on the wooden chest and drops his backpack next to them. "So, how are you feeling?"

"I'm okay, just tired. Can you open the window?"

Natua throws it open then sits back on the chest. In the silence that follows, he wrings his hands. "I'm sorry about what happened," he says finally.

"Not your fault," she replies, keeping her responses short and hoping he'll leave soon to go talk to her father like all the other visitors have this week. Though, from the sounds of it, talking to Papa is the last thing Natua wants to do right now.

"Listen." He fiddles with a strap on his backpack and avoids meeting her eyes. "About what we talked about at the tree—"

Ari's fingers find the edges of her bed sheets and rub them nervously. She's afraid to look at him in the silence that follows.

"Can we talk about it some other time?" Her voice is gentle, apologetic. She'd acted rotten towards him that day. And yet he'd come back that night and helped her anyway.

"I just need to know..." he hesitates. He speaks his next words carefully, handling the syllables like bits of broken glass. "Why are you really trying to keep me out of your family?"

Unwelcome tears prick at the corners of her eyes. She wipes them away with closed fists. "You don't wanna be my brother." She tries to sound determined but her voice trembles.

"Why not?"

She looks towards the door and lowers her voice. "Think about it. My brothers are all dead."

Natua scrinches his face up in confusion. "What's this all about, anyway? You think your family is cursed or something?"

Ari shakes her head. "No, it's not like that. I mean, it could be I guess, but I don't think so."

"Then what's wrong?"

"Close the door?" she asks. After it swings closed, she whispers, "I couldn't bear if something happened to you."

"It'll be fine. I'm fine."

"I know, but it's not just about you. My dad..." She closes her eyes and, despite her best efforts, a few tears escape and roll down her cheeks.

Natua gulps. She feels bad for making him squirm, but he's the one that wanted to talk about this.

"My dad is like, trying to replace Henri and Oscar, and it makes me really mad that he thinks he can do that." She opens her eyes, hoping they aren't red.

"I'm sorry," he says. Ari can tell from his quiet tone and the way he refuses to meet her eyes that he's fighting the urge to run from the room. "I didn't mean to pry."

"No, it's okay—you deserved an explanation and an apology. I hadn't sorted out how I felt about it when you showed up at the tree, and then I was so mean."

"Hey, I get it. I don't know what I would've done in your shoes." He heads over to her and gives her a hug. "I'm sure things'll work out either way."

She leans into him. Her next words are muffled because she speaks into his stomach. "What's that?" He pulls back.

"I'm really, really sorry. You think we can just forget it ever happened?"

"Already done." He pats her hair awkwardly then heads back to his spot on the wooden chest. "Anyway, uh, we got our science tests back today."

"How'd you do?" She sniffs and wipes at her face with her hands. She's feeling drained—especially since she didn't tell Natua the whole truth *again.* But no one can know her secret. She's glad Natua isn't going to press her any further.

"Fine, but you did better." He fishes some papers out of the front pocket of his backpack and hands them over.

"I got a 95? No way," Ari says. She attempts a little smirk.

"Yeah way," he replies. "I only got a 77."

"Shoulda paid more attention to the teacher and less to the back of Paulette's head, huh?" There's a brief twinkle in her eyes.

"I can't help it." He shrugs. "She's amazing."

Ari rolls her eyes. "Whatever."

"I also brought you something else." He leans over to dig through the overstuffed backpack.

"Oh god, don't tell me they're going to make me do homework while I'm stuck at home."

"No, no, it's nothing like that. Well, I mean, they are, but that's not what I'm talking about." He pulls out half a roll of duct tape. "When I gave your grandma your tape player, it looked like it was in kinda rough shape. I figured if you had something to hold it together, you might be able to get it to play again."

Ari scooches closer to the foot of the bed so she can take the roll. "Thank you." Her voice is soft and low. She places the duct tape on the bedside table, wedged between the Walkman and her crepe. "I think that'll work."

"Great." Natua flushes, a bit sheepish at the gratitude, and turns his head. "Now, come on, let's go eat on the veranda. Just because the doctor told you not to dance doesn't mean you're chained to a bed."

"I know it doesn't, but getting up makes me really tired."

"You don't have to go to school until you're better, so what difference does it make if you're tired? I also did bring you some homework, so you should at least enjoy what's left of the day before you realize how far behind you are on the French reading."

"Ugh, I don't even want to know."

"Come on, Ari." He gestures towards the door, undoubtedly trying to get into the fresh air on the veranda, away from the stale sweat and sleep that's invaded every corner of her room. The open window didn't really help as much as she hoped.

"All right." She slides her feet to the floor and throws the blanket back, revealing a pair of ratty pajamas.

"I know it's only your veranda, but you really can't go out wearing that," Natua eggs her on. He scoops up the two leftover crepes from their spot on the chest. "I'll close the door behind me so you can put some clean clothes on."

Reluctantly, she agrees, but she's past the point of caring. She's felt numb about everything in the last few days, and she's exhausted from telling Natua most of the reasons she's against the adoption. But she gets dressed anyway for his sake, easing into a pair of cargo pants and a crinkled T-shirt. She grabs the walking cane Pop Tama left for her on Monday before heading out on the veranda.

"See? That wasn't so hard." He speaks around a mouthful of crepe from his spot in a cushioned lawn chair.

"Yeah, yeah," Ari replies and sinks into her father's rocker with a sigh. "Papa says thank you for the crepe, by the way. The egg and ham ones are his favorite."

"Where's yours?"

"Oh, I forgot it in my room."

"Want me to go get it?"

"No, forget it—I'm not that hungry anyway."

"Are you kidding? You don't really have to be hungry to eat one of Mr. Osferaii's crepes. They're too delicious to go to waste."

"Good point," she replies. "If you wanna grab it, feel free to stop by the fridge to get yourself something to drink. We've got coconut milk, water, tea, and maybe some soda in there."

"Thanks." He heads inside and Ari can hear him clattering around in the fridge and looking for glasses.

When he re-emerges onto the veranda, she's staring off into space at the trees outside of the closed-in patio. He clears his throat and motions towards the crepe, which is balanced precariously on top of two glasses of tea.

"Thanks," she mumbles as she grabs the crepe. She nibbles some more and takes a delicate sip of the tea, but she stays silent. Natua takes the hint and looks off into the distance between bites of crepe. They watch wordlessly as the sun disappears behind the trees.

Half an hour later, no-no flies are swarming the porch light. He stands up, crumpling the paper wrapper from his crepe. "I should probably head home. If you need any company when your dad starts flying again or whatever, you know you can always give me a call."

"Thanks."

"Want some help going back into the house?"

"No, I think I'm going to stay here for a little bit."

"Okay. Good night Ari."

"Night, Natua. Thanks for everything."

"Anytime."

She watches him walk down the steps and cross the dirt driveway towards Fare. He turns to look back at her. Even though she knows he can't tell where she's looking, she averts her eyes anyway. She stays there, staring into the darkness, until Papa calls for her frantically. He'd forgotten she was still outside.

•   •   •

"Henri, don't fly today." She tries to step towards the pilot's seat but something is stopping her.

Henri ignores her and continues going through his pre-flight checks.

"Henri, check the radio!" He doesn't look her way, long dark hair falling carelessly over his eyes. In his rush, he forgets to look underneath the radio transmitter, and doesn't notice the loose wires. Somewhere in the engine, a fuel leak is dripping towards doom.

"Stop!" she yells, still unable to move any closer.

He hesitates before pulling the cockpit door closed. "Please, something's wrong!"

He starts the plane and taxies to the end of the small runway.

"Henri, you have to stop! Henri!" Tears spill onto her face.

He turns and stares her down. "You could've stopped this."

"I'm sorry—I didn't know what would happen!"

She can feel the air getting stuffier, can see sparks bursting to life underneath the faulty radio.

"It's still your fault."

The plane is about to erupt into flames when she wakes up, horror and guilt building in her stomach. A plane drones on in the pre-dawn sky overhead.

Later that morning, Ari gets out of bed of her own accord and manages to eat a few orange slices for breakfast. There are dark circles forming under her eyes—the nightmares she thought she had left in the past were back. She hasn't slept a full night even once in the past week. Manu doesn't comment on how poorly the girl must have slept as he cleans up from breakfast. Instead, he acts delighted when she asks for his help going into the yard.

Ari inches her way onto the veranda using Pop Tama's cane. Manu steadies her as they navigate the steps to reach the patchy lawn. They make their way towards the side of the house, where the family burial ground is located.

"I want to stay here for a little while," she says. She's a bit out of breath from exerting herself.

"Do you want me to bring you a chair?"

"I can just sit on the ground—it's no big deal."

"I don't think so. I'll grab a chair."

"Okay."

"Are you steady enough for now? Can I let go?" He gestures down to her arm.

"Yeah, I just needed help with the stairs." She shifts her weight onto the cane.

"Don't fall, please." He rushes back to the veranda and grabs a plastic lawn chair. When he returns, she still hasn't moved.

"See, Papa? I'm fine."

"Good. Here's a chair for you when you get tired." He sets it up just behind her.

"Thanks."

Inside the house, the phone rings. "Sorry, let me go answer that," Manu says.

"Don't worry about me," she replies. "I'd like a few minutes alone anyway."

"I'll check on you in five."

"I'm okay, really. You'd better go answer before they hang up."

Manu kisses her forehead and heads in. She takes a seat and leans the cane against the chair. In front of her is an unassuming headstone for Mama and her baby brother Oscar. The two were buried in the same casket. Henri is next, in Papa's place because he died with no home or family of his own.

"I'm sorry, Henri." Ari addresses her older brother's stone. "I should have done something while I still had the chance. You deserved a better sister."

She turns to her mother's grave marker next. "I wish I was a better daughter—that I honored your memory instead of bringing shame to it. You are a better mother than I ever could have asked for. I'm sorry I failed you and Papa, and I'm sorry I haven't told anyone what really happened that day."

She chokes up. "I just can't bear to know what Papa would think of me, if he knew what kind of person I actually am. If he knew what I let happen to Henri. He blames so many people for what happened—how would he react if he knew it was really all my fault?" Ari covers her face with her hands and leans forward, elbows on her knees. "I'm sorry," she whispers. She cries, her hands clammy in the still, humid morning.

. . .

Manu manages to answer the phone on the fourth ring, expecting another sympathetic call where he says "thank you" and "we're very grateful" a lot, without really knowing how much of it he means. He's surprised to hear Angela's voice on the other end of the line.

"Angela, how great to hear from you! We saw Natua just yesterday and he sent your well wishes."

She asks after Ari and tends to pleasantries, but Angela's voice sounds strained. Manu is expecting the call to end when she says, "Listen, I'm very glad she's okay—Ari's a good kid. But I didn't call to have the same conversation that half the island has already had with you. We have something else to discuss."

"I see," he says without seeing. "Is everything all right? We are incredibly grateful to you and to Natua for helping us track her down—of course, you are both welcome to our home for dinner whenever you wish."

"Oh, Manu, don't worry about that. I'm more concerned about what my son told me earlier this week about your intention to adopt him. I certainly don't appreciate hearing that through the kids when that's something you and I ought to discuss before anyone else. Or did you want the entire island to know before me?"

He's caught by surprise and his throat catches. "Ahem—excuse me—of course I understand that, Angela. I had meant to call you about that the very night Ari went missing, in fact," he says, "so I'm sorry you had to hear it from someone other than me."

"That's funny, because your mother-in-law said you were heading to dinner over there the night she went missing."

"Right," he says. "Sorry, I'm still a little mixed up about everything. I asked Ari about it first because I'd wanted her to be on board before anything else happened. She must have told Natua about it before her accident."

"His name is Ignacio," she responds, her tone edgy. "And I also don't appreciate how you blamed him for getting your daughter into trouble."

"I'm not sure what you're talking about."

"You said it yourself. He could be trouble if I'm not careful. He's too adventurous for his own good."

"Oh, that's not what I meant by that at all—he's a great kid. We both know that."

"*I* know that," she says, "but apparently you only know that when it's convenient for you."

"Please don't take anything I said that night to heart—I was worried sick about my daughter."

"And looking to blame my son?"

"No, no—"

"Yes, it'd be a lot easier for you to ignore the fact that your daughter needs more attention than you give her if you can just blame her problems on my son. What is it that makes him such a lost cause to you, anyway? Ari doesn't have a mother any more than Ignacio has a father, yet you think you have the right to judge my parenting?"

"No, of course not," he replies. "I think that his future—"

"Exactly, you have no right. He's a good, kindhearted kid with a bright future ahead of him. Now tell Ari again that I hope she feels better."

"I wi—"

He's cut short by a dial tone on the other end of the line.

•   •   •

Ari's drying her tears when she feels Nona Alii's warm, wrinkled hand on her shoulder. "I miss them too," Nona says quietly. "I feel Henri's presence on the wind, and I listen for your mother's laughter in the brook behind my house, but it's never enough. No parent should ever live to see their child or their grandchild die."

Ari wipes at her nose with the sleeve of her T-shirt. "It's so hard without them, Nona."

"I know." She crouches next to the chair, a hand on Pop Tama's walking cane. "If your mother were here, she would tell us both not to cry. She would tell you, especially, to enjoy every minute of life that you can."

"That's kinda tough right now, since I can barely even walk. All I can do is think about how much I miss them."

"I miss them too, but don't let that pain steal what happiness life still holds—it won't make anything better, including your health. You're a strong young girl, and we are all here for you." She stops, then adds, "I'm here for you."

"Can you tell me what Mama was like when she was a teenager?"

Nona smiles. "She was a hell-raiser, that's for sure. She started running around with your father behind my back when she was just a slip of a thing, barely older than you are now."

Ari giggles. "Why did she sneak around? I thought you liked Papa."

"Oh, I do... now. But your father was a reckless young man. His plan back then was to join the military and fight his way into earning a living on the mainland—back before the *métropole* chewed him up and spit him back out on island shores. He never planned on coming home. No mother in her right mind would want her baby girl to go off alone, only to end up a widow because of someone else's wars."

"But we're a part of France, Nona."

"Yes, but their fights are not the same as our fights. You'll see that someday."

"Right." Ari's not sure she will.

"Life doesn't always work out the way we expect it, baby girl," Nona continues. Ari feels her grandmother's eyes on her. "I never thought I would lose my precious Amy so young, and I certainly never expected to end up being such great friends with your father."

"I'm glad you did though," Ari says. "Become friends with Papa, I mean."

"Me too, sweetie. Me too." Nona looks towards the gravestones. "You can't spend your whole life looking back—Henri understood that after your mother's passing. We honor them by moving on, no matter how scared we are to keep going without them. Henri had a lot of your father's bravery in him. A lot of his recklessness, too."

Ari's eyes are red when she meets Nona's gaze. "But I'm afraid to forget about them."

"No one ever said to forget about them. Henri never forgot your mother, and your father holds onto both of them—and Oscar—in his heart. But you can't spend your days pining away for something you will never have." Nona shifts a bit.

"I know."

"Is that what bothered you about your dad adopting the boy from the village?"

"Nona, I don't want to talk about that right now." She eases out of her chair, annoyed that even this simple task has become a challenge. "Did Papa send you out here to soften me up about that?"

"Don't be silly, my dear. We both just want to be here for you. There's no need to get worked up."

"Ugh! He did put you up to it, didn't he?" She grabs the cane and huffs. "I'm sick, and all Papa can think about is trying to fill the hole Henri left behind." She attempts to storm off, sighing when she reaches the veranda steps.

Nona is right behind her with a steadying arm. "I didn't mean to upset you, you know."

"Yeah, I know. I just don't understand why Papa thinks that Natua can just replace the sons he lost. It doesn't work that way."

"I don't think that's what he's trying to do."

"He can say whatever he wants, but I don't buy it. I get it, no parent should have to live through their kid dying." She pauses on the second step, already out of breath. "But he shouldn't pretend any old kid on the island can replace Henri."

"I really don't think that's what he's doing, okay?—Careful on this step."

"I'm serious, Nona. When he said he wanted to grow our family, I asked him if he meant dating, and he acted like he couldn't replace Mama, but Henri was a different story."

"Your father is trying to help someone he knows you're close to. He will always miss Henri, and he knows no one will ever replace him. He's only hoping he can make a positive difference for the people still living on this island."

Ari grunts out a dissatisfied *hmph*.

"I would've done the same, if your mother had died so young like that." Nona's voice is gentle as she continues, "But I didn't have to, because she left me with two precious grandchildren to help raise. Now let's get you inside."

. . .

Later that morning, after Alii leaves to grab some necessities Manu needs from the market, Ari's classmate Etienne knocks on the screen door. Manu calls for her to come in.

"How are you, Ettie?"

"I'm fine, Mr. Fonua, thanks. How's Ari doing today?"

He doesn't want the girl to be offended in case Ari refuses to see her—Ari was still upset last time he checked on her. "She's really tuckered out by all of the company and she's still recovering, but you're welcome to visit." Ettie nods. "Let me head in first to see if she's awake."

"Of course," she replies. Her ashy blonde hair is piled precariously on top of her head and it wiggles as she talks.

"You can take a seat at the countertop." He gestures towards the barstool he's been using to work from home. "Sorry about the mess."

"Oh, it's fine! I'm not here to pick on your house." Her voice is warm and clear.

Manu raps on the closed bedroom door with his knuckles. "Hey honey, can I come in?" He waits a second then heads inside to find Ari huddled under the blankets, tired from the trip out to the backyard but still awake. "Riri," he says. "You've got company."

"Send them away," she says. "And please stop calling me that."

He sighs. At least she isn't yelling at him. "Are you sure? It's Ettie—I thought you two were close."

"Yeah... fine." She exhales, blowing a few stray hairs out of her face. "Give me a few minutes and I'll be out. I'll meet her on the veranda."

"Okay." He backs out of the room and closes the door. To Ettie, he says, "Would you like something to drink? I've got some soda in the fridge."

"Sure, sounds wonderful!"

He hands her a chilled can. "Why don't you head out onto the veranda? Ari will be right out."

"Is she okay? If it's a bad time, I can come back later."

"No, no, you're perfectly all right. She could use the fresh air and the company," he says. He doesn't mention that Ari's refused to see almost anyone for more than five minutes the entire time she's been home aside from Natua. The boy brought her a crepe and some duct tape—not to mention a week's worth of homework. They barely even spoke. Yet somehow, he did more for her spirits than anyone else.

. . .

Father and daughter pass a quiet dry season together, settling into a new rhythm and religiously avoiding the topic of adoptions. Manu goes back to work at both the town hall and the airport, conducting surveys about snacks at youth cricket games and having flashbacks every time he sees the runway that claimed Henri's life. He and Ari return to the hospital monthly for additional IV treatments and testing—a time-consuming process that drains both of them.

Although worries about Ari fracturing her pelvic bone or the disease progressing never leave the back of his mind, Manu beats back the anxiety and instead chooses to celebrate every step of her gradual recovery. Within a few weeks of coming home, she gives up using Tama's walking cane completely and goes back to school. By the start of the wet season in November, she's even allowed to take up dancing again, though the doctor at the clinic continues to bar her from watersports.

During this time, Manu is slowly asked to do more and more for the municipal council. He drafts all three of his proposals for how the new safety department should be organized in hospital waiting rooms.

He also becomes increasingly concerned about Ari's nightmares, which are happening almost every night. Between a few of his regular flights to Pape'ete, he talks it over with his old friend Oriata, who's been the airport groundskeeper for as long as Manu can remember.

"I don't understand it," Manu tells the man as they inspect the edge of the airport's sole runway together. "She had a few bad dreams right after Henri's crash. We both did. It was an awfully traumatic thing for anyone to deal with, and she was so young and so close to her brother. But she hasn't had them like this for years."

Oriata bends down to stroke the grass. "After the crash, the grass at that end of the runway was scorched for a full season. But you know what was funny? The rest of the grass started to flag after a while too. I spent weeks trying to coax it along with different things. It hadn't experienced any of the side effects of the crash directly, and I couldn't figure out what was wrong."

"How did you bring it back to life?"

"It might have had something to do with the heat from the explosion or maybe a change in the soil conditions, but I never quite figured it out." He stands back up and breathes in the salty ocean air. "The only thing that fixed it was time. Once the scorched grass had been replanted and taken root, the rest of it slowly turned around on its own."

"Time... we've had plenty of it, but it never seems to be enough."

"Some pain never goes away," Oriata agrees.

"But Ari needs to make her peace with things somehow, Ori. If she isn't able to rest well, I don't know how she'll be able to fight this disease."

"That is a problem. Have you tried giving her herbal teas before bed?"

"Yes, of course. She falls asleep perfectly fine, but she's screaming herself awake within a couple of hours." He yawns. "And she's not the only one waking up for it, trust me."

"Mmm." Ori falls into silence, no doubt thinking about the day of the crash. Henri was a precocious young pilot. In fact, he was probably the youngest pilot the airport has ever employed, before or since. A large part of that was because of Manu. The boy would come to work with his father when Manu was running postal shipments, and the girl would occasionally do the same with her brother. There was a running joke among the flight crew that the boy knew how to fly before he could even walk.

"It could be guilt that she lived and he didn't. The day of the crash, I found her playing in the cockpit unsupervised." Ori tells Manu how upset she'd been when he sent her home for violating the rules.

"I didn't realize she was going to ride with him that day—Henri didn't tell me he was going to take her, and he always mentioned it before letting her go with him."

"Maybe he hadn't invited her," Ori suggests.

Manu lowers his gaze to the grass, now lush and healthy beneath his feet, before he responds. "Ari and Henri became very close after Amy passed. Ari probably guessed that if she showed up out of the blue, Henri would cave and let her tag along." He shudders at the realization he nearly lost both of his children in a single day. "Thank God you sent her away."

"Yes, thank the gods indeed."

At this, Manu nods slightly. "Thank the gods," Manu repeats, eyes travelling over the vast and empty northern horizon.

. . .

Ari's nightmares and diseased bones leave her exhausted all hours of the day, and Manu frequently entertains her visitors while she's napping. It would be far too rude to turn them all away. Besides, he needs as many distractions as he can find, and this is the best way to fill the empty hours between his work schedules.

It's pouring rain one solitary Sunday afternoon when there's a knock on the door. "Come on in," Manu calls. He's expecting to entertain yet another one of Ari's snorkeling girlfriends for an hour or two until she wakes up from her nap with a wild look in her eyes and Henri's name on her lips.

Instead, Natua walks in, hair and clothes *drip dripping* on the scuffed floor. "Do you have a towel?" he asks, avoiding Manu's eyes. The boy has more or less kept his distance from Manu ever since Ari fell sick, though he's constantly walking Ari home from school and trying to cheer her up.

"Of course." Manu gets up and grabs a clean towel from the chifforobe next to the bathroom. "Can I get you a cup of tea to warm you up?"

"No, no, I'm fine," Natua says. "I just stopped by to see how Ari's doing today."

Manu points his chin towards her bedroom. "She's sleeping right now, but you're welcome to stay for a while. She'll probably wake up within the hour."

The boy takes a look outside. The rain has intensified and the clouds are turning dark.

"Okay," he says reluctantly. As he's toweling himself off, Manu sees a shiver run down his spine.

"Here, let me warm some water for a couple of cups of tea. Or would you prefer a cup of coffee?"

"If you're having tea, then that's fine."

"I'll drink whichever you prefer."

"I don't really care."

"Tea it is, then." Manu busies himself with the kettle and the mugs so he doesn't have to admit he feels as awkward as the child does.

When the drinks are ready, the two sit across from each other at the tiny kitchen table and fiddle with their tea, avoiding conversation for as long as they can. But eventually, all milk has been added and all sugar stirred in.

Manu decides that since this discomfort is, in a way, his fault, he should be the one that dispels it. "Ari is lucky to have a friend like you," he starts off. He blows on his tea and takes a small sip. "I appreciate how much you've been there for her."

Natua shrugs. "That's just what you do for your friends."

Manu waits until the boy meets his eyes before he says, "I miss teaching you two the dances. You are probably the only person who ever could've gotten Ari to take it seriously."

In spite of himself, Natua giggles. "Come on, she doesn't take it seriously at all and you know that."

"Oh, that's not true. She puts on quite the show about not caring, but she was practicing a lot before she fell ill." His smile fades at the memory. "She wanted to show you up or at least stop giving you ammo to tease her with."

"Well, she's got a long way to go for that," Natua replies. The boy fights back a smile as he struggles to remain cool and detached.

"She most certainly does."

The two fall into another uncomfortable silence. Manu stirs his tea absent-mindedly as he thinks through what he wants to say next.

"Natua, listen, I'm glad we have a moment to talk, just the two of us. I don't know exactly what Ari told you before her accident, but I never meant to offend you or your mother." The boy is staring into his mug as Manu continues. "I only wanted to help you—you're such a promising young lad. I'd hate to see that promise wasted because you have to drop out of school to make ends meet."

Natua still doesn't meet Manu's gaze, but he swallows a lump in his throat and nods.

"My mom does all that needs to be done," he says. There's a hint of defiance in his voice.

"Yes, she does. I admire her for that—I know firsthand how hard it is to raise a child alone. I can't imagine handling everything she does while being so sick."

"It's just emphysema. It's under control."

Manu's voice is impossibly soft and gentle. "But for how long?" He gestures towards Ari's bedroom with his open hand. "Illnesses wreak their havoc whether we're ready for them or not."

Natua shrugs again, and there's a cough from Ari's room. "Thanks for the tea," he says. "I'm going to go see if she's awake now."

. . .

Just before the council disbands for Christmas holidays, Ari's doctor informs them that Ari's bones are almost completely normal, and testing shows the disease itself has gone into remission only five months after its discovery.

"Hey, that's great!" Manu grins.

The doctor cautiously agrees. "With this type of cancer, you do still need to follow a healthy lifestyle and come back regularly for testing. Remission is not the same as a cure. Though it is wonderful news, you both need to be aware that the cancer can return at any time. That is why monitoring is so important."

Despite the doctor's ambivalence, the pair are relieved and look forward to having extra time at home over the holidays. Manu splurges on a fancy dinner in 'Uturoa, and the two head home in jolly spirits. The next weekend, Nona Alii and Pop Tama throw a party to celebrate, with chicken, three kinds of fish, and fruits and vegetables galore.

Neither Ari nor Manu spoils the festivities with any mention of the doctor's warnings. They've tacitly agreed that today is a day to be happy, and both father and daughter are ready to throw themselves into the emotion after so many trying months.

. . .

One unseasonably cool Saturday afternoon towards the end of the wet season in March, Manu hears Ari pad through the house much slower than usual. He's wondering if, God forbid, she's already having some sort of relapse. He's researched the disease and quizzed her doctors half to death, and no one can give him an answer he likes about how long remission will last.

He has a vision of his daughter celebrating birthdays in the hospital, of never being able to see far enough in the future to live outside the shadow of myeloma. She's always loved being in the water. She talked for weeks about the problems facing the ocean after doing a unit about it in her science class last year. What if his baby girl is never healthy enough to surf or dive again?

He knows that would kill her long before the disease could finish her off, and he's fighting back tears when she walks onto the veranda with a full bowl of soup. He grins and blinks away his wet eyes the best he can. *Don't stress over problems before they even exist.*

Except for moments like this one, life is back to normal. Natua has gotten into the habit of walking Ari home from school every day, but Ari doesn't need the assistance anymore. Many days, he stays at the Fonua house until evening falls. The kids practice their dance routine on the lawn. On dry, clear days, they even head up to the docks north of the village to fish.

Manu senses that the boy is no longer angry with him over the adoption issue. The boy continues to be reserved around him, but Manu doesn't blame him. Angela's illness is a ticking time bomb, and no one knows when the countdown will reach zero. Manu understands that he's probably an unwelcome reminder of that none-too-pleasant truth, so he avoids asking too often after Angela's health.

Angela, who didn't speak to Manu for over a month after their tense call, has started phoning again as well. At first, she was looking for more detailed updates on Ari's health than the "okay" that Ignacio provided, but gradually her and Manu's stilted conversations gave way to more comfortable chitchat. After Ari went into remission, he'd expected the calls to stop, but the weeks go by and she continues calling.

Manu is happy that their friendship is on the mend but doesn't mention anything about the adoption. He'd said what needed to be said to the boy, and from the friendly tone Angela strikes in their conversations, he knows Natua has spoken to her about it as well. Manu considers the issue closed—he's better off only caring for one child anyway.

Once he and Angela are back on truly good terms, he asks if she and Ignacio are ready to take up that dinner invitation he had extended so long ago. To his delight, she invites him to come to her home and offers to make her famous *uru* dish.

The dinner is going smoothly and the kids are talking about a new school project when Angela stands and clears her throat.

Manu sees Ignacio's eyes cloud over. His easy grin evaporates like a puddle on a hot sidewalk.

"I have an announcement to make. I hate to darken such a nice evening, but there's something Ignacio and I need to say." Angela pauses for a moment and fingers one of her necklaces. It's a simple black key hanging from a silver chain. Manu recognizes it—her mother had left it to her in her will, along with some sort of riddle nobody could solve.

"The pension has been a part of my life for as long as I can remember, and I've never wanted that to change. But life doesn't always work that way. We've been losing traffic to the bigger resorts for years, and my health just isn't what it used to be." She coughs into a napkin, almost as if for effect, then continues. "We've decided that it's time to close the pension."

Manu's shock registers in an involuntary gasp. "Are you sure there's no other way?"

She nods. Her glassy eyes reflect the low light from sconces lining the tiny dining room in the back of the pension. The business may be closing, but she still refuses to use the guest dining area for personal affairs. Some habits are just too hard to break.

"I can't do it alone, and I've already had to let our chef and groundskeeper go because of business. It wasn't an easy decision," she says, dabbing her eyes, "but it had to be made."

"We're so sorry, Angela."

"What are you going to do now?" Ari asks from the other end of the table. Manu shoots her a look for such an insensitive question, but she only shrugs her shoulders at him.

"I'll be eligible for a disability pension through the government, and in a few years, Ignacio will be out of school and able to work. We'll be fine."

"That must have been an incredibly tough choice," Manu acknowledges.

"Yes, it was," she says. "But there was one more tough choice that I needed to make." She sits back down and puts her hands in her lap, as if unsure what to do with them.

"Back in June, when I heard you wanted to adopt my son, I was furious. I thought you were trying to say I was a bad mother. But now, I see things differently."

Ignacio motions for her to go on, his eyes moist. He doesn't speak. His mother continues, "If you are still open to it, we would be very happy if you adopted Ignacio."

In spite of his newfound reluctance to take on any extra responsibilities, Manu hears himself saying yes.

PART II: SIX YEARS LATER

Chapter 5

"*Ia or'ana*," Ari says from her spot behind the counter of the airport's tourism booth. She repeats the greeting in French and English. Then, she hands the woman and her husband a pamphlet about Huahine's historical landmarks.

The couple are dazed from their long flight but the woman snatches the pamphlet. "You speak such good French!" she exclaims.

"Yes, that's because I am a citizen of France," Ari responds. She reaches back to re-do her ponytail, hoping the motion will hide her annoyance. It needs to be fixed anyway—Ari recently decided to cut her hair to her shoulders, but the style makes it that much harder to tame.

"Then how in the world did you end up in a paradise like this?" the woman asks, gesturing behind her, where a wall of windows highlights the ocean view.

Ari sighs. "We are in French Polynesia...?" Her voice rises in pitch, and she raises her eyebrows ever so slightly.

"Well, there's no need to be rude. Come on, Bert, grab the bags, would you?" She stalks off, high heels clicking to announce her every move.

Ari watches them head towards the exit. No doubt their prearranged taxi is waiting to pick them up and take them to their air-conditioned hotel as quickly as possible, while the lady and her husband complain about how hot it is.

She'd begun working the booth during her last year of high school at Papa's suggestion. He thought it would be nice to go to work together on Thursday afternoons—him to take a business flight and her to work the booth. And it was nice, for a while. Two years later, Ari can't stand dealing with tourists, though the occasional surfer boy stops by and makes her laugh.

Her dream is to study ecology at the University of French Polynesia, but with her father's election campaign to the General Assembly just completed, he needs help recouping some campaign costs first. In exchange, he promised to pay for her apartment and registration fees at university.

As she talks another particularly airheaded couple through how to find the taxi waiting for them less than twenty meters away, she daydreams about what she could do with a degree. She imagines figuring out how to clear the garbage patches growing in the far reaches of the Pacific or diving in the ocean every day to examine endangered reefs, waterproof notebook and pencil in hand. Her first genuine smile of the day blossoms on her face as the last passengers filter outside.

A few minutes later, her father strides through the lobby, briefcase in hand. He looks distracted, doubtless thinking about the bill he's been drafting to address needed nuclear cleanups. He hadn't cared quite as much about the Municipal Council, but he seems to enjoy the larger scale of the Assembly. *And the nice restaurants in Pape'ete too,* she thinks as she notices how much rounder his belly has become lately.

During dinner last night, he kept talking about what a difference his safety department idea all those years ago had made on the island.

"What happened to Henri will never happen again," he said. "We've actually legislated that kind of carelessness out of the airport."

"That's great," she'd replied, unease gripping her stomach.

"Those French officials they send our way every now and then might not care about the safety of our people, but our internal guys do a phenomenal job now at keeping those planes up to date. And since that's taken care of, I have bigger fish to catch."

He paused to savor a cool sip of wine. "I don't know how officials let all the violations slip that ended up taking my poor boy's plane down—or who was crazy enough to leave exposed wiring in a cockpit—but it won't ever happen again."

She nodded, unsure of what to say. This was the thousandth time they'd had this conversation, and it was still putting knots in her stomach. And, like always, Papa was too absorbed in his success story to notice.

. . .

Manu heads outside for lunch after returning from another island, recapping the particularly productive meeting he had this morning with several fellow Assemblymembers. Before the clock even strikes noon on this blistering Saturday, the tarmac is so hot his shoes are in danger of melting to it.

He ignores the exhaustion spinning a headache behind his temples and sits down in the sparse grass, taking a swig of lukewarm water from an insulated thermos and wiping the sweat from his forehead. It's a tough job, but he's satisfied with it now that he's seen the difference politics can make in the lives of his people. In the life of his family.

As he munches on his chicken sandwich, he looks off in the distance. The heat is shimmering in the air over the tarmac. Just like it had that day, after the fire reached the fuel tank. His breath catches in his throat, and he coughs on a bit of bread.

Most people would have left the airport far behind after what happened. But not Manu. The runway may hit him like a truckload of bricks every time he travels, but he hesitates to transition to lengthy boat trips and move completely past the airport.

And look at all of the good that has come of it—there's a focus on safety and inspections from the local government that most islanders never imagined possible. There are fewer accidents. People's lives are being saved. This is what he's supposed to do.

. . .

"Ari, can you refill the watersports and hiking pamphlets? There are boxes for each in the storage closet." Irene's voice carries all the way from her office in the back, where she runs a small travel agency and takes care of the business's bookkeeping. She mostly handles hotel bookings for local politicians like her father, though there's also the occasional tourist who shows up without an itinerary.

Ari ducks behind the curtain separating the so-called "back" from the rest of the booth. The knack Irene has for knowing exactly what needs to be done is uncanny. She doesn't even look and yet somehow, she's always right.

The storage closet smells like glossy paper and makes Ari want to sneeze. She grabs the boxes on top, hoping they're the right ones as she hefts them out to the booth.

She drops them on the floor and a few pamphlets flutter to the ground... for hotels in Pape'ete. Both boxes are stuffed with the same pamphlet. "Crap," she says, hoisting the boxes back up and turning around.

As she twists, her shoe catches the edge of one of the pamphlets and her feet go flying out from under her. "Ouf!" Papers scatter everywhere and the boxes land on top of her with a *flump.*

"Are you okay?" She can hear Irene shuffling out of her office.

"I think so," Ari calls. She tries to roll onto her side, but a searing pain rips through her right leg and she cries out.

Irene emerges from behind the curtain and takes in the mess through coke-bottle glasses with bright red frames. "Ari, are you all right?"

"I don't know," she says, a note of panic creeping into her voice. "My knee really hurts."

"You look okay—maybe you just bruised it. Here, let me help you up. Take my hand."

"Aaooo!" Ari lets go and sinks back to the floor.

"Could you have sprained it in the fall?"

"I don't know. Listen, can you go outside and get my dad? He came in on the 11:45. I think he's having lunch on the lawn."

"Are you sure? I feel like I shouldn't leave you alone."

"We're in the middle of an airport and somebody propped the doors open again. Just go. Please."

Irene nods and speed walks to the front. She's not even running, but Ari can hear her panting already. Her many baubles jangle as she rushes through the entrance and yells as she nearly bumps into her father, who was already rushing in.

In an instant, he's crouching next to her, asking where it hurts.

"Papa, something's wrong with my knee." She points at it. There's no blood or obvious break visible through her khaki clam diggers.

"Can you bend it?"

"I don't know." She tries, but tears spring to her eyes. "No."

"Irene, can you call a doctor?" The woman disappears behind the curtain as Manu turns back to his daughter. "How about your foot? Can you move it?"

She wiggles it back and forth, but before her father can move on to the next test, she whimpers, "Papa." He stops and looks into her eyes. "It feels like my stomach felt, before..."

The vein in Papa's neck pulses slightly, but his voice stays calm. "We are going to call the doctor, and he's going to figure out what's going on, okay? But don't go there—it's useless to get yourself worked up over something like that. We don't even know what's going on."

She nods and steels herself against the injury. "Fine."

"Hey, at least it won't take long for you to get to the transport plane." Manu chuckles.

"Not like last time," Ari replies, wishing he wasn't trying so hard to lighten the mood.

"Try to relax. Those boxes look heavy, so I'm sure it has nothing to do with any of that. Just put it out of your head."

The myeloma has been in remission for almost six years. Ari hopes with all of her being that her time hasn't run out.

· · ·

Ari isn't checked into the hospital on Ra'iatea until the middle of the night, and a scan reveals a fracture across her right knee cap. The doctor applies a stint and a nurse collects several vials of blood before Ari ends up in a room.

She swears it's the same room she had when she knocked her head, but Manu's determined they were on the other side of the courtyard. They debate for over an hour on the topic as they try to distract themselves from the bigger question hanging in the air.

"The nurse's station was just outside the room on the left," Manu says. "I must have passed it a hundred times. There's no nurse's station on this side."

"And I know that the courtyard opened up to the right from my spot in the bed. All these rooms are set up the same—it had to have been over here. Just look out the window."

"Come on, they can change which way the beds face any day and then it would open on the right over here instead of the left," Manu replies.

"They barely have enough staff here to take care of the patients, and you think they're wasting time arranging furniture?"

The adrenaline rush from the afternoon is long gone, and Ari's eyes are drooping despite the banter. Manu pats her hand.

"You should get some rest."

"I want to be up when the tests come back," she mumbles. "I don't wanna be left out of the loop."

"I'll nudge you," he promises. "They probably won't come until morning anyway. Now go to sleep if you can."

A few minutes later, both of them have drifted off, their fears temporarily bested by exhaustion.

• • •

"You're going to have to undergo drug therapy, I'm afraid." The doctor who comes by the next morning flips through her chart as he talks. He has dark hair and deep brown eyes. Ari would have normally registered his looks as quite attractive despite his short height, but right now, she's too busy fighting the panic rising in her stomach.

It's not worth getting so upset over. The myeloma can't be undone, but at least it can be treated.

"When do I start that?" she blurts out. She's not sure she wants to know what kinds of drugs they will need to put in her body to help her recover.

"The treatment I'm recommending for you will need to be shipped in from the mainland—I've checked every hospital in the islands, and no one has it in their stocks right now. So, treatment will begin as soon as they arrive."

"How long should that take?"

"I sent the order out this morning, so they should be here within a week or two at the absolute latest."

Ari looks to her father to see if Papa has any questions of his own. He catches her eye and she nods.

"I'm presuming we aren't considering radiation for an option, then. Are these chemotherapy drugs?"

"Yes, they could be considered that. However, it's not an IV treatment—these medications are both oral pills that can be taken at home."

"That's good. How long will she have to take them?"

"That will depend on how Arietta responds to the dosages—she will need to take them until either the myeloma goes back into remission or they stop working and we switch them up."

The doctor turns to face Ari. "The drugs will come and go in cycles. You will take them for three weeks, then take a week off before starting again."

Ari tries to keep her voice steady as she asks, "Am I going to die?"

Without taking his eyes off of the doctor, Manu folds his daughter's hands into his.

"People with myeloma at this stage usually have a prognosis of three to five years," the doctor replies. "But, most people with myeloma are two or three times your age. You're very young and much healthier than a typical myeloma patient. Those are the biggest allies you can have against this illness.

"Starting you on treatments as soon as the drugs arrive will help you get the best outcome, but don't worry too much in the meantime. Stress is like an anchor. We might need some to keep us in place, but too much could sink us."

He sets down his clipboard and extends his hand for a handshake. "It's tough but think of it this way—the more time you spend worrying over survival rates and the like, the more energy you're wasting on something you can't control. All you're doing is robbing yourself of a chance to be happy."

She shakes his hand. "Good advice," she mumbles, though she doubts she'll be able to heed it.

"We'll call to set up your next appointment as soon as the lenalidomide comes in," the doctor says.

"Are there any natural remedies that she can try in the meantime?" Manu asks.

"Well, nothing that has been confirmed by enough studies for me to officially recommend. However, there has been promising results from patients who take turmeric. It won't cause any harm if you're interested in trying it."

"Would I have to get that here?"

"You can if you'd like, but you should also be able to get it from your primary care doctor or the chemist's. It doesn't require a prescription."

Manu looks to his daughter. "Is that something you would want to do?"

She shrugs. "If I have to wait for the other stuff to come in anyway, then yeah. Let's do it."

Ari boards the boat home with her father a few hours later, supplement bottles and information packets in her lap. There won't be any celebratory dinners tonight, but she's glad to get away from the sterile hospital hallways and sympathetic doctors bearing bad news. She breathes in the salty air, eyes closed against the bright ocean glare as the doctor's voice repeats in her head... *Stress is like an anchor. Too much will sink us.*

• • •

An array of friends and family stop by over the next few days to wish Ari well and offer their support. Natua, who works for the bakery delivering everyone's morning bread, stops by each morning on his way through. He changes up his route so that their house is last and he can have breakfast with them once his day is done. Even being the last house, Natua arrives by 6:30.

"It's almost too early to operate a wheelchair," Ari jokes each morning when he arrives.

"Almost, but not quite," he shoots back. "Now let's eat! The bread's still nice and warm."

They gather around the small kitchen table, which Manu has pulled away from the wall to accommodate the space Ari needs in the wheelchair.

"Do they really let you wear that thing to work?" Ari points at his red FIFA jersey.

"Temata doesn't care. Chances are nobody'll even see me in it."

"Yeah, because most people have the sense to stay in bed until a decent hour."

He shrugs. "The rest of us have the best breakfast and the best work uniforms." Angela had given him the jersey for his last birthday and he's worn it nearly nonstop ever since.

"Do you even have any other clothes?" She gestures at the jersey. He's worn it three times in the past week alone.

"Hey, these are Spain's colors! Gotta represent."

Ari rolls her eyes. "Right. How 'bout you represent the bakery and pass me some of that bread?"

. . .

After dinner with Manu and her grandparents a few nights later, when most visitors have already come and gone for the day, Ari hears a knock at the door with the telltale sound of bangles ringing in the night.

"Come on in," she says, wheeling over to the door from her spot by the couch.

Irene opens the door and bends to give her a hug. "How are you doing?"

Surprised by the display of warmth, Ari gradually raises her arms and hugs her boss back. "I'm doing as good as I can," she says as Irene releases her, "though I'm really tired of being stuck in wheel chairs and crutches."

"Oh, I'm sure. I broke my ankle a week before my first wedding and let me tell you what, that was the pits!"

"Yeah, sounds like pretty bad timing," Ari agrees, wondering how many more weddings Irene had—for all of her jewelry, she doesn't wear a wedding ring. Ari turns her chair towards her family and introduces Nona and Pop to Irene.

"Wonderful to meet you both," Irene says, "and it's always good to see you, Manu."

She's carrying a red and white striped tote bag, which she plops on the floor. "Listen," she says, "I feel real bad about what happened." She roots around in the cluttered bag.

"It wasn't anyone's fault," Ari says. "That would have happened to me anywhere."

"I know," she says, standing back up with a few papers. "But it happened on my watch."

She offers Ari the crumpled pages. "When you get better, I want to do something for you. I can tell by the way you hoard the international pamphlets that you're curious about the world."

Ari's eyes widen as she reads through the sheets. "Irene, you can't do this—"

"Nonsense! I'm a travel agent, and you work for me. Not only can I get you discounted flights, but I can write them off later as a work expense. So, when you're better, you pick a spot on the map and I'll book you a flight there, no questions asked."

"Really?"

"Of course! It might have to be last minute, but you have a boss who's willing to give you a couple of weeks off on short notice." She winks.

"Papa, did you hear that?"

He gets up and walks over to shake Irene's hand. "You don't have to do that, Irene—you're a great friend."

"Oh, don't be silly," she says, "It's the least I can do."

"Have you eaten yet? We just finished dinner, so I could fix you a plate," Manu offers.

"I shouldn't, but it smells absolutely delicious in here! I simply have to try it."

. . .

Excitement over Irene's offer takes a backseat over the next two weeks, as Ari waits less and less patiently for the hospital's call. Every time she gets worked up, she closes her eyes and takes three deep breaths to calm herself down. When that stops working, she ups it to five deep breaths, then seven, then ten. *Stress is an anchor.*

When the deep breathing isn't enough, she thinks of meditation exercises and curses her banged up knee. She works on arm and shoulder stretches, then takes out an old ukulele she hasn't touched in years and practices the few traditional songs she still remembers how to play.

The wheelchair Manu had brought home for her is a bit too wide for the house, and she keeps knocking into the narrow doorways. As the days come and go, her nerves tighten further and further until they are a coiled spring. *Stress is an anchor. Can't let it get me down. Stress is an anchor.*

One Tuesday when she's about to burst, the phone rings.

"Hello? ... Yes, that's me—who's this? ... I see."

She fiddles with a pencil as she listens.

"What do you mean, delayed? It was supposed to be here a week ago and I need it now... I don't care if your plane was held up. Send it on a different plane! You know how many flights come here from the mainland every damn day?"

"You've got to be kidding me," she says after she hangs up the phone. She slumps back in the wheelchair and then gets hit by a wave of guilt. It wasn't the man on the phone's fault that her medicine was delayed. *What is wrong with me?*

After giving herself a minute to calm down—and take her turmeric for the day—she realizes that she didn't even give the man a chance to explain or tell her when the drugs would arrive. Ari groans. Hopefully she can track him down again and find out. She dials the hospital's number and goes through a maze of automated options before connecting to a motherly-sounding woman with a warm voice.

"You want to know what?" she asks. "Who did you say you were?"

After 10 minutes, the woman determines she can't help Ari, so she transfers her over to a different department.

"Hello, this is Georges," a man's voice says, interrupting the jazz solo that was playing for her on hold.

Thank god, the same guy as before!

"Hi, my name is Arietta Fonua, and someone called me earlier to let me know the medicines my doctor ordered have been delayed."

"Yes," the man replies wearily. "How can I help you?"

"Well first, I wanted to say I'm sorry, because I was rude before," she says. "Now that I've had a chance to calm down, I realize it wasn't cool of me to take that out on you."

There's continued silence on the other end of the line, so she keeps going. "And I was also wondering if you could tell me when I can expect the medicines to arrive?"

"Let me see," Georges says, typing away with barely an acknowledgement of her apology. "I don't have a date in my system yet, but it depends on why the shipment was delayed."

"I thought you said the plane was held up."

"The shipment was held up," he corrects her. "I'm not sure why—sometimes it's due to an item that's out of stock from our primary supplier, sometimes it's because the shipping manifest doesn't match the order."

"Can you find out why for me?" she asks, doing her best to keep her attitude friendly.

"I'm working on it," he says. She can hear him typing some more, and then he says, "Can I put you on hold? I need to check with my supervisor on something."

"Uh, okay." She stares at the clock above the memo board, its tiniest hand smoothly counting away the seconds as she listens through the rest of that jazz solo. After five minutes, she's done her deep breathing exercise four times. She's working through it a fifth time when the line gets picked up by a different man with a deeper voice.

"Hello, Ms. Fonua?"

"Yes, hello?"

"We've determined that this medicine was delayed because it was back ordered by our primary supplier. Someone has already contacted our secondary supplier right now to get things rolling with them."

"So when will they get here?"

"I'm truly sorry for the delay. Assuming they have it in supply—and they should—we're looking at about two weeks."

"Oh." She tries to hide her disappointment. "That long?"

"Again, I'm so sorry for this delay. The particular treatment your doctor ordered isn't one we use very often, but we are working on getting it as fast as we can."

"Okay." She takes another deep breath for good measure. "Thank you for your time and have a nice day."

As she hangs up the phone, her hands are shaking. *Stress is just an anchor.*

Chapter 6

Now that the waiting game has restarted, Ari and her father distract themselves by talking about where they would like to go.

"How about Hawai'i?" Manu suggests one night. He takes a sip of coffee and waits for her answer.

"That would be fun, but it wouldn't take much longer to get to Japan. I've always wanted to see Tokyo," she says. They're sitting on the couch together, a dusty globe on the table in front of them that Manu dug out of Henri's old closet.

"Yes, Tokyo sounds good. Or..." He spins the globe. Dust flies everywhere and gives him a case of the sneezes. "Excuse me! We could go to Norway and watch the northern lights."

"Oh, that would be cool," she says. "Or we could go to England to see Buckingham Palace."

"Or New York to see the Statue of Liberty."

"What about the Taj Mahal in India?"

"The Pyramids?" Manu suggests as he rotates the globe. His hands crawl across continents as he imagines the possibilities.

"Machu Picchu?"

"Mayan ziggurats?"

"The Eiffel Tower?"

"Agh," Manu says, "I'm sick of the *métropole*. The French don't care about us here, so why would they care about us there? Maybe we could try the Vatican instead."

"Sounds like a bore. I'd rather go to Greece to see the Parthenon."

They go on like this for hours, circling the world a hundred times in their imaginations, wondering where this trip could take them and if Natua would be able to leave his mother behind to come—between the jet lag and ensuing days of exploring on foot, Angela certainly wouldn't be able to handle the trip.

During all of their discussions, neither Manu nor Ari broach the subject of how long it will take to get the myeloma under control. The cast on her knee is due to come off in a month, so Ari focuses on that instead. "We could go once the dry season hits in May," she says. "I know I've got to take it easy for a couple weeks after my cast comes off, but by then my knee should be fine."

"That would be nice," he says. "We can miss the first few rounds of tourists and instead be tourists ourselves."

"I like the way you're thinking!" she replies.

"But, of course, we'll have to take it one day at a time. I'd rather not push you too far when you're still healing."

"Right." Her mood turns somber as she considers the other health conditions that could cause her problems three months down the road.

"Let's just take it slow and not plan anything until we're sure we're ready." Manu grabs his empty mug and heads to the kitchen for a refill. "Want some tea?"

• • •

Despite her father's advice, Ari calls Irene a few days later and asks her to look out for flights heading to Iceland for "sometime in May."

"Oh, Iceland—what a great choice! That sounds so fun," Irene gushes. "You'd better apply for a passport now to make sure you get it on time."

Right. Suddenly, the whole trip becomes a reality for her, and she wonders what she should pack. *There might even be snow there!*

"Just make sure you wear comfortable clothes on the plane," Irene continues in the matter-of-fact tone she reserves for customers. "You'll be in the air for around 30 hours."

At the thought of boarding an airplane and spending hours upon hours trapped thousands of meters in the air, Ari's breath becomes ragged and her stomach curls into knots. Although she knows it's her imagination, the smell of smoke fills her nose and stings her eyes.

She is standing next to the kitchen table leaning on a crutch when the room starts spinning. Irene's voice pierces through.

"Are you all right Ari? Honey?"

She shakes her head vigorously to rid herself of the episode and then her crutch slides and scrapes along the wooden floor. She catches herself with a hand on the table just as she's convinced she's going to fall and then settles uneasily into a chair.

"Yes, Irene, I'm fine." Her voice trembles in spite of herself.

"Okay." Irene doesn't sound convinced.

"On second thought, I'm not sure I'm ready to plan this trip yet. Just the thought is exhausting me."

"Well, you let me know when you're up to it. There's no rush on anything, you know."

"That's true. Thank you again for offering to do this for us. You don't know how much it means to me."

"You're welcome, Ari. I just felt so bad seeing you like that that day. I want to make it up to you."

"There's nothing to make up for," Ari says, "but thank you all the same."

"I still feel awful."

"It's okay," Ari replies.

"Anyway, let me know what you're thinking once you're feeling up to it."

"I will. Do you think you'll let me come back to work the booth next week? All I need is a chair—and maybe a free pass on the heavy lifting."

"Are you sure you're ready for that? I don't want to see you push yourself too hard. You've got to get your rest."

"Funny, everyone seems to be saying that to me lately. I'll be fine, though, I promise. I know my limits, and right now I need something to do." As if to punctuate her words, she absent-mindedly twirls her frizzy hair around one of her fingers.

"If you say so. And hey, there's four flights coming in next Wednesday—I could use some help in the afternoon."

"I'll be there."

After she hangs up, Ari lays her head on the kitchen table and exhales loudly. How can she take a trip if the mere thought of boarding an airplane gives her a meltdown?

"Can I come in?" a voice at the door interrupts her thoughts and she sits up.

"Natua, just open the door," Ari calls.

He's announced himself like that for years. Manu had told him once, shortly after the adoption *tamaaraa*, that he wasn't allowed to knock on the door anymore—this was his way around it.

She's still sitting at the table, and she orders her hands to stop shaking before he sees. Maybe she shouldn't have answered him quite so soon.

He opens the door and strolls in. "You say that, but what if I walk in and someone's walking around naked or something? Nobody wants that," he says with a chuckle.

"You know that neither of us do that." She tucks her hands beneath the table into her lap.

"You can never be too sure," he responds.

"Don't be ridiculous," she snaps.

He stops and takes a long look at her face. "Are you okay? You look like you've seen a ghost."

"Um, yeah, no," she mumbles. "I'm okay."

"Don't wanna talk about it?"

"Nope."

"I can't help it if I worry about you. Is it your knee?"

She sighs. *I hate it when he's like this.* "No," she says. "I just got off the phone with Irene."

"Your dad was telling me—didn't she offer you two some crazy all-expenses paid trip?"

"Yeah, that's the problem."

He tilts his head in confusion. At her silence, he urges, "Well, go on!"

"Listen, I thought it would be really great and I've always wanted to travel."

"And...? It will be."

"I don't know what happened. Irene was talking about how long the flight would be to go to Iceland, and my head started pounding. I got dizzy, and it was like I could smell the fire all over again, and..." She looks up from her still-trembling hands, tears filling her eyes. "And I don't think I can fly."

"Oh."

He sits in a chair next to her and takes her hands in his. In her disappointment, she hardly registers how natural the gesture feels. "You've flown before, though, right?"

"A helicopter ride when I was passed out doesn't count."

"Maybe Irene can book a boat trip then."

"Oh, and get stuck with a thousand bored tourists complaining about the buffet? I don't think so."

"Have you ever tried a shorter flight? We could try going to the *Heiva* or maybe the Ma'ohi Sports Festival on a plane, see how that goes."

"I've never even stepped foot on a plane since that day. I don't know if I can."

"Don't let someone's generosity stress you out—if you don't want to go, then don't. Irene was only trying to help, I'm sure."

"But Papa is really looking forward to this trip. It's the kind of family getaway he's talked about for years."

"Maybe Iceland is a little much, but I'll bet you could handle a quicker ride. What about the Cook Islands or the Marquesas? Those aren't nearly as far away."

Ari shakes her head. "I don't think I can do it." She pushes his hands away and grabs her crutches to stand up. "Just drop it, Natua. Please."

"I'm sorry. I don't like seeing you this way."

"You think I want to be like this?" She raises her voice.

"I only want to help," he murmurs.

"Well, there's nothing you can do."

. . .

The next morning, the hospital finally calls to tell her the treatments have arrived. "Oh, thank god!" Muscles in her face relax that she hadn't even realized were tense. They schedule her to come in the next morning, so she gives her father a ring at the town hall to let him know the good news.

Shortly after he lets her know that he's finalized their travel arrangements and gotten the day off to accompany her, Ari's doctor calls the house.

"We're all set for tomorrow at 8, correct?" Ari asks.

But instead of confirming her appointment as she'd expected, the doctor says with a sigh, "We will have to reschedule the treatment for another time."

"Why? Is everything okay?"

"They've sent the wrong dosage," the doctor replies.

"Can't I just cut the pills or something?"

"It's the opposite, actually—you'd have to take half of your supply in a single day. The decimal point is in the wrong place."

"You're going to have to reorder the medicines from the mainland, aren't you?"

"I'm afraid so. I'm still going to have you come in so we can get a few tests done and check to see whether the myeloma is progressing."

"And if it is?"

"The most important thing is not to worry. Don't stress your body with anxiety—make sure all of the energy you have is being used to fight the disease."

"Okay, that makes sense," Ari says, but inwardly her heart is racing. *He didn't even answer my question. This must be bad.* She listens as someone explains to her for the third time that the right drugs should arrive in one to two weeks. She tries not to scream at the doctor and keeps her tone as level as possible.

"I'll see you in the morning," she says. For the second time in as many days, she is emotionally exhausted by a phone call.

She takes a nap. When her father comes home and shakes her awake, she can tell from the look on his face that she was yelling about Henri in her sleep again.

"Are you all right?" he asks, eyes shining.

She blinks against the bright afternoon light. "Just a bad dream," she says. She sits up and runs a few fingers through her tangled hair.

"Right," he says, his voice soft. "What would you like for dinner?"

Ari tells him about the mix-up with the medicine but tries to keep her tone positive. She doesn't want him any more concerned than he already is. She feigns a smile between bites of grouper.

"I'm sorry honey," he says once she's finished explaining what happened. "I wish I could fix it. I hate having our hands tied like this."

"I know. It'd almost be faster for me to take a flight to the mainland and pick 'em up myself." She tries to play the suggestion off as a joke, but her eyes are a little too focused on Manu's reaction.

"Don't be silly. Those French doctors would make you wait forever just to get seen, the snooty little bastards."

"PAPA!" Ari bursts out laughing. "Have you forgotten that *we* are French?"

"You know what I mean," he says stubbornly. "They only call us French when it's convenient for them. The rest of the time, we get treated as second-class citizens."

She rolls her eyes. "Fine, have it your way. But our doctors are the ones making me wait an awful long time."

"That's not their fault. It's because the French have to ship your medications here. You see where you fall on their priority list."

"Whatever, Papa." She gives up, knowing he'll never budge when it comes to this particular argument. "We're still going in tomorrow for an exam, so don't forget."

"Of course. I took the entire day for you, my dear."

• • •

"It's time to go," her father calls the next morning.

"Right, I'm coming," she says. "Just have to grab my crutches."

The two head to the docks in the jalopy. They're nearly late for the boat because Manu drives at a snail's pace to avoid the bumps in the road.

"You don't have to baby me, Papa," she says as they crawl through the deserted streets of early morning Fare.

"What are you talking about?"

"A pothole isn't going to kill me."

"I don't want to bother your knee," he replies. "I just want you to be comfortable."

"I'd be more comfortable if you weren't walking on eggshells around me all the time," she snaps.

"There's not much I can do to help you feel better," Manu responds. "I'm only trying to do what I can."

"I know, but I don't want you to go out of your way like this." She gestures towards the road Manu is currently weaving around. "Just, you know, be my dad and everything will be fine."

"That's what I've always done. Even when you don't appreciate it."

There's a playful glint in his eyes when he purposefully slows to a crawl over a speed bump by the school. A smile brightens her voice as she says, "Love you, Papa."

"I love you too, Riri."

"Now let's go!"

After a quiet boat ride, the doctor draws blood and sends Ari to get an MRI done.

Manu ends up sitting alone in a bland white waiting room with six-month old magazines, twiddling his thumbs as his daughter gets ushered around to different parts of the hospital.

He considers how Ari snipped at him over his driving. *Those damn mainlanders can't get anything right, even with her life hanging in the balance. Of course she's stressed out. But I have to do something, and what else is there to do?*

While he's not bothered by the sharp tone she'd taken that morning, he is troubled by her recurring nightmares. She tries to play them off as nothing, and he lets her, but he can hear her talk and even yell in her sleep multiple times every week—sometimes more than once a night. The dreams are always about Henri.

The bags under her eyes are dark enough to give him serious concerns, but he's not sure how to deal with it. She's had nightmares about that day on and off for years, but ever since the incident with her knee, it's been almost nonstop. He vaguely recalls the last time her nightmares occurred this often—it was shortly after she was diagnosed with myeloma.

She really dodged a bullet that day thanks to Oriata. That could be bothering her somehow—maybe she thinks she could've done something to save him if she'd been on board. Even though that's complete nonsense. The only thing that would've happened is I would have lost her too.

He shudders at the thought, then ponders the facts some more. Manu knows better than to expect Ari to talk to him about the nightmares, so he decides to discuss them with the doctor at the clinic back on Huahine. The genial, professional man might be able to get her to open up or refer her to someone she can talk to. He speculates whether the church pastor would be helpful, but then dismisses it. Ari hasn't gone to church since he stopped insisting.

He doesn't care how the issue gets resolved, as long as it gets addressed before the stress and lost sleep affect her ability to fight the cancer. *Since she can't seem to get those damn drugs, she needs all the other kinds of help she can get.* The last thing Ari needs is to be followed around by nightmares at the very points in her life when she most needs to focus on resting and getting better.

When his daughter is returned to the waiting room by a quiet nurse, she sits next to her father in silence and flips through a magazine. They're the only ones in the microscopic waiting room.

"How did everything go?" He immediately feels stupid for asking the question.

"Fine, I hope." She looks up from her magazine. "Guess we'll find out when they bring us the results."

"I'm sure they'll find out you're doing great. You haven't been showing even half as many symptoms as when we came in here five years ago."

"Just one," she says, pointing to her cast.

"Mm."

She goes back to her magazine. Manu wishes he had thought to bring work with him from the office to distract him from his nerves, which are coiling in anticipation of the worst—again. Instead, he grabs an old issue of Time and reads an interview with some recently famous American businessperson. *Look at how clueless they are. Let me tell you about hard times.*

Chapter 7

Natua has had a full-time job delivering bread ever since graduating from high school. He'd started delivering part-time on the weekends after Angela closed the pension, but Manu and Angela had both insisted he finish high school before going full-time.

His route covers the southeast corner of Fare, including the Fonuas' house. As he finishes up, he wonders whether they're going to need their bread today. Uncle had mentioned they were taking the first boat to Ra'iatea and spending the day there. Natua doesn't like the idea of wasting the bread if they aren't going to be around to eat it.

He's lost in thought when he walks up to Wan's house. Despite his mother's urging—or perhaps because of it—he and Wan aren't particularly close. Natua's classmate has always seemed so sure of his goals and how to accomplish them. Recently, he finished a two-year business degree so he could be ready to take on more responsibility at his family's grocery. When pressed on why he didn't go for a four-year degree, he said it wasn't necessary for his plan. Natua won't admit it, but he's a bit intimidated by the certainty and intensity with which Wan lives his life.

Wan is also one of the few people who is routinely awake before Natua drops off their morning dough, though the grocery doesn't open until 09:00. Today is no exception. The kitchen lights are all on and a kettle is singing for tea.

As Natua opens the squeaky bread box, he hears a voice.

"Hello?" he calls.

There's shuffling in the house, and then Wan appears at the door. "Good morning Natua," he says with a bow. "You're right on time—I was just starting to think about breakfast."

Natua shifts on his feet a bit uneasily. "Oh, good. By the way, were you talking to me a minute ago?" Wan is one of the few people from his graduating class that lives alone. Most of the others are either still at university or staying in their parents' homes (like he does) to support and care for the household.

Wan turns to pull the warm bread out of the box. "I didn't mean to disturb you," he says. "I was practicing my Mandarin."

"Always got a project, don't you?"

He shrugs. "This is one I should have started a long time ago. After all, how can you find your place in the world if you don't know the language of your own people?"

"Huh, you've got a point there," Natua replies. Instantly, he forgets about the Fonuas' bread. For the rest of the morning, he can't stop thinking about Wan's words. And where he might find a Spanish teacher.

. . .

A few hours later, a doctor, clipboard in hand, comes into the room where Ari and Manu are waiting. "I'm afraid I have some bad news," he says. He is a French man with a thick, graying mustache and heavy Parisian accent.

Both father and daughter put their magazines back on the room's one tiny coffee table and fold their hands neatly in their laps. Two pairs of anxious brown eyes await his news. He clears his throat.

"A second lesion has formed in your left shoulder, suggesting that the disease is advancing despite the turmeric supplements you're taking. You will have to brace it and avoid lifting anything heavier than 2 kilos with that arm."

Ari glances at her shoulder in dismay, but when the doctor pauses, she meets his eyes. "Does that mean I can't use the crutches anymore?"

The doctor nods. "Yes, you should stick to using a wheelchair until your knee heals enough that you can walk without crutches."

She groans. "Great." Manu envelopes her hands in his own, and the doctor takes that as his cue to go on.

"Because of the breakdown in your clavicle, calcium levels were quite elevated in your blood. There has also been a significant drop in your kidney function. While these complications are not entirely unexpected given your diagnosis, we had hoped to avoid the loss of kidney function at this stage."

"Okay, so what's going to happen now?" she asks.

"Our first priority is to get your kidneys back to normal before lasting damage is done. To do that, we are going to put you on several medications, including a fairly common steroid known as prednisone."

"Is there anything I can do to help?"

"Your job will be to take the prescriptions exactly as directed and to stay extremely well-hydrated. You'll have to drink between 2 and 3 liters of water every day to have any effect on your kidneys. You will also need to avoid ibuprofen and caffeine of any kind, including tea, coffee, and chocolate."

"How long will I have to do that for?" Ari keeps her questions basic to avoid confronting how overwhelming the situation is. *If only those treatments had come on time...* She doesn't allow herself to finish the thought, instead forcing herself to listen to the doctor.

"The medications are designed to help bring down the levels of calcium in your blood. As they begin to work, we will monitor for the return of kidney function. The first thing we will do is have you follow up with us in two to three weeks' time for a blood test. Where we go from there depends entirely on how you respond to treatment."

"Treatment—I should be coming back here in a week or two for chemotherapy to treat the myeloma, right? Is this condition going to stop me from getting those medicines?"

"It shouldn't, no. In fact, the sooner we get your myeloma treated, the better it should be for your kidneys."

"Why is that?"

"Myeloma creates abnormal proteins in your blood, which can sometimes bond with normal proteins in your kidneys. If this bond forms, the combined proteins become too large to pass through your kidneys and can form a blockage.

"As we treat the myeloma, fewer of these abnormal proteins should be created. Then, those blockages won't have a chance to form as quickly and—as long as your body responds to the other medications—any existing ones should dissolve, allowing your kidneys to work normally again."

"Will these medicines need to be ordered?" Manu asks. He hasn't said anything up to that point, and his words manage to sound both gentle and commanding at the same time.

"No, we have them in stock in the hospital pharmacy. There's already a script waiting for you."

"Thank god," Ari breathes.

"I'll have a nurse take you down there," the doctor continues, "and I'll have someone check on the arrival date of the chemotherapy drugs so we can get you scheduled before you leave today." He jots down a quick note on his clipboard.

"Thank you, doctor." Ari leans forward in her chair and extends her hand.

He takes her hand gingerly, then shakes Manu's hand and excuses himself. "The nurse will arrive shortly," he says before he leaves the room and heads down the hall.

After they are once again left alone, she sighs. "Well that was the worst Tuesday I've had in a while."

"Tell me about it."

They're still catching their breath from the news when the promised nurse, a Ma'ohi man in faded aquamarine scrubs, arrives to escort them to the pharmacy. He's pushing an empty wheelchair, which he steers over to Ari's seat. "Ms. Fonua?"

She slowly shifts into the chair, careful not to put any weight on her left shoulder as she does.

"Let's get you folks to the pharmacy."

The nurse deposits them in front of a sterile white counter hedged in on all sides by glass. At the service window, a friendly pharmacist in a lab coat goes through each medication in detail and helps Ari schedule when to take each one, starting with the steroid.

"You can always call us or consult with your local doctor if you have any questions about how to take them." The woman pushes on the plastic frame of her glasses. "And be sure not to forget the prednisone—you can have withdrawal symptoms if you are too inconsistent in taking it."

"That doesn't sound pleasant," Ari says.

"Joint pain, nausea, weakness, lightheadedness— definitely not pleasant," the pharmacist agrees. "If you have any severe side effects, such as pain, extreme fatigue, or a high fever, you have to call your doctor right away."

"Okay." Her voice sounds defeated already.

"And hey—chin up, my girl." The woman waves her finger in the air like it's a magic wand. "Just because something could have a side effect, doesn't mean it will."

"Right. Thanks, ma'am."

After a quick stop to put Ari on the books to receive counseling on the chemotherapy regimen and pick up the pills in two weeks, they emerge from the hospital into the humid afternoon.

"Remember when I was a kid and I said I wanted to go to different islands all the time?"

Manu turns to her and his eyes shine. "Like it was yesterday."

"I didn't mean like this."

He stops walking. "Then let's do it the way you meant."

"What?" She tries to maneuver the wheelchair to face her father, but then sighs and settles for simply turning her head.

"I don't have to go back to the office until tomorrow, Ari. Imagine for a moment you're 10 again—what do you want to do on an afternoon trip to Ra'iatea?"

"Hmm... paddle boarding," she says with a sigh. Despite the wistfulness in her voice, a smile blooms on her face. "We could go on one of those cheesy guided tours of the marae."

"I'm not sure there are any in the city—we might have to go south to O'opa."

"Ah, okay. Let's do something here then. What about the park by the coast? I've heard it's got amazing views."

"Sounds perfect. I'll get us a cab."

The two spend the afternoon alternately wandering around the coastal gardens and relaxing on—or, in Ari's case, next to—the wooden benches placed under fresh-smelling Tahitian lime trees.

Towards the end of the day, Ari puts a hand on her father's forearm and takes a deep breath of the salty ocean air. "Thanks, Papa. I needed this."

"We both did," he says, smoothing her hair with his fingers. He looks out over the lagoon at the neighboring island of Tahaa, at the open water, at the clouds dancing in the pale blue sky. "Is this more of what you'd had in mind as far as traveling goes?"

118

"Yeah, it is."

. . .

Ari and Manu board the last boat home and Ari falls asleep on the harsh wooden bench. Her leg is stuck awkwardly out towards the vessel's rusted railing. Manu briefly considers waking her or trying to tuck her leg in, but the other islanders and few tourists on board the half-empty boat have given them all the space they need.

In the failing light, Manu watches as the coast of Ra'iatea fades and with it, their lighthearted afternoon of exploring. He wonders how many more memories like that he'll be able to make with his daughter. His eyes sting with the sudden realization that hospital visits will probably start to consume more and more of what precious time they have left together.

Inaudible underneath the boat's whirring engine, Manu talks—at first to himself, and then to God. "What did we do to deserve this?" he wonders. His whole life has been spent in service of his people. He even served the French in their military. He's given up so much for the safety and well-being of others.

"It wasn't enough to take away the mother of my children? Both of my sons? Are You really going to take her too?"

His quasi-prayer ends with an anguished, "Why?" The wind carries his voice over the wide waves, in the opposite direction of the home that already seems empty of Ari's carefree presence. Pink sunset fades into blackness and he weeps, his questions left unanswered.

. . .

After his assessment, Natua's tutor nods approvingly. "You can understand Spanish very well for someone who's never tried learning it before."

"Thanks," Natua replies. "I guess it's similar enough to French that I can catch some things."

"Yes, that's exactly it—in fact, there's a name for that. It's called receptive multilingualism."

"Cool. So I'm like halfway done learning it, right?"

The tutor dismisses the thought with a wave of his hand. "Learning another language isn't as simple as that, but it will help. Now, let's get started." He hands Natua a thick textbook. "This is yours. Study it on your own to improve your ability to read and write, and then in our lessons, we can focus on speaking and going over anything you didn't understand."

"Perfect. I'm more worried about being able to speak than anything else anyway." He realizes in that moment that learning Spanish was never just about knowing the language of his father. "I'm planning on going to Spain someday."

"Very exciting stuff. Going to do anything special there?"

Natua's eyes brighten as he talks. "I have some family living there. I think it's time I tracked them down and paid a visit."

The tutor grabs a pen and a worn pocket planner. "Then we shouldn't waste any time. Can I put you in for lessons on Monday mornings? Maybe 10 o'clock?"

"Yeah, that's perfect. How soon can we start?"

"I have time to give you your first lesson now, if you're up for it."

Natua nods. "Let's do it." He sips on his coffee, glad they'd decided to meet in this café. He spent a solid year of high school pretending to study here for the *baccalaureate* exam. It only made sense he'd break out the books again in one of their booths, just like old times.

Chapter 8

"Would you listen to this?" Manu calls to his daughter from his spot on the couch, where he's watching the evening news with Natua. "They've upgraded Winston twice since last night—it's a category 4 now."

Manu turns the volume up on the TV as he talks.

"That storm's over by Fiji, right?"

"Oh yeah, it's nowhere near us," he replies, half-yelling over the news anchor. "Those poor schmucks better get ready for a beating though. They're saying it's on track to be the strongest cyclone the Pacific's ever seen."

She emerges from her bedroom with one crutch situated haphazardly in her right armpit. "Wow, that's awful!"

"Thank goodness we don't live in Fiji," Natua says. "Take a look at this monster, Ari."

"Yeah, I'm coming." She makes her way slowly across the room. Because she can't put weight on her left shoulder, she has to choose between walking lopsidedly on one crutch or using the wheelchair.

Just as she sits, the TV goes to a commercial. Ari groans. "You've got to be kidding me!"

"I've seen sea turtles go faster than you," Natua teases.

"Well, they are very quick in the water so I'm going to take that as a compliment."

"I wouldn't," he says. "I was talking about on the beach."

"Hey! Papa, do you hear this?"

Manu smirks. "It did take you a while to get over here," he says. "But don't worry, my dear, your cast comes off in just a couple of weeks."

"Yeah, thankfully. Besides, I'm sure if either of you ever end up in a cast, my pace will suddenly look a whole lot faster."

"Right you are," Manu says as he stands up. "In the meantime, I'm going to grab something to drink—if you want anything Ari, I'll make sure you get it before the late-night news."

"Oh, ha ha."

"Actually, Uncle, I'd like a soda if you have one," Natua pipes up.

"Sure thing."

"Thanks," Natua calls.

Manu gave up on convincing Natua to call him Dad years ago, back when the kids were still in school.

I have a father, Natua had said. He never raised his voice, but his tone was firm.

Have you ever spoken to him? Has he ever taken care of you? Manu pushed.

That doesn't make me any less of his son. I don't even know if he realizes I exist—not exactly hard to be a bad father if you don't know you have a child. I'll find him one day. Then you'll see.

. . .

On Monday morning, the phone rings. Ari is getting ready to go to a coffee shop to meet her old diving buddy Etienne and she hobbles over to the phone on one crutch, hairbrush caught in a snarl near the crown of her head.

"Yeah, hello?" Her face tightens. "Oh my god, again? At this rate, I'll die before I get those damn pills!"

She pauses and listens to the voice on the other end of the line. "I work at an airport—flights originating in France almost always lay over in LAX. Winston's by

Fiji… Well, none of our flights have been delayed or canceled, so why is this one?"

Ari sighs. "I don't care if there's another storm forming off to the west, that plane doesn't have to fly anywhere near there to get here! … Oh, it does, does it? Well that was a stupid plan given the time of year." She scoffs and hangs up. *I don't care when they think those medications will come in. They'll probably never get here.* She takes a deep breath and dials Irene.

. . .

Ari shows up at the coffee shop an hour later, glad she's there ahead of Ettie. Maybe a good cup of coffee will get her into a better mood before her friend arrives. "The usual, but make it decaf today," she tells the barista at the counter. "Can you just bring it out to me when it's ready?" She juts her chin to indicate her lone crutch.

"No problem," the man says with a wave of his hand. His parents own the café, which was the first place on Huahine to offer internet access. Years later, it's still a popular place to study. She, Ettie, and Natua spent hours together here during high school while they were studying for the *baccalaureate.*

That's why it seems natural to her that Natua's here now, though he's sitting at a back table with someone she doesn't recognize. He catches her looking at him and holds a notebook in front of his face.

Ari starts and her balance is thrown off-kilter. "Natua?" she calls.

He excuses himself from his friend and walks over to her. "What are you doing here? You never come here on Mondays."

"What? How do you know that?" She tilts her head at him quizzically.

"Because—oh, never mind. Can you just forget you saw me here?"

"Natua, why are you being so weird?" She forgets about her foul mood in favor of satisfying her curiosity. "Wait, are you seeing someone?"

"Huh?" He laughs uneasily. "I'm not...uh..." he trails off and holds his hands up.

"All right, sure." She decides to play it off, but then she notices a Spanish textbook on the table he just left. "Oh, you're learning Spanish? That's cool—why would you be embarrassed about that?"

"Look, I'm not embarrassed. Just do me a favor, and don't tell Mama about this, okay?"

"I won't, but I'm confused. Why not?"

He speaks in hushed tones. "Think for a second about why I would be learning Spanish."

"Well, it's important to know the language of your people, but I'm sensing something else is going on."

"It started like that—listen, I don't need the entire café to hear this, okay?" He sighs and shifts his weight from foot to foot. "I decided I'm going to go to Spain to track down my dad. I have a name and a ring he left my mother. I think it has his family crest on it or some shit like that."

"Won't she understand?"

He gives her a look. "Are you serious right now? All our lives you've heard her tell me that he won't give a damn about me. Her and Uncle both. And there's no way she'll let me take his ring—it's her most prized possession."

"Right... so, are you expecting that he'll want you in his life after all these years?"

"I have to know for myself. What if he's out there somewhere, wishing he had a son and not knowing I exist? Or what if we never meet because we're both sure the other one hates us?"

"Natua, you are one of my best friends, so I have to be honest. Are you prepared for the possibility that your mom and my dad could be right?"

"I am, but it's not the only possibility. Stranger things have happened than a father reuniting with a son."

His eyes harden a bit as he speaks. Ari knows it's a touchy subject, so she changes tack when she says, "No matter what happens, you shouldn't go alone. What if it doesn't go well and you have to deal with that by yourself?" Ari resists the temptation to lay her free hand on his arm. Instead, it hangs uselessly at her side.

"Who's going to come with me? I can't put Mama through that, and you—you can't even think about boarding a plane without a panic attack. Anyone else would either tell Mama about it or wouldn't be able to afford the trip."

She clears her throat and lowers her voice. "Actually, I have something to tell you. My medications got delayed—"

"Oh, again?" he interrupts, sympathy in his voice. "I'm so sorry, Ari."

"Yeah, again. So listen, you know how Irene offered to send me on that trip?"

"Mhmm."

"I called her today and she's booking me a short trip to Paris. She said there was one leaving next week I might be able to get on."

"You can't even sit through a ten-minute flight!"

"I will die waiting for those pills to get here. I'll take a sleeping pill or something to get through it. I don't care. If I can just get to the *métropole*, I can get free hospital care as a citizen of France, and they'll have the medications I need in stock because they aren't waiting weeks for these pills that are apparently so hard to ship."

"Why not go somewhere closer, like New Zealand or Australia?"

"My English isn't all that great. You know that. I can't risk the possibility of misunderstanding stuff about my health."

He nods. "So how does your dad feel about this?"

She hesitates.

Natua lowers his voice. "You haven't even told him, have you?" When she shakes her head, he takes a step back and laughs. "And you thought I shouldn't go on my trip without my mother's blessing? God, Ari... this isn't even remotely the same."

She ignores the chastising. "We both know what Papa will say. They can't even handle a cold shower—how're they going to handle my health?"

"Oh come on, that has nothing to do with anything."

"Haven't you heard the way he talks about the safety officials they send here? Or the nuclear waste they left on some of the other islands?"

"Well yeah, but—"

She cuts him off. "He's convinced that they don't care about us. That they're taught not to care about us. Besides, they can't even get two bottles of pills here in a month and a half. He'll just say that their doctors won't care enough to help me either."

Natua shakes his head but before he can speak, the barista taps Ari lightly on her good shoulder. "Where would you like me to put your drink?"

"Oh, I'm sorry, you can put it right there." She gestures to a table that's situated in front of a sofa.

"Listen, I should go back to my lesson," he says.

"Wait, there's something else I wanted to say."

He looks up.

"I don't plan on going alone. I want you to come with me."

"What? But I told you I have to go to Spain, and I'm not even close to being ready. My Spanish sucks even more than your English."

"Right, but I can get you all the way to Paris through Irene at a huge discount—then all you have to do is get an extra layover and you're there. I can meet back up with you after I get my medications sorted out and you have some time to find your dad. Think about it."

He tilts his head to one side and then the other. "It would be way more affordable to do it that way. And then at least you wouldn't be flying alone. What about my Spanish though?"

"Does your mom speak Spanish?" she asks pointedly.

"Um... not really."

"Then the one person who counts will be able to understand you."

"I don't know if counting on everyone else being able to speak either French or English is a smart move."

Ari shrugs. "Americans do it all the time."

"You've got a point I suppose, but I've always thought I would be better than that." He sighs and gives in. "Are you sure Irene's okay with it?"

"I'll talk to her."

"And your dad? He was really looking forward to this trip."

"I know, Natua, but he won't get it—he'll only try to stop me. At least this way, we won't have to fight over it, because I'm not changing my mind." She charges on, a plan falling together as she speaks. "I'll tell him we're going to go watch the inter-island athletic competitions—I think the basketball team is playing in Bora Bora next Saturday. And hey, maybe I can tell him we're going to stick around a little while to look around, check things out. That'll give us some time."

"You're sure you're ready for this?"

"I don't have a choice—I'll die waiting. What about you? Are you ready to meet your father?"

He stares off into the middle distance. "As much as I'll ever be. Let me know when we leave. I'll have to make arrangements with Temata for the bakery."

"I will. I'm working a shift at the airport this afternoon, so I can touch base with Irene then."

"Are you going to be okay travelling with that thing still on your knee?"

She holds her leg out and examines the worn cast. "I have to be."

. . .

Ari no sooner sits down with her mug than Ettie breezes in, practically radiating joy. She waves at Ari, who tips her head at her friend before taking a sip of her coffee.

Ettie gestures with her hands about the coffee and the small line that's formed. Ari sets her cup down and waves her on. The pair have developed their own brand of pseudo sign language over years of scuba diving together, and it saves them a lot of yelling in the din of busy cafés, bars, and clubs.

Although she doesn't admit it to herself, Ari's glad to have an extra few minutes to think through what she and Natua just decided.

"What's on your mind?" Ettie asks when she settles in a wingback chair across from Ari. She blows steam away from her frothy mug and looks at Ari expectantly.

Ari tries to push away her thoughts to focus on her friend. "I'm jealous of your caffeine."

"Yeah, that's brutal. How long do you have to lay off it?"

"Until my kidneys are back to normal."

"Good thing Irene doesn't ask you to work the morning flights."

"Tell me about it."

Ettie takes a measured sip of her drink and Ari feels like her friend can see her every secret written all over her face. "That's not what's on your mind though."

Ari shakes her head. There's no use trying to hide anything from Ettie. "You know me too well," she says.

"So... spit it out."

"I can't. Too much of it isn't about me at all."

Ettie raises her eyebrows. "Juicy." She holds Ari's gaze.

"Stop it! I'm not telling you."

"Then don't."

They spend a moment in silence until Ettie speaks up. "Okay, if you're not even going to ask me how I'm doing, that means you have to share." Before Ari can protest, she adds, "Those are the rules."

Ari groans. The rules they'd made up as kids always seem to work in Ettie's favor. "Fine, but you can't tell a soul."

. . .

When Natua arrives home a few hours later, he mentally makes a list of what still needs to be done before he's ready to go to Spain. He knows he'll have to save getting the ring for last, so instead he boots up the computer in the back room to continue his clandestine search for his father.

He's made a list of men living in Spain who might have made the trip to Huahine 21 years ago, and he's been slowly eliminating the wrong ones as he hunts down more information about each.

Could you be from Granada? The old computer whirrs and beeps its way through pages and pages of search results and websites before Natua finds out that Armando L. da Costa of Madrid is only 16 years old. He crosses out the entry in his notebook with a shake of his head.

Only four left. *Please be him, please be him*, he thinks as he tracks down another Armando, this time living in the Pyrenees Mountains near Andorra. But information about the man is scant—all Natua can find is a birth announcement from a digitized newspaper. He has trouble understanding the Catalan he mistakes for dated Spanish, but the year is clearly wrong. *He's old enough to be my grandfather.* He crosses off another entry.

He's able to eliminate the next thanks to an active social media profile showcasing the man's first trip outside of Europe, which appears to have been a stay in Africa late last year. Natua crosses him off the list as well.

Only two more.

Natua pauses. What if the man isn't even on this list—what if there's no record of him on the internet? How can he go to a foreign country to track down his father without even knowing where to go?

His stomach tumbles as he wonders whether he'll be able to track him down by sometime next week. *Just breathe, Ignacio, breathe.* He's staring at the last two names on the list when it hits him. *The ring!*

Mama keeps the ring on a glass shelf next to her bed, and even though it's all he has of his father, Mama rarely lets him touch it or even look at it. It's a strange-looking piece of jewelry, with an ornate setting that is indelibly tarnished from decades or even centuries of wear.

He tries to picture the engravings along the wide-set band—Mama has always said they were part of his family crest. Maybe he can use that to track down his father's entire family. Maybe...

"What are you up to in there?" Mama's voice carries across the room from her spot leaning against the doorway.

"Oh, just looking for something," he replies. He wills himself to be casual as he closes the open search window and flips his notebook to a blank page. She would go ballistic if she knew what he was doing, and there's no time to waste on arguments.

"Find it?"

"Uh, no, not yet."

"Make sure you turn that thing off when you're done. It sucks electricity like nobody's business," she scoffs. "Damn Americans and their wasteful inventions."

"Of course, Mama, I will. How are you feeling?"

"Quite well," she says. "I think I'm going to head down to the kitchen to fix myself some hot tea. Can I get you some?"

"Thanks, but I'm fine right now."

"Suit yourself," she says as she hobbles down the hallway.

Once she's gone, Natua breathes a sigh of relief. *That was too close.* He grabs his cell phone and sneaks down the hall towards his mother's room. The door is closed. He waits until he hears the clanging of mugs in the kitchen before he turns the knob and slips inside.

He only has a few minutes, but he has to move slowly. The room is cloaked in gloom thanks to his mother's blackout curtains—a holdover from the glory days of the pension, when she tried to maintain her privacy while surrounded by wandering tourists. He tiptoes over to the window to open them when his foot connects with a bedside table.

"Shit!"

The noises in the kitchen stop. He holds his breath for what must be an eternity. Finally, the kettle sings and silverware rattles against ceramic. His eyes adjusted to the darkness, he opens the curtains to let in a slit of afternoon sunlight.

Quickly, he opens the camera on his phone and scans the glass shelving unit for the ring. *Where is it?* He hears her coming down the hall when he spots it in a pile of traditional jewelry.

He separates it from the others and takes a photo, but it comes out too blurry. Knowing he won't get another chance if his mother finds out why he's snooping, he hurriedly snaps another. The footsteps have stopped. He's out of time.

He walks over to the door and takes a breath. When he opens it, she's nowhere in sight. Natua closes the door carefully behind him and slips his phone back in his pocket. "Mama?"

"Oh, there you are!" She shuffles out of the computer room. "You left that damned machine on."

"I wasn't done with it yet, Mama. Just stepped out for a moment."

"Hmm." She frowns, a mug of tea steaming in her hands. "Well, make sure you don't forget to turn it off when you're finished."

Whew. Natua goes back to the computer and, as soon as he's sure he's alone, uploads the photo to the old desktop. *I'll find you yet, Armando.*

. . .

It's Friday, and Natua is just finishing his delivery route for the bakery when his cell phone vibrates in his pocket. His heart races. *Could it be him?*

Instead of the email he's hoping for, it's a message from Ari. "Tuesday's the day. I convinced Irene to make your ticket half-price and swore her to secrecy about the whole thing, but you need to pay her a 50% deposit before we leave. Hope that's okay. Also, Papa's cooking breakfast if you're hungry."

He types out a reply as he walks back down the driveway. "If Tuesday's the day, I've got a few things to take care of. We can do breakfast in Paris."

Chapter 9

"No, this is too much," Robert says. He looks up from the proposal Manu's printed off for him and speaks over the Tahitian café's reggae music. "I can't put my name on this."

"France needs to take responsibility for their nuclear waste, Robert. Not just in name, but in action."

"I'm telling you—this is too far, too fast." The man takes a sip of his tea.

"The testing stopped 20 years ago, and we've still gotten nowhere. It's time for that to change."

"I know, but we have to tread carefully in order to get what we want. You remember what happened a few years ago, right?"

He's referring to a resolution that was very similar to the one Manu is proposing now. It had passed in the Assembly, and then the new president's supporters boycotted it and shut everything down until it was thrown out. "Yes, of course. That's how I know the people are ready for this."

"One step at a time. The president still has plenty of friends in the Assembly. Maybe even more than he did back then."

"What would you propose instead?"

Robert leafs through the pages again. "Take out all of the language about declassifying military secrets related to the testing, the estimated costs, and the timeline for disposal—you know these things take time, and if we make things too difficult, it will never pass through their greasy hands."

"Without all of that, there's nothing left to the proposal!"

"Wrong," Robert replies. "There's still accepting responsibility."

"After all these years? That's not enough." Manu drains his coffee mug. "We need to make a stand and commit to the health of our islands. Not just make a nice-sounding statement with no action behind it."

"You're right, but we have to start somewhere. It's easier to build on later if the responsibility has already been accepted. Here, let me get you another cup of coffee." He stands and heads towards the counter.

Manu shifts in the hard wicker chair, uncomfortable with stripping all of the details from his proposal. But he had called Robert precisely for this kind of perspective, however much it frustrates him. This is the first piece of legislation he's written for the Territorial Assembly, and he only let his aide check it over for the legal terms.

Robert returns with a steaming mug of java and Manu thanks him. "If you think that will put us on the right path, then we can adjust the wording about the timeline."

The senior politician sits and grabs his pen. "Legislative change is not a sprint, my friend, but a never-ending marathon. Let's get to work."

. . .

Back on Huahine, Ari is at the chemist's looking for a sleep aid. When she finally finds what she needs, it's too high for her to reach. "Excuse me?" she calls.

The old man who runs the shop surfaces slowly from behind the counter. Ari can practically feel the pain in his joints as he struggles to straighten his back.

"Yes, little one?"

"I need that white and orange bottle up there." She points.

"Aah, got a case of insomnia, have you?"

She looks down and decides to roll with the

lie. "Yeah."

"This is a good one to help you." A metal stool scrapes against the tile floor as he drags it over to the shelf. "It's all natural and helps flush caffeine from your body for a better night's sleep without using harsh drugs."

"Huh. I've been avoiding caffeine anyway, so that's good to know. How much is it?"

He heaves himself onto the stool and leans towards the price tag. "Ahh, looks like it's 2,000 francs." He glances down at her. "Is that okay?"

"Yes, of course," she replies. She takes the bottle he's holding out for her and walks with him to the cash register. The man is barely moving, and she pulls a couple of crumpled bills out of her pocket as he makes his way around the worn wooden counter. "Thank you."

Ari slips the bottle into her bag, hoping the medicine will work without interfering with the prescriptions she's still taking for her kidneys. *Not that I have much of a choice,* she thinks with a hint of bitterness. It should never have come to this. She shouldn't have to get on a plane—not now and not ever—unless it's on her terms. And yet here she is, rushing home to finish packing for a trip she should never have had to take.

Tomorrow's the day.

. . .

Manu and Robert have just sat down to dinner in Pape'ete with an Assemblymember named Diane. She's serving her first term, like Manu, and Robert has taken both of them under his wing.

They've just finished drinking a toast to the islands when his phone dings in his pocket. "Excuse me," he says as he unlocks the screen.

Hey Papa, Natua got some last-minute tickets to the basketball game in Bora Bora this weekend. I think we're going to head over early so we can get in a bit of sight-seeing. Don't be surprised if I'm gone before you get back tomorrow.

He looks up at his colleagues. "Just my daughter."

"Hasn't she been ill? How is she feeling?" Diane asks.

"She's doing fairly well but we've been waiting on some medications to arrive from the mainland. It's illnesses like hers that make passing this bill so important—not just for me, but for all of the other families out there who have been impacted by the testing."

"I can't even imagine what you and your family are going through," Diane says sympathetically.

"Things are a bit tense in the house but we're holding it together," Manu replies. "Seems one of her friends has convinced her to take a short trip while we're waiting for the latest batch of meds to come in."

"Oh, that will be good for her," Robert says. "It doesn't do anyone any favors to sit around and worry."

"My thoughts exactly." To Ari, he writes back, *That's great, honey. Take your mind off of things for a little while. When are you planning on coming back?*

Just then the food arrives and he slips the phone into his briefcase. The trio take their time, enjoying the meal and drinking quite a few more toasts to the islands.

After Robert excuses himself to find the restroom, Diane turns to him and says in a serious tone, "Do you need another co-sponsor for your bill?"

Manu shakes his head to clear the buzz from his brain. "You wanna talk politics *now?*"

She sighs. "I didn't want to say this in front of Robert because it would offend him. I know he's working with you on the bill, but to be honest, I don't know if I trust him on this issue."

Manu giggles through the tipsiness. "He's the whole reason I ended up in the Assembly. Why wouldn't I trust him?"

"He had an in with quite a few of Fritch's supporters—about that bill that was overturned. He could've broken the deadlock, but he sat by and did nothing." She leans closer to him and her words come quickly, in a fierce whisper. "Promise me you'll look into it."

Manu's face scrunches up as he tries to focus on Diane's words. "I'm sure he did what he thought was best. He's a good guy."

"He is. But promise me you'll look into it anyway."

Manu slurs out an affirmative response.

She shifts away from him and resumes a warm, conversational tone. "What a wonderful evening this is turning out to be!"

Just then, Robert claps a hand on Manu's back. "Hey, hey, it's my two favorite new co-workers! How about a toast?"

It's not until Manu awakens the next morning in his hotel room with a pounding headache that he notices Ari never mentioned when she would be coming home.

• • •

Beep. Beep. Beep. Beep. Alarms are sounding in the cockpit, and there's a faintly acrid smell in the air—burnt hair, maybe. Ari dashes out of her seat, towards the front of the plane.

"Miss, you can't go in there." The flight attendant speaks politely, but puts a hand firmly on Ari's shoulder to stop her.

Ari brushes her hand away. "What's going on up there? I need to make sure everything's all right."

Just then the door to the cockpit opens, and the pilot appears. He's wearing his favorite green khakis and an incongruously formal starched shirt. "If anything goes wrong, I'll know why."

"Henri... no, I'm so sorry." She steps back, as though from a gut punch.

"Sorry doesn't change anything, Ari. Ariiii!"

"ARI!"

Natua shakes her awake, an alarm clock beeping uselessly next to the guest bed. "Come on, our flight leaves in less than an hour. We've gotta go." At her stricken expression, he adds, "You going to be okay?"

She swallows her misgivings. "I have no other choice. Give me five minutes and we can go." She hits a button on the clock to quiet the racket.

Natua backs out of the room and pulls the door closed behind him. Through the door, he says, "We can eat in the car. A taxi is already on its way."

To make things easier for their early morning flight, Natua had convinced Angela to let Ari spend the night in one of the pension's unused rooms. Ari had been surprised at how well-kept the place still was, with only a fine layer of dust over cobwebs in the high corners of the room.

She sits upright in bed and lets her feet dangle towards the floor as she collects herself. *It was just a dream. People fly in and out of the airport every single day. It's going to be fine.* She practices her deep breathing exercise twice and then changes into loose-fitting slacks and a gray tee shirt. She tosses her cell phone into her bag and heads for the door.

At the airport, Irene is ecstatic to see her off. "You will love Paris," she gushes, bangles accentuating her words. "Make sure you head to the Marais—they have such gorgeous art galleries in that district! Mmm." She shakes her head in enthusiasm.

Ari smiles wordlessly.

"You take good care of her, young man," she says, turning to Natua. "Paris will not be easy to navigate with that cast on her leg." Half to herself, she adds,

"Can't even wait to get a cast taken off. The impatience of youth!"

"Thank you for this, Irene," Ari finally says. The appreciation in her eyes is genuine. She hopes it hides the panic rising in her belly.

"Of course, of course." Irene chuckles lightly. "This is what we do for our friends."

"Seriously, thanks Irene," Natua says. "Anyway, we should probably start heading towards the plane, since my gimpy friend here will take a little longer to get over there than normal."

"Ha, yes, she will! Safe travels my friends!" Irene waves them off and heads back to her booth.

Once they are alone, he turns to Ari. "Are you sure you're all right?" He sees the panic, even if he doesn't know what to do about it.

She swallows hard. "Yeah. I think I just need some water."

"Well, let me take your bag and once we get over to the lounge, I'll refill that water bottle in my backpack."

Ari makes a face. "Just don't refill it from the fountain by the bathrooms—that water always tastes rusty. The best fountain is the one in the back corner."

"You got it," he says. *Whatever it takes.*

A few minutes later, with Ari settled, he sets off towards the fountain in the back corner. He fingers his father's ring in his front pocket as he walks.

Having Ari spend the night had helped keep Mama distracted. She always insists on preparing breakfast for her guests, no matter what hour they need it, and while she busied herself in the kitchen that morning, he had slipped into her room and taken the ring.

Natua had posted its image on forums all over the internet in French and broken Spanish, but no one's stepped forward to claim it just yet. His plan is to stay with Ari for a few days, and then hopefully get a lead on his father's whereabouts and go from there.

He fills the water bottle, then takes a couple of swigs. *Mm, that is good.* He tops it off, then looks out towards the runway. It makes him uneasy to think Ari might have a panic attack in the air, but like she said herself, she's out of options. She's planning to take a sleeping pill to get through the flights from Tahiti to Paris, but she's going to have to stay awake until they get to Tahiti. It's this first flight—only a hair over 30 minutes in the air—that could be the most difficult.

His stomach tightening, he heads back over to Ari and passes her the water bottle. "Drink up," he says, trying to keep his tone light. "Don't want you getting dehydrated in the air."

She sucks in her breath and closes her eyes. "Can we not talk about flying right now?"

"Sure," he replies easily.

"Thanks." She takes a long drink. "You're right though, I do need to keep hydrated. I'm on those stupid drugs for my kidneys, and I need to drink a boat load of water every day to make sure the treatment actually works."

"What kind of boat is loaded with water?"

"What?"

"I'm serious," he says with a twinkle in his eyes. "What kind of boat is loaded with water?"

"One that's already sunk," Ari replies grimly.

"Hey now, don't start with the doom and gloom. This was your idea."

"I know, and it's probably the dumbest idea I've had in my entire life."

"Nah." He gestures towards the half-empty bottle she has a death grip on. "Taking vodka to school was way dumber."

She giggles. "Fair enough, but it was senior week—they're lucky I showed up at all!"

"You and your 'water bottle' showed up all right... made quite the impression on the principal, too."

"Oh my god, I never told you this, but the worst part was when they called my dad in. He had to leave *a council meeting.* They called him right in the middle of the meeting and they had to adjourn so he could take my drunk ass home. The entire council heard what I did." Her grip loosens on the bottle, and the crumpled plastic pops back into place.

"Oh really? Ouch."

"I was so embarrassed, Natua, you have no idea."

"Oh, I think I know. You hid in the back of the classroom as much as you could the rest of the year."

Ari laughs, her eyes staring into the middle distance. "And, of course, all the council members thought it was hilarious, so they joked about it for months."

"Yeah, that was definitely your dumbest idea."

"Thanks," she replies sarcastically. "Like you never had any dumb ideas."

He laughs. "No, I did. Like choosing you to be my dance partner when we were learning all those traditional routines with your family." Natua shakes his head, hair falling over his eyes. "Should've gone with your grandma."

"I got better at least. No more chicken dancing for me." Her eyes sparkle, but her body is still tense in the plastic seat.

"How's your knee?" He points to the cast.

"To be honest, I think I'm sorer from the cast than the fracture at this point."

"How much longer do you need to have the cast?"

"Just two more weeks, as long as it's healed the way it's supposed to." She sighs. "Since I have a bone problem, that's not exactly a given."

"I'm sure it'll be fine—if it doesn't hurt anymore, that's gotta be a good sign."

"You'd think, but things haven't been going the way I need them to lately."

"Lighten up, Ari. The sun will come out tomorrow," he croons.

She puts up her hands to stop him and laughs.

Natua grins—only five more minutes until boarding starts and she's doing great. He's beginning to think that maybe this will work out after all.

Chapter 10

Ari's glad Natua is going with her—she knows if she had been alone, she'd already be in a taxi heading back home. Even with him distracting her, she feels like she might throw up from the anxiety. The boxy shape of her beat-up Walkman in her backpack comforts her just enough to talk herself down.

I've watched people come in and out of this airport for years, and they were none the worse for wear. Just because I only fly during rainstorms when I'm half-dead doesn't mean anything. She stops herself from even thinking about Henri and fakes a smile for Natua's sake.

She's trying to decide if it would be better to stay in the airport until the last minute or board right away and get it over with, when a flight attendant walks behind the check-in area and announces boarding for first class passengers to the empty lounge.

"Are you okay?" Natua asks, grabbing her hand.

She shakes her head almost imperceptibly. Now is not the time to be sharing her feelings.

"Ari Fonua? Is that you?" The flight attendant's smile is dazzling even from Ari's chair several meters away. Ari wonders how much money she spends to keep her teeth so perfect.

"Moehara? How are you?"

"Wonderful! So good to see you," she says, dropping the fake voice she reserves for passengers. Then she asks, "Is everything okay?"

Great. Another person I have to pretend to be okay for. Before she can answer, though, Moehara continues, "If you need any help getting onto the plane because of your leg, just let me know. I can call for an aisle chair or have someone carry your luggage on for you."

"Oh, that," she says. *Duh.* "We've made it this far on our own. We should be able to get on without too much trouble, right Natua?"

"Right," he replies, "that's the hope. If we need anything though, I'll give you a holler."

"Perfect!" A few businessmen approach, and she returns to her job and her bright falsetto. "I need to see boarding passes and photo IDs, please."

Ari looks down and is surprised to see her hands are shaking. She takes a few deep breaths, hoping to calm herself down. *I can do this.*

"Are you going to be okay?" she whispers to Natua in a last-ditch effort to distract herself. "You were always afraid of heights as a kid."

He giggles. "I'll be fine. I don't know if you noticed, but my fear was pretty much limited to when Mama asked me to get the ripe coconuts."

"You've got to be kidding me," she groans. "How many times did I do that chore for you?"

"Hey, it's not like I wasn't afraid," Natua replies. "At least in a banyan tree, you can hold onto branches and stuff on the way up."

"You and I both know how to climb a palm tree— don't go giving me that excuse now. It's all in the feet."

"I know, but letting go so I could pick the coconuts still freaked me out."

Ari rolls her eyes. "I think the work is what bothered you."

"Anyway," he says, "to answer your question, I'll be fine."

The businessmen have passed through the metal detectors and disappeared out the door, and Moehara turns back to them. "I know it's still a few minutes before first class is done boarding, but nobody else is here—these early morning flights are either completely packed or half-empty, and you lucked out today. If you want to get on the plane now, you'll have a few minutes to manage those stairs without anyone getting in your way."

"That's really sweet of you, Moe," she replies.

"You sure you're not too tired from the walk over here?" Natua asks Ari.

"Now's just as good a time as any," she says. "Let's go, coconut boy."

"Very funny," he says drily before addressing Moehara. "I'll just bring up the passes and what not for both of us, if that's okay. Wouldn't want Ari to stand on that leg too long."

"Of course. Not a problem," she says. "Are you sure you don't want help with your carry-ons?"

"I think we've got it," Natua says as he digs through his backpack for his wallet. Ari hands him her documents, and he squeezes her hand reassuringly when he takes them.

Moe is efficient at her job, and before Ari can fully prepare herself, she's on the stairs, pulling herself up by Natua's arm for dear life while the guy who works security stands guard behind her. "This was a mistake." She tries to whisper, but she has to raise her voice to be heard above the breaking waves.

"I don't know what you're talking about—you're doing great." Natua loosens a few of her fingers from their death grip. "Though I'm pretty sure you've cut off circulation to my hand."

"Oh, sorry." She laughs, but instead of coming out lighthearted, it sounds desperate.

"Just think—in less than an hour, we're going to be safely in Pape'ete. And once you've done one flight, what's one or two more?"

"Right." She focuses on penguin-walking up the stairs so she doesn't lose her balance.

Natua reaches the top, and it's time to step onto the plane. Ari feels the blood drain from her face, but to her relief, the captain looks nothing like Henri. He's dressed in a formal suit and jacket, a pair of golden wings pinned to his lapel.

"Welcome aboard. My name is Stephan and I'll be your pilot today."

"Great, we're glad to meet you." Natua speaks for the both of them, guessing Ari might not be able to. He moves to let Ari go up the aisle first and he shakes the pilot's hand.

"Nervous flier?" The pilot asks.

Natua points a thumb in the direction Ari hobbled off in. "The worst."

"We'll make sure the cart's fully stocked with wine before we take off," he replies with a wink.

Natua moves on and sees that Ari's past the curtain into economy class. He presses forward, backpack awkwardly bulky in the narrow aisle, but when he moves into the rear of the plane, Ari's nowhere to be found. *Oh no...*

He tries to turn around, but his backpack catches on the seat behind him. Without a second thought, he whips it off and throws it in a seat. "Ari?" he calls tentatively. That's when he hears a plastic door *click clacking* against a wall.

Ari emerges from the lavatory, patting down disheveled hair before wiping at her mouth. "Sorry I disappeared," she says as she wobbles towards him. "Lost my stomach for a minute there."

"You had me worried you ditched, though I don't know how you could've."

"No, didn't ditch." Her words fail to sound as carefree as the smile Natua knows she's faking.

"Here, let me take your bag." He holds out his hand.

"Thanks, Natua." She passes it over. "For everything."

He turns away to put the bags in the overhead bin and hopes she doesn't notice his sheepishness. "No problem," he mumbles. After fiddling with the bags for a minute, he moves down the aisle and exclaims, "Oh, you should take a seat!"

"Relax, I'm not exactly an invalid. Besides—" her tone darkens, "we're going to be sitting a lot over the next 24 hours."

"Don't be so dramatic," he says, tired of tiptoeing around her fears when this whole thing was *her* idea. "You're going to sit on your ass until you are exactly where you need to be, so just chill."

"You're right," she replies, but her tone is unconvinced. She had requested the window seat for this first flight so she can look outside and distract herself with the ocean view. Natua sees that she's lost in thought staring at the water, and he only hopes that strategy will continue working once the plane leaves the tarmac.

Other passengers slowly fill in the back of the plane, and Natua's pulling out his phone to turn it off when it lets out a small *ding.* He has an email about his father's ring. He sucks in his breath, and the sound breaks Ari out of her reverie.

"I thought I was the nervy one today," she says as she turns towards him. "You sure you're all right?"

Natua turns his phone away, wanting to navigate this moment on his own. "Yeah, everything's fine." At her insistent stare, he adds, "Seriously! I thought I forgot my wallet in the lounge, but I'm sitting on it."

She shakes her head, amusement fading as she turns back to the window.

Let's see what you have to say for yourself, Armando. But when he opens the email, he quickly realizes it's not from his father. It's from someone named Mariana who claims the ring belonged to *her* father. He's obsessed for most of his life over finding the man, but he hadn't stopped to consider what other family he might stumble across. He furrows his brow at the thought of a half-sister, and types out a reply in stilted Spanish just as Moe walks through the curtain and asks everyone to turn off their electronics.

. . .

When Moe reappears and runs through the safety checks, it's all Ari can do not to bolt. She knows that if there's a problem with the plane, a plastic oxygen mask and a seat belt aren't going to go very far. *I wonder how many times Henri listened to that drill from the cockpit.*

It's the first time that day she's allowed his name to cross her mind. She's felt his presence with her ever since she boarded the plane, but she still hasn't decided whether that's a good thing or not. After all, what happened was her fault. Even if it was a mistake, it was one she didn't fix—and now she can never undo the damage. She wonders if the dead can forgive. If Henri would want to forgive her.

The thoughts are brief, but they distract her until the seatbelt light turns on with a dull *bing,* the sound muffled as though it's filtered through the layers of emergency supplies stowed in every spare crevice of the plane. *Not that any of them do any good. If it weren't for a malfunctioning seat belt, Henri might still be alive. Or maybe if it weren't for me...*

The plane begins its short taxi towards the runway, and she doesn't even realize she's grabbed Natua's hand until he leans over and says, "Do you know if Moe's single?"

She drops his hand just long enough to give him a playful smack on the arm. "Is that really what you're thinking about right now?"

He grins, but his little joke isn't enough to stop her stomach from turning to knots as the plane begins its steep ascent. She finds herself holding her breath and counting the seconds after liftoff. She doesn't let herself breathe until she's hit 43—the number of seconds it took for Henri's plane to become engulfed in flames after he started the engine. At 44 seconds, she knew he was gone forever, his spirit lifting off for heaven from the northwestern corner of the island.

. . .

Natua tries to watch Ari carefully throughout their flight but his thoughts keep drifting towards Mariana. He had been purposefully vague in the posting about the ring, and now he finds himself wondering how to break this news to her.

I should really talk to Armando first, not my sister. My sister. The phrase feels foreign to him, so he looks up the Spanish words on his phone. *Mi hermana. Nope, still weird.*

The flight seems much longer than the 40 minutes Irene had printed neatly on their itinerary. Natua may be nervous, but he's impatient to get to Europe and finally start to build the relationship with his father—with his whole new family!—that he's always dreamed of.

Natua doesn't notice how shallow Ari's breathing has become until she's on the verge of hyperventilating.

"I've gotta get outta here," she says. She pushes past him to stand in the aisle.

"Where are you gonna go?"

"I've gotta get outta here," she repeats.

That's when he notices the wild look in her eyes. "Ari, relax, please—you're freaking me out."

"I can't—I never should've done this, I deserve—" she cuts herself short, voice choking on a sob.

"Look at me. Ari—look at me." When her eyes finally meet his, he sees the desperation of a trapped animal. "I want you to listen to me."

She swallows hard. "Mhm."

"We are in Tahiti. Just you and me. Can you picture that for me?"

She shakes her head and clears her throat.

"Yes, you can. Just close your eyes and imagine it." He waits until her eyes flutter closed before continuing. "We've already landed. Everything is fine. We're off the plane. Nothing bad has happened. Are you with me?"

"I think so."

"We're in Tahiti, and we just sat down to have dinner. You ordered *uru* and mahi-mahi. The server is on their way with a second round of drinks. Can you smell it?"

She shakes her head no.

"Just think about how *uru* smells when my mom makes it, with that thick coconut sauce you love on the breadfruit. The fish is slathered with *taha'a* vanilla sauce. Can you smell it now?"

"Yeah." Her leg twitches—she's still itching to run.

"Your drink is here. What did you order again?"

"Uhh... maybe a Tahiti Drink."

"That's right, you love Tahiti Drinks, despite the stupid name. Imagine you're having a sip of it now—how does it taste?"

She cracks an eye open. "This is ridiculous, Natua."

"Work with me, Ari. What's it taste like?"

She huffs and closes her eyes again. "Like a Tahiti Drink. It's sugary. I guess it tastes like pineapple with, uh, a bit of passion fruit mixed in. You can't even taste the rum."

"Can I try it?"

"Natua, I know what you're doing."

"Please, let's not make a scene in the restaurant. Can you sit back down with me? I don't want to eat alone."

"Fine." She continues to stand, stock still.

"Hey, open your eyes." Natua motions to the seat beside him. "Aren't you forgetting something?"

All of her muscles tense at the suggestion. "I can't do that."

Just then, Moe begins making her way down the aisle towards the galley in the back of the plane. "Is everything okay?" she asks in her customer voice, still six or seven seats away.

Ari snaps her head up and starts backing down the aisle, away from Moe and Natua and their seats.

Natua catches Moe's eye and winks. "I was just telling Ari how Paris would be so much more fun if I had someone *real special* to share it with. If you ever end up on a transatlantic flight, you should call me."

"Uh... right," Moe replies.

"Na-tu-a," Ari scolds. "Stop making poor Moe uncomfortable." She walks back towards him to continue the scolding. "I can't believe you."

Crisis averted. Ari's still staring at him, so he feels the need to keep up the charade. When Moehara walks by, he whispers, "Call me," and puts his hand near his ear in the universal sign. Ari groans, but she's back in her seat and their first flight is almost over.

. . .

They have to wait until well after nightfall to board their next flight, and both of them are relieved to get away from the tension of the airport. Ari takes a deep breath and flexes all of her muscles one by one after they walk out into the morning sun.

"Now I really want some mahi-mahi."

"It's too early for lunch, but I'm down for seeing a few sights and then grabbing some food."

He intends to tell her about Mariana during their first meal in Tahiti—and then their second—but something keeps holding him back. He tells himself he's just waiting for the right opening to mention it, but he knows that isn't the reason at all.

After a full day wandering around Pape'ete in a cast, Ari hardly needs the sleeping pill. She crashes in a hard plastic chair in the lounge next to the gate and she only wakes long enough to board. *Thank god for sleep aids just the same.* He's avoided looking at his phone all day, but he knows he has a new message waiting from Mariana. He breathes a sigh of relief when he sees she's switched to French.

Hi there Ignacio. I was wondering if you would be able to mail the ring to me? My P.O. box is below. I'd really appreciate it, and I'd be more than happy to wire you the cost of shipping.

He resists the temptation to slap himself. He hadn't thought this through at all. If he gives up the ring *and* doesn't get the opportunity to meet Mariana, he'll never get another chance to find his father. Not to mention that his mother will be bone-shakingly angry when she finds out what he's done. No, mailing it just won't do.

But in dropping her P.O. box, Mariana has given him exactly what he needs to plan his next step—the city where she and maybe even the man they both call father currently reside.

. . .

When Manu flies back into Huahine later that week, he's wondering if Robert was the right person to ask to co-sponsor his bill. He can't remember much of their dinner on Monday thanks to the free-flowing drinks, but he remembers a vague sense of discomfort and scraps of a conversation that don't make any sense.

Even aside from his feeling that something happened that night he should remember, Manu's disappointed in the man's efforts to weasel the meat out of what he's come to think of as the responsibility bill. He'd hoped his old friend would risk a bit of boldness for his sake.

"Hey Moehara," he calls to the flight attendant. "Grab me a Hinano from the galley?"

"Sure," she says. She flashes her brightest of smiles and disappears into the back of the plane.

Upon her return, she pops open the beer and pockets the cap. "Did you want a glass today?"

"You know better than to waste plastic on a guy like me," he says lightly. "I'll just take the bottle, hon."

She passes it to him, and she's about to walk away when she stops. "Hey, aren't you Ari's father?"

"Yes, I am," he replies. "You know her from her post at the airport?"

"Yessir," she says. "In fact, I just saw her a few days ago boarding a plane to Pape'ete."

"You mean Motu Mute—she was headed to Bora Bora."

"Hmm... I'm sure I was working the Pape'ete route." She pauses to think. "Well you know firsthand how busy they keep us—I hardly know one route from the next some days!"

"How was she looking?"

"She was a little nervous, but her friend seemed like he was taking pretty good care of her."

"He's a good kid," Manu responds. "I don't know how he managed to get her on a plane. I thought they would take a boat over."

"He was a bit cheeky for my taste, but it seemed to relax her—I never knew she was so afraid of flying. Anyway, enjoy your Hinano, Mr. Fonua!"

He downs the bitter beer as Moehara makes her way back to the galley. He might not be afraid of planes like his daughter, but flying has never come easy for him as passenger or pilot. He only flies because it helps him feel closer to his son. And that's worth the pain regardless of how it threatens to consume him.

PART III: AWAY

Chapter 11

The next 21 hours are exhausting for Natua and Ari, despite Ari's abuse of the sleeping pills in her carryon. Their journey is marked by a layover in LAX and two more panic attacks before they finally leave airplanes behind for their lodgings in Montmartre. Irene had booked them a tiny hotel room with two rock-hard beds and a locker for any valuables they've brought along.

Natua scoffs at the locker. The only thing he has worth stealing is the ring, which he keeps in his front pocket or slipped loosely on his index finger all hours of the day. Ari quietly deposits her mom's ancient Walkman there, and he curses himself for making fun of the locker.

Despite having slept on the overnight flight, both Ari and Natua are hit by jet lag thanks to the 11-hour time difference. The first thing they do in Paris is nap on the uncomfortable beds. Ari suggests lunch when she gets up a few hours later.

"Look who's finally awake," Natua teases. "I was worried you'd turned into Sleeping Beauty or something."

"We've been in Europe for less than a day, and you're already comparing me to some Sleepyhead No-Spine? Next thing you know, you're going to start smoking cigarettes and investing in electric cars."

Natua guffaws. "Well, we are in the *métropole* now. Gotta fight the smog, you know?"

Ari rolls her eyes. "I'd rather just focus on finding a decent restaurant," she replies. "What're you in the mood for?"

"I think I want some beef," Natua says. Cows are scarce in the islands, making beef the most expensive meat in Polynesia.

"Ohh, living large I see." She laughs.

"Hopefully," he says. "Now let's go."

Ari is winded by the time they walk down the three flights of narrow stairs to the street.

"You all right?"

"Don't worry about me. Let's figure out where that metro station is, eh?"

When they finally get on a train, the cars are so crowded the pair can barely breathe, much less sit down. The jerking starts and stops make Ari cringe, so they get off after a couple of stops at Gare de L'Est.

"You'd think someone might give up a seat for the girl in a cast," Natua grumbles as they emerge onto the city streets.

"My leg doesn't bend very well in the cast, so there wouldn't have even been enough room for me to sit. Besides," she adds wistfully, "we aren't in the islands anymore."

"No kidding. Hey—there's a little restaurant over there. Wanna try it?"

"Sure. We can even sit outside."

"Why would we sit out here? It's freezing! Besides, think about all the car fumes and secondhand smoke."

"Killjoy," Ari mutters. "Fine, inside it is then."

Natua's impressed by the steak he orders, but Ari is disappointed in the shrimp.

"What did you expect? We're way too far inland for decent seafood."

They make small talk, and Natua is trying to decide whether he wants to bring up Mariana yet when Ari asks, "Have you had any news about your father?"

He nods, mouth full. He washes down the last few

bites of steak with a much bigger gulp of beer than necessary before replying. "I actually got a response about the ring, but not from him."

"Who then?"

"His daughter." He pauses, as if it's the end of the world.

"That's really cool," Ari replies lightly. Then, "Wait, are you not okay with having a sister?"

"It's just so weird," he says. He's relieved to finally talk about it. "I mean, what if I had never reached out, and I have this huge family that I never knew I'm a part of?"

"Right, but you did reach out. What did she think about having a new brother?"

He gulps down more of his beer and avoids her gaze.

"You can't put that off forever, Natua. You have to tell her."

"I know, I know, I'll tell her. I'm just not ready right now. It's going to be so awkward."

"That's fine. Just make sure you *do* mention it—the sooner the better." She sips her water before adding, "Are you sure she's real though, and not some poser on the internet trying to get something out of you?"

"Huh. No..." he trails off. He'd gotten so caught up in the existence of Mariana that he hadn't considered whether her existence could be a ruse. "How would I know though?"

"If it's really her father's ring, then she should have photos to prove it. Ask her for one."

"And then I'll have a picture of my father too. Ari, you're a genius!" He pulls out his phone and starts typing. "Give me a second. I'm going to email her right now."

• • •

While Natua is busy with his phone on the slow restaurant Wi-Fi, Ari strikes up a conversation with the waiter who stops by to refill her water glass.

"Can you tell me what's fun to do in this area?"

He gives her a tiny smile. "You are in Paris, *n'est-ce pas?* Then you must see the Tour d'Eiffel and the Arc de Triomphe."

"Right, but what kind of things are fun in *this* neighborhood?" She points to her leg. "I don't feel like going very far."

"Agh! I see. There is a haunted house a couple blocks that way," he says, gesturing vaguely, "but I'm not sure if they're open this time of year. My personal favorite around here is the street art place, but their biggest thing is walking tours." He looks pointedly at her leg and lets his gaze rest on it a beat too long before meeting her eyes. "Obviously not your preferred activity."

"No, definitely not," Ari agrees, waving a hand dismissively at her cast. "Anything a little more sedentary nearby?"

"If you're looking for a place to relax and take in the city, the park behind the restaurant is a great spot. It backs up to the canal."

"I would love to see some water," she replies, though she's not sure a canal counts.

"Where are you from, exactly? Your accent is charming."

Ari's cheeks warm at the compliment. "We are visiting from the Society Islands."

The waiter grows more detached after she pronounces the word "we," as if he hadn't been waiting on their table for the last half hour and hadn't noticed Natua's presence. "The canal may be a bit disappointing to you then," he replies before moving abruptly to another table.

"What was that all about?" Natua looks up from his phone.

"I think he was flirting with me," Ari whispers excitedly. "A Parisian guy! Flirting with me!"

Natua rolls his eyes. "Oh please, it's probably part of his job. Get silly women like you to come back over and over again to buy more lunches from Fabio over there."

"Fabio is an Italian name," Ari scoffs. "He looks more like a 'Pierre' to me."

"Are you done drooling?" he asks. "Or are we going to have to stay here all day until pretty boy finishes his shift?"

"Very funny. He was telling me there's a nice park out back with a view of the canal."

"What canal?"

"I don't know!"

"I'm not interested in sitting around in the freezing cold where ol' Fabio goes to woo women."

"Oh, stop it. Now tell me more about Mariana." Her eyes light up with excitement.

"For starters, she lives in Seville."

The pair continue their conversation about Mariana long after leaving the cozy lunch spot. Ari convinces him to stroll through the park the waiter had recommended, and she sees on the map that there's a hospital located a few blocks away, across the canal. "You should book your flight soon so you can get a better rate. We can head over to the hospital today and see about getting me that medication, and then you can be on your way. If that goes well, I might even be able to go with you!"

His voice is uneasy when he replies, "But what if I can't determine if she really is who she says she is? I need to be sure."

"Na-tu-aaa," she groans, "don't put this off because you're scared. I'm sorry I said anything."

"No, I'm glad you did because I wasn't thinking about it that way."

"I'm sure it'll be fine. Besides, you need to go to Spain to find your father anyway. Might as well investigate this lead in person."

"How?"

"Stake out her P.O. box or something! Haven't you read any good detective novels? This is part of the process."

"This isn't a detective novel. I don't want to get robbed or beaten up."

"Just try to stay in public places. You'll be okay."

"Easy for you to say," he says, brushing aside a stray lock of hair that's swaying in the bitter March wind. "What do you think—off to the hospital? I can't stand the cold of this place much longer."

"Off to the hospital," Ari repeats with a sigh, wishing she had paid the extra fee to bring a wheelchair along.

. . .

"If you have an emergency, I'm going to need you to check into our Emergency Department—I can't help you here." The receptionist pushes on the red-framed glasses that keep sliding down her thin, severe nose.

"Please," Ari replies, squirming under the woman's steely gaze. "If I don't get the medications I need, I'm going to die."

"Is that so? Why didn't you get those medications from your doctor?"

"I've been waiting over a month for the damn pills to get to the islands! But since no one here seemed capable of putting them on a plane, I decided to come retrieve them myself before this stupid disease gets any worse." Agitated and no longer caring about being polite, she points to the bulge of the cast underneath her pants. "You think this is the way I want to live? You think this isn't important enough to treat?"

"I'm sorry to hear you've been having trouble getting what you need from your doctor," the receptionist says, "but you can't just walk into a hospital demanding pills and expect them to be handed to you." She stares Ari down as if she was a drug runner. "A policy like that would create chaos and transform Paris into the city of addicts. You need a referral from an oncologist or you can head back to the Emergency Department and wait to be seen there." She looks down her nose at Ari. "Last I checked, the wait time back there was about six hours, and there's no guarantee you'll be seen by an oncologist today."

Natua has been hanging back but he comes closer now. He strikes a conciliatory tone when he says, "Is there really nothing you can do for her? We've travelled a long way and she's running out of time."

The woman sighs and reaches up to smooth an imaginary flyaway back into her tightly wound bun. "What I can do for you is offer you a chair in our Emergency waiting room or provide you with the name of an oncologist you can call. Would you like me to send someone up with a wheelchair?"

Ari steps back from the counter and turns to Natua. In Tahitian, she asks, "What should I do?"

He looks down at her knee. "Are you up for staying here half the night to be seen by staff who are only experts in broken bones?"

"I didn't come here to be put on some fancy doctor's waiting list," she replies stubbornly.

"You don't know that you'll be put on a waiting list."

"So you think I should call the cancer doctor, even though I already know what medications I need?"

"What you know doesn't matter if they don't listen to you." He motions slightly towards the receptionist, who is scowling as she waits for them to finish their conversation. "Besides, you've never gotten a second opinion to make sure that *is* what you need."

Ari measures her words and takes her time more than usual because of the receptionist's appallingly bad manners. Still in Tahitian, she tells Natua, "You do have a point. Besides, if they want to make me wait too long, we can always come back and sit in the Emergency Department then."

"Yes. Hopefully after we've had some dinner."

Some of the tension in Ari's face loosens. "It's a plan, then." They turn back to the receptionist, only to find that she's taking care of someone else. "Wow, these people's rudeness knows no limits," she adds. The receptionist waves them to the back of the small line that's formed.

Natua groans. "Seriously."

"Maybe Papa was right—maybe they really don't care." She picks at her fingernails and wonders if this whole trip was a mistake.

Natua shakes his head. "You know we aren't in the islands anymore. Things were bound to be different in the *métropole.*"

"You mean they only care about saving *real* French people."

"Ari, jeezus, no need to be so dramatic. I think we just went about this a little backwards—we probably should've made you an appointment with a doctor instead of just waltzing into a hospital like this."

Ari looks unconvinced. "That woman wasn't even taking me seriously. Whether we walked in the wrong door or not shouldn't matter," she says. "I've already waited far too long for that treatment. But you're probably right about the second opinion—it's a good idea to see a specialist if I can get in."

The receptionist has taken care of the line of people in front of them and now she motions them back over. "Here's the card for the best oncologist on the east side of the city," she says. "Be sure to call right away so you can talk to someone. His office closes at 15:00 hours on Wednesdays—that's 3PM," she adds, as if they don't use the 24-hour clock in the islands.

"Thanks for the information," Ari says. "Do you know how long his wait list is?"

The woman's steel-faced expression somehow grows even colder. "I don't work for him," she says. "If you want that information, you'll have to call his office yourself and ask."

"Oh, of course." Ari slides the card into her pocket and hobbles towards the wide glass doors.

"Cheer up," Natua says. "Give the doctor a call, and then let's take a taxi and go check out some of that tourist crap Irene put in our itinerary."

A small smile forms below her troubled eyes, like sunshine during a rain shower. "If you insist. Just give me a minute." She heads for a row of empty chairs along the half-wall that separates the reception area from the hospital's tiny café.

Ari takes a deep breath, pulls out her phone, and dials.

A polite-sounding man answers the phone in crisp French.

"Yes, hello, I was hoping to make an appointment to see Dr...." She glances at the card. "Dr. Barreau?"

"Your name and date of birth?"

Ari gives him the information, and there's a small pause. She can hear clicking as the man types her information into his computer. "I'm sorry, you're not in our system?"

"No, I'm not a current patient," she says, her voice quickening. "But I need to see an oncologist. I have myeloma and I have come all the way from *Polynésie Française* to get the best medical attention I can, and I'm only in Paris for a week. There's no time to waste getting me on a treatment plan."

"You're not even a patient here, and you want to be seen immediately?" His voice is carefully controlled, but the incredulity still stings.

"Yes," she says, unsure of herself now that he's questioning her. "I went to the hospital, and they said I could call you or sit in the waiting room all night."

His tone softens when the fear creeps into her voice. "We aren't technically receiving new patients right now, but since you're only in the city for a short time and seem to have some exceptional circumstances, let me see if we can't make something work. I'm going to put you on hold, but don't go away."

Soothing piano music fills her ear. Natua is a few meters away staring out the window, lost in his own thoughts. Ari realizes how much she's come to depend on him in this strange city. How easily she would have drifted away without him.

When the man comes back on the line, he tells her that a last-minute cancellation has opened up their only time slot for the next three weeks. "Do you think you can be here Friday afternoon? Say, 14:00 hours?"

She lets out a sigh of relief. "Of course. Thank you. I will see you then."

• • •

Manu is taking his breakfast on the veranda when the phone rings. "Hello?"

"Good morning Manu, it's Robert." It takes a second for Manu to recognize the tinny, faraway voice of his colleague.

"Robert?" The man never calls him at home, especially so early in the morning. Manu checks his watch—he isn't planning to head into his office for at least another hour.

"I wanted to let you know as soon as I could—our bill is going to be heard for arguments at the very next meeting of the Assembly!"

"What? That's great news!" He breaks into a huge grin, then stops. "Wait, doesn't our next session start on Tuesday?"

"You bet it does," the Assemblymember replies. "But I think the bill is ready. You think you can prepare opening arguments by then?"

"I've been waiting for this moment all of my adult life," Manu responds. "As co-sponsor of the bill, will you say anything?"

"I'll be your backup," he says. "So send me a copy of your remarks when you get them on paper."

"Perfect," Manu replies. "This is my highest priority, so I should have them to you by Friday afternoon."

"That's wonderful," Robert's voice is calm and measured in contrast to Manu's obvious elation. "I'll let you get to it then."

Manu is too excited to finish the rest of his breakfast and he talks to himself as he cleans up. "Ari will be so excited to hear this." He grabs his cell phone to text his daughter. He starts a message but he's so caught up in figuring out what to say about his bill that he doesn't finish it. A few hours later at the office, Manu remembers and deletes the half-written text. No need to bother her now. *I should let her keep her mind off things here for a few more days.*

. . .

By the end of the afternoon, Ari and Natua have snapped a selfie at the top of the Eiffel Tower and toured the Arc de Triomphe and even seen the Mona Lisa—although this last activity takes quite the toll on Ari's bum leg.

"All this walking and standing around for a painting this big?" She gestures with her hands as she talks, her voice incredulous. "Mainlanders really are weird."

They get lost on their way out of the museum and Ari stops for a breather at the bottom of a majestic marble staircase. "Now this is worth stopping for," she says. She's pointing to a stone statue on a landing halfway up the stairs. The statue could have come from the bow of an ancient warship—perhaps from the Vikings. Its state of decay speaks of an authenticity that the well-preserved paintings lack from their orderly spots in glass cases or behind impeccably restored frames.

The winged woman stands victorious on top of a pile of stone. Her head and arms have been lost to time, but the sculptor had caught her in midstride, robes flying like they're being whipped by the ocean wind. Her total height is enormous—people milling around her on the landing don't even reach the top of the stone platform she so easily dominates.

"Wow," is all Natua can manage.

"Yeah." They both pause to take it in for a moment before Ari breaks their silence. "Could you go up there and read the plaque for me? I want to know more about her."

He complies and shoots her a text with a photo of the information. Ari opens her phone and is about to start reading when she decides against it. *I know all I need to know just by looking at her.*

When he gets back, he asks lightly, "Can you read it or you want me to tell you what it said?"

"I'll read it later," she responds, still enraptured by the work of art. "Can you just tell me what her name is?"

He pulls out his phone and references the photo he took. "They call her the Winged Victory of Samo... Samothrace?" He struggles with the pronunciation.

"Winged Victory. It suits her." Her voice is faraway and dreamy. With newfound energy, she says, "Actually, I think I'm going up there to take a closer look for myself."

"You sure? I don't think we go this way to get out."

"Oh, I'm sure." Having caught her breath, she takes on the stairs with determination in her eyes. "She's exactly what I needed from this stuffy old place."

By the time Natua and Ari sit down for dinner that night, it's much later than they'd intended and both of them are starving. Natua picks an unassuming, poorly lit restaurant that seems oddly packed. Ari raises an eyebrow over the choice.

"What? They have 5-star Yelp! reviews."

"Fine," she says, "but if it doesn't live up, then you aren't allowed to decide where we eat anymore."

"It's a deal," he says and makes a show of shaking her hand. "And if it does, you need to stop questioning me so much."

"Oh, get over yourself," she responds. "I only question you when you need it."

He shrugs. A few minutes later, a server brings them to a table.

Ari shifts in her chair uncomfortably before stretching her leg out. She tries to keep it tucked under the table, but her shoe keeps edging into the aisle.

"What are you staring at?" Natua asks finally, breaking the relative silence enveloping their table.

"My leg," she replies absent-mindedly.

Natua follows her eyes to the outline of her oversized calf pressed tightly against the gray fabric of her slacks. "Holy smokes, Ari! You should've told me it was bothering you before it got this swollen. We could've headed back to the room hours ago."

"It doesn't hurt that bad," she says. "Besides, I wouldn't have wanted to miss that statue in the Louvre."

"Which one? We must've seen three dozen."

"You know. The one at the top of the stairs." Her eyes dance as she pictures it. "Winged Victory."

"Oh, that's right," he says. "We could've saved that for tomorrow though—I mean, come on, look at you."

"It's not that bad," she argues. "It's these pants. They're designed to be a little snug anyways." He gives her a pointed look that says *I don't believe you*. Ari continues, "I'll rest tomorrow, promise."

"Fine. But jeez Ari, next time don't let it go like that!"

"It doesn't hurt," she says, then, "You worry more than my dad."

"Ao!" He clutches his chest as if the words have physically struck him. "That's a low blow!"

"What's gotten into you?" She laughs and takes a sip of her water. "You're even goofier than normal."

"Just having a good time, that's all," he replies easily. "Speaking of your dad, have you talked to him since we left?"

"No." A guilty tone sneaks into her voice. "He's probably worried sick, huh?"

"It wouldn't hurt to check in. I'm going to text Mama now."

He pulls out his phone and is about to press send when Ari says, "Wait!" He looks up at her. "What time is it back home?"

"Oh, good catch. It's 11 hours behind, right?"

"Yeah, I think so."

"Well, it's not super early there. I'll just um, change dinner to breakfast." He grins sheepishly.

"Oh my god, Natua, you nearly ruined our whole alibi!"

"I know, I know. And almost gave my mother a heart attack." He pauses and his smile turns somber. "She can't handle that kind of stress these days—that's exactly why I had to tell her I was headed to Bora Bora."

"At least we made it here. So far, so good."

"And that calls for a toast." He picks up his wine glass and motions towards hers. "To the long way we've come."

She clinks his glass and a shadow moves across her face. "And the long way we still have to go."

When they arrive back at the hotel after couscous that lives up to the 5-star reviews, Ari immediately announces she is completely, utterly exhausted. Though she's in a rush to get to bed, she spends quite a bit of time in the bathroom struggling to change out of her slacks. The swelling in her legs isn't limited to the area around her cast, but seems to have covered the entirety of her lower extremities. Even her feet are puffy.

She finally peels off the disobedient pants. By contrast, her loose pajama shorts are a breeze to slip into, though they don't fit very loosely on this particular occasion.

Ari makes a beeline for bed after she emerges. "Bathroom's all yours," she mumbles to Natua. He grunts back a reply, but he isn't paying any attention to her or her swollen legs—he's staring at his phone.

. . .

Ari may have taken an absurdly long time in their on-suite bathroom, but Natua hardly cares. Mariana wrote back to the message he sent her at lunch, and she attached a photo of their father.

Natua is glad he's alone when he first opens it. He lets out a gasp, and then a low whistle.

There, right in front of him, are the grainy lines of an old family photo. *His* family. A youthful-looking man, maybe in his late twenties or early thirties, is holding a smiling woman with impeccably teased hair in his arms. The photo doesn't show much of the man because the woman's puffy dress takes up most of the lower half of the frame, but it doesn't matter. His complexion is a shade or two lighter than Natua's, but the man's features are a carbon copy of his own, down to the wavy dark hair framing his face.

The man's hands are grasped loosely around the woman's stomach, and the ring is unmistakable. So are the bright gold wedding bands on their left hands, glinting in the midmorning sun.

Natua takes in every bit of the photograph slowly, purposefully. He hadn't even bothered to read the email before getting assaulted with this piece of his history. *No wonder Mama's always told me to leave him alone. She had to have known.* Ari's breathing in the bed next to his has deepened and slowed before he remembers to read Mariana's message.

Hey Natua, I hope this settles any doubts for you. These are my parents on their wedding day. I don't ever remember the ring because he lost it on a trip when I was just a child, but I'm sure you can agree we are talking about the same piece of jewelry.

Yes, he can agree. He's glad he hadn't called the ring his father's in the listing, but how can he say something now? *Yes, hi, I'm actually your brother. Care to arrange a family reunion between me and our cheating bastard of a father?*

His finger slips on the screen and he gulps. There's more to her message.

I'm leaving the country next week for work. When I get back, I was hoping to give the ring to my mother as an anniversary gift. Think you can get it to me by Saturday?

He knows he's going to get there on time before he even finishes reading the words, but he's just as sure that Mrs. da Costa will *not* like the gift he's bringing for her. Not one bit.

Chapter 12

"What do you mean all of the flights on Friday are booked?" Natua asks into the phone the next morning. He's called several different airlines to book a flight to Seville, but he's having trouble finding a last-minute seat. "No, no, I'm not interested in first-class seats for a two-hour flight—I don't care if it's spring break! You have four flights a day and not one pair of economy seats on any of them?"

"Having tough luck?" Ari asks from her spot in bed after he hangs up in frustration.

"Apparently everybody is heading to Seville this weekend," he says glumly. "Everybody but me, that is."

"Have you asked about single seats? I know I was talking about going with you, but I don't have to. We can meet up again here for the flight home once you're done, if you want."

"I don't like the idea of leaving you before you've been seen." His voice takes on a protective edge.

"I'll be fine. Better than ever, really, once I get those drugs."

"Still, I don't like it."

"I would've done this alone if you hadn't come. You might as well finish what you came here for."

He sighs. "You're right. I hate it, but you're right. I'll keep looking."

Twenty minutes later, he's talked to every airline that flies out of Charles de Gaulle and Orly, and the only seat available is on a flight that leaves later that afternoon from Charles de Gaulle.

"You think I should take it?" he asks Ari. His phone is pressed to his shoulder.

"Yes!" She talks with her hands as she says, "It's not like you came along just for me. I only ask that you meet up with me here for our return flight on Monday."

"I wouldn't dream of making you fly alone! I promise we'll get on that plane together."

"Then you should study your Spanish while you still can. You're going to need it awfully soon."

He nods. "Sorry about the delay," he says into his phone. "I'll take that economy seat. What time did you say the flight leaves?"

. . .

It's another quiet morning at the pension. Angela tries to take it easy. Even getting herself out of bed can leave her breathless on the bad days. She's spent the last two hours preparing and nibbling on her breakfast, and now she's faced with the monumental task of cleaning up after herself.

"I thought those kids were going to be back by now." She stands. "He knows I can't handle things like I used to—not for this long." She huffs. "But kids will be kids. At least he didn't run off for no reason. Poor girl needs something to do besides worry and wait."

Her whole body shakes when she coughs. She has to grip the edge of the table so she doesn't lose her balance.

"Though she isn't alone in this world without him."

Angela's been irritated for the past several days. After the kids left, she noticed Armando's ring missing from its place next to her bed. She never touches it, just keeps it in her jewelry dish exactly where he left it.

"A parting gift for my sweet," he had said in thickly accented French as he plopped it among her earth-toned baubles. All these years, it's shone like a beacon—or a mirage. She still doesn't know if it lights the way ahead or if it's been leading her astray in a vast and empty desert all these years.

That day, it had taken all of her willpower to resist asking him to take off his *other* ring, to pawn it and stay with her forever. She'd been afraid to ask because she was sure she had known the answer. *Island women are exotic playthings, not life partners*, she had thought bitterly.

She's hoped with all of her might that she judged him wrong, that he'd come back to her someday. His continued, deafening absence has told her all she ever needed to know. Notwithstanding, she's never moved on... just in case.

Angela still treasures the ring and the hope she lets it represent. She looks at it and imagines all that could have been. If she stares at it long enough, she can almost convince herself that Armando is in the kitchen fixing himself a morning espresso. By now, his dark waves are tinged with gray and his fair skin thoroughly tanned. They spend dozens of sunny afternoons in their bedroom behind the blackout curtains. They have a running joke about the tan lines that sit just below his hips from designer swimming trunks.

But now the ring is gone. "He better not have pawned it for an airline ticket," she growls to herself. Her grip on the table turns her knuckles pale. She'll have to search his room and see if she can find it.

"First things first, I suppose. I should clean this up." She stacks her dishes in a neat pile and then hobbles towards the kitchen. The distance feels much farther than it ever has. Her ragged breathing echoes around the pension's empty halls, disturbing the calm morning.

She stops to lean against a wall in the front hallway, the once bright yellow stucco faded from years of scrubbing. She remembers the day she applied it, not long after her parents retired. Angela had been determined to turn the pension's dismal prospects around and make it a top destination spot. That was back when she had her strength. Now, Angela shakes her head at the memory. Instead of leaving her son a brighter future, she's run the place into the ground.

In her distraction, a tea cup slips off her precarious pile and breaks into a thousand pieces on the cool brown tiles. "*Merde.*" When she adjusts her footing to bend down and grab one of the larger pieces, a sharp fragment finds her bare heel and she cries out.

Angela loses her balance and the rest of the dishes crash around her. Her ragged breathing becomes dangerously slow. The pension is filled with an all-consuming quiet.

. . .

Ari reassures Natua she'll be fine on her own what feels like a thousand times between when he books his flight to Seville and when he's scheduled to leave early that afternoon.

They walk out of the hotel together and Ari insists he get a decent lunch before he heads to the airport, even though she's too nervy to eat much herself.

"Come on—it'll be my treat." They choose a quiet café advertising hot cocoa and an assortment of hot soups.

He stalls as long as he can, but the time for him to leave comes all too fast. Ari hides her concerns about fending for herself behind a mask of humor and nearly pushes him out the door when she runs out of jokes. Alone in the restaurant, she watches as he crosses the street and descends into the metro.

Once she's sure he can't see her anymore, she takes a deep breath and lets her fake smile crumple. Thank goodness they didn't go very far from the hotel. Blocks stretch to the size of islands in her mind without Natua to lean on. She already feels adrift in this frigid ocean of concrete and cobblestones.

He has to do this. I don't need him. I don't need him. I don't need him. But she does need him, and no amount of pretending is going to change that. On her own, she doesn't know how to make sense of this foreign, half-frozen city that isn't supposed to feel foreign at all.

. . .

Natua's stomach does somersaults as he heads down the dirty stairwell into the metro station. Now that he doesn't have to be strong for Ari, he finds his own anxieties overwhelming. His fingers tremble as he inserts a paper ticket into the machine, and it takes three tries before the light turns green and he can move further into the subterranean station.

He resists the urge to get off at the next stop and take the train heading back to their hotel, or to get out and just walk on street level where he can breathe. Instead, he grips the metal bar on the underground train as he travels where only the dead should stay.

He gets off at Gare de L'Est to change trains. The lunch hour crowd pushes him this way and that through the station as he looks for the train that will take him the rest of the way to the airport. Panic knots itself through tensed muscles as he fights his way through the press of the throng.

He can't find the right platform, so he gives up and flows along with the suits and tourists. But people are going every which way, and no one seems to care that they're cutting in front of him or pushing up against him beyond the occasional thrown *"pardon."* He's wandered through most of the terminal before finding the blue signs that point the way, and he dashes through a small break in the crowd.

On the dingy platform, an icy breeze makes him shiver. An ancient homeless woman squats next to a wall and chants for coins. Even half a dozen meters away, he can recognize the stench of poverty.

The entire station reeks of it. Inside his pocket, the few euros he has feel heavy with his guilt.

He walks closer to the woman, his breathing shallow out of necessity. Her sweater was once a lovely shade of cream—here and there the original color shows through the patches of grime that have accumulated from her life in the metro. A small suitcase rests on the ground between her legs, and she holds out a coffee cup with trembling hands. The few euros at the bottom of the cup clink together from the jerky motion.

She doesn't look up as Natua approaches. He's shaken by the absence in her eyes. There is no hope, no sadness, no desperation. Only an emptiness that stabs at his heart.

"Here you go, *Tantie*." He drops a few coins in and hopes to earn a smile, to ignite a bit of gratitude or even hope in the woman's eyes. But she doesn't acknowledge him, just continues with her monotonous chant.

By the time the train rolls in, he's glad to get away from her and board the first train he's managed to grab a seat on. As he settles onto the bench's torn plush cushioning, he decides it's time to suggest Mariana meet him face to face. To show her why, he includes a quick snapshot of his face with the message.

He hits the send button and immediately regrets it. Not wanting to know what she's going to say, he turns off the phone. *I'll check it once I land*, he promises himself. It's not like what she says can stop him now. He's going to find their father, with her help or without it.

At the airport, security is a bit more relaxed than it had been on the flight into Paris. He gets to keep his shoes on, but they make him throw away a plastic water bottle he'd forgotten about in his backpack. Natua's taken his seat on the plane before he gives into the temptation to turn his phone back on.

No new messages.

I really should've waited to bring that up. Didn't she say there was some sort of anniversary next week? Talk about bad timing, Natua.

He turns the device back off. Maybe she hasn't responded because she's talking to their father. The man is about to discover the truth at last.

. . .

After Ari gets back to the hotel that afternoon, she has a hard time convincing herself to go back out for dinner. *People don't eat out by themselves for dinner. It's weird.* But late that evening she gets hungry, and the idea of eating alone in her empty room seems too sad for words.

She hobbles back down the stairs to the street level with her bag over her good shoulder. Deciding against dealing with the discomfort and sacrilege to the earth that the metro represents, she hobbles north. Despite having been in the city for a few days now, she still marvels at the chilly March air that seeps into her thin hoodie and makes her breath visible. It's strange to see this proof that she's alive, floating out in front of her. Stranger still is how quickly it disappears.

Ari plans to duck into whatever restaurant she finds first, but it still takes several blocks and what feels like an eternity before she happens on a café with dim lighting and a cozy atmosphere. *Good. I won't look out of place eating by myself if people can barely see me.* She heads in and gets a table near the back.

Once the server heads off to the kitchen with her order, she takes a long swig of the ice water in her glass. Her legs are even more swollen than yesterday despite the bed rest. She wonders whether the wine she'd had with dinner the night before is messing with her meds.

Only one more day until I get the pills that will actually make a difference. She's given up on the turmeric, but she pulls out her other medications and takes some with what few bites of her meal she chokes down. She misses the fresh seafood and the many ways she can eat coconut in the islands.

Her steak is covered in a green sauce she doesn't recognize, but partway through the meal she starts to feel woozy. The server must see it in the slump of her shoulders because he stops by her table with a concerned look on his perfect, pale face.

"Is everything okay with your dinner, *mademoiselle?*"

"It's fine," she says. "It's not that."

"Is there anything I can help you with?"

"No, no," she replies, waving him off. "It's fine."

But it's not fine. After paying for food she felt too sick to eat, Ari embarks on what feels like a never-ending journey back to the hotel. She tires out quickly, and stops several times to rest on shockingly cold metal benches placed underneath dormant or possibly dead trees.

The air feels biting, but when she reaches up to brush her hair out of her face, she's surprised by the heat of her forehead. It's nearly midnight when she finally sees the sign advertising the tiny hotel Irene had chosen for them.

Her knee is aching, but rather than stop *again*, she presses on. She's waiting at the crosswalk when the nausea is replaced by an exhaustion beyond anything she's ever known, and the world fades into nothingness.

. . .

After the plane lands, Natua realizes with a pang that he has no idea where he's going. He's in a strange city and barely knows enough Spanish to ask for directions. He certainly doesn't recognize enough to understand the answer.

Doesn't matter. Can't ask for directions if you have nowhere to go. So, he boots up his phone and sees with relief he has a new message from Mariana.

Hey Natua. I'm not sure why you need to meet in person, but if you insist, you can find me and my boyfriend in front of the post office on Av. de la Constitución at 18:00 hours tonight. Can you let me know if that works for you? And remind me, how much do you want for the ring?

He glances at the clock in the upper corner of his phone. He has plenty of time as long as he doesn't get lost.

He exits the airport and hails a taxi while typing a quick reply. *I'll be there. I'm the one wearing the green tee shirt and yellow jacket.*

"See you soon, sister." The words still sound foreign to his ears. He gets into a cab and tells the driver where to go, then stares out the window in silent awe.

These are the streets my father walks. The city may be strange, but it belongs to him in a way Paris and its cold, cigarette-strewn sidewalks simply never will. His heart beats quick against his chest as they maneuver the narrow streets towards the post office where his sister will be waiting.

Natua pays the cabbie and steps out onto the sidewalk. There's a stone bench a few meters from the entrance and a bus stop across the way. Both are empty, and he doesn't see anyone that matches his mental image of Mariana. So, he heads to the bench and plops his bag on it so he can wait for her. Thankfully, the city doesn't have the same frosty air as Paris, though it's still quite chilly by island standards.

He's just pulled out his phone to check his messages when a kid on roller skates speeds by and yanks it out of his hand.

"Hey!" Natua calls. They're in the middle of a busy street, but nobody stops and it's too close to 18:00 hours for Natua to leave. And so, the little thief gets away with it.

He sits down next to his bag with a sigh. As an afterthought, he loops his arm through one of the straps just in case *that* decides to grow legs and run off too. He's still cursing himself for his luck when a young woman in heels *click clacks* up to him, uneasy boyfriend in tow.

"Are you Natua?"

When he looks up, her face pales. "Oh my god."

He offers his hand and in Spanish that he's been practicing all day, he says, "It's nice to finally meet you, sister."

"It's... it's nice..." she trails off and then takes a seat on the bench next to him, her squared shoulders deflating. "My God. I—I didn't know."

Her boyfriend is an older but stylish man in an expensive-looking pea coat, and he's the one to switch to French and suggest that they head to a nearby restaurant for some coffee.

"Yes, I need coffee." Mariana has recovered slightly, but she still looks like she's seen a ghost. "Do you drink coffee, Natua?"

"Are you sure that's going to be strong enough?" He smiles uneasily. "I knew this would come as a shock, but I didn't expect to find anyone through this exercise but my father."

The couple exchanges a quick look before Mariana says, "Well, surprise!" Her laugh is nervous. "You found me instead. There's a great tapas bar a couple blocks from here—let's make ourselves comfortable over there and then we can, um, get to know each other!" She's trying to stay enthusiastic, but the effort shows.

Natua regrets the offhanded way he's thrown her entire world into chaos, and he's thankful they've decided on a bar. *I could use a little alcohol myself.*

As they walk, Mariana introduces her boyfriend Francisco. "Nice to meet you," the man says with a wave.

"Pleasure's all mine," Natua responds. "I'm sorry I didn't think to prepare you better for this ahead of time, but didn't you get my picture?"

"What?" Mariana pulls out her phone. "You mean this?" She opens her email and Natua sees his subway snapshot. It looks a lot darker and blurrier than he remembers.

"Huh, it looked fine on my phone," he says. He goes to pull it out of his pocket and then curses under his breath.

"Everything okay?" Mariana's tone is high-strung, like her laugh. Despite the genetics written so clearly on his face, she still seems unsure about what he wants with her.

"Yeah, it's fine. Some kid on roller skates snatched my phone while I was waiting for you."

"That's terrible!" Francisco leans forward to catch his eye. "You have to keep a watchful eye on practically everything these days. In fact, just the other day, someone stole a diaper bag from my cousin Sebastian—he's living in Madrid." He turns to Mariana. "Did I tell you that, Ana? It had Sofia's favorite binky in it and a week's worth of formula. He was *encabronado.*"

"I'd be mad too—formula is expensive!"

"Yeah, it's a terrible thing when people have to steal to feed their children," Natua adds.

Mariana and Francisco both look at Natua in surprise, as if they hadn't even considered the motivation behind the theft. After a beat, Mariana says, "Well, I'm sorry that happened to you. We can show you where to buy a new phone later tonight or we can meet up tomorrow."

"Actually, I'd rather just wait until I get back home to get one. SIM cards, you know?"

"Right, right, I didn't think of that," Mariana replies. "Oh, here's the restaurant."

"You *have* to get the sangria," Francisco chimes in as they take their seats in a comfortable corner booth.

"Let's get a pitcher for the table," Mariana suggests.

"That's a great idea," Natua agrees. After they order, the food arrives quickly.

Mariana takes a long drink of sangria. "Where did you say you're staying? I should probably take down the number if your phone was stolen."

Natua takes another bite of the cheese and bread he'd ordered so he can think through his answer. He doesn't want to sound like a beggar but he has nowhere to go.

He swallows. "Actually, I was wondering if you knew of any good places around here. I uh, only flew in about two hours ago. I didn't reserve anything in advance because I was waiting for a lead before flying in."

Mariana's cheeks are already flushed from the alcohol and her face scrunches up as she thinks. "You didn't just fly here all the way from Tahiti, did you?"

"No, no." He chuckles. "I was in Paris with a friend." He's always resisted calling Ari his sister, and he's not about to change that now—even if the feminine *amie* raises a few eyebrows in mixed company. "It's a long story," he adds at her expectant look.

"Of course. I don't mean to pry," she says. "Did you want some more gazpacho?"

The trio dine in true Seville fashion, with plate after plate of tapas and multiple pitchers of sangria. Finally, though, Natua can't take any more of what has become quite comfortable chitchat.

"I don't mean to be insensitive," he starts, "but when can I meet my father? I know this is a lot to take in—it is for me too—but I've come a long way and waited a long time. Is there any way you can call him, maybe have him meet us here? I can only stay in town for a few days, and I want to spend as much time with him as I can."

"I—uh—"

"Ana." Francisco takes her hand. "It's okay."

She refuses to meet Natua's eyes. "I don't know how to say this but... He's not coming."

Sangria and anger both warm Natua's cheeks. "This isn't your decision." He points a finger at her. "I need to hear from him tonight!"

She shakes her head and her eyes are filling with tears.

"You don't know what you're asking kid," Francisco says. To Ana, he whispers something in a comforting tone that only stokes Natua's rage.

"Of course I know what I'm asking for!" In his anger, Natua switches to Tahitian and ignores the feeling in the pit of his stomach that something is wrong. "I've been asking for this my entire life, and I'm not about to let you people stand in my way!"

"Natua." Mariana's voice is soft. A solitary tear slides down her cheek. "You don't understand—Armando died six months ago."

Natua doesn't remember standing up, but this blow knocks the wind out of him and he falls back into his seat. The anger dissipates.

"What happened?"

"A boating accident in the Mediterranean. It... it wasn't pretty." She sniffles. Francisco offers her a clean napkin to use as a tissue.

"Can you take me to his resting place? Please."

"Of course."

"I'm sorry," he adds. "I didn't know."

"How could you? Mama did all she could to keep it out of the news." She blows her nose. "She's an incredibly private person, and we all wanted to grieve on our own terms, without reporters snooping around for a story."

She drops some bills on the table and stands. "Come on." She reaches out for Natua's hand. "We'll get you a place to stay tonight, and then tomorrow we can go pay our respects together. As a family."

He takes her hand and the three head off into the night. They find Natua a second-rate hostel near Mariana's apartment and bid each other goodnight. He heads up the rickety elevator alone.

Natua drops his bag on the floor and takes a seat on the bed, head in his hands. All this way and it doesn't even matter. He's too late.

Chapter 13

Manu had expected this speech to write itself. He figured he'd have to cut material down after letting his emotions play out on the page. But all of the years spent fighting the *métropole* have taken their toll on his spirit. His voice. The blinking cursor mocks his silence. His experiences simply refuse to be wrapped into neat sentences and tidy paragraphs on the computer he uses at the office.

So, with Thursday afternoon sliding by, he leaves early. He needs to do this a different way.

"Finalize the travel plans for next week and then you can close up for the night," he calls to Peter, the enterprising young aide fresh out of some fancy European law school.

"No problem, Mr. Fonua." Peter beams. "I'll leave the itinerary on your desk so you can take a look at it in the morning."

Manu says goodnight and heads out, his briefcase lighter than ever. Its only contents are a clean copy of the bill, some blank paper, and a tape recorder. He isn't going to let anything distract him until this is done.

At home, he puts on shorts and heads out to the side yard in his bare feet, papers rolled up to hold a pen and the recorder.

"My love, you've always known how to put my thoughts into words." He plunks on the ground in front of Amaru's gravestone and starts the recorder. "What would you say about this?" He sets the stapled text of the bill on the ground like an offering.

He picks up his pen, poised to write, but nothing happens. "It's the most important thing I've ever done for our people—I need your help to get it right."

A moment passes in silence, then he sighs. "This entire journey began with our own family. Remember the trip we took all those years ago? You were out to here with Ari." He gestures as though his wife is in front of him and not a decade in the ground. "If only we'd known how much those weeks would cost."

His thoughts drift to Henri, and the safety department Manu had created when he first started in politics. He'd had to stay on top of it for over a year before everyone at the airport was consistent with their checks. How much energy would he need to put into making this bill a reality? Into fighting the entire *métropole* and its legacy of destruction?

When sunlight fades to dusk a few hours later, Manu heads inside. He may not have everything figured out just yet, but he's managed to scribble out an introduction that ought to move the hearts of the most hardened politicians in the islands or even the *métropole*.

He settles into his favorite work spot in the house—the palm tree counter that divides living room and kitchen—and he's replaying the tape to help him sort through what he ought to address next when the phone rings. The thought of the kids alone in Bora Bora flashes through his brain and he rushes across the kitchen to grab the handset.

"Hello?"

He's greeted by an unfamiliar voice. "Mr. Fonua? It's about Angela Raina."

"Is everything all right? Who is this?"

"This is Afaitu. I'm at the pension—Angela's out cold and an ambulance is on its way. Can you call Natua and tell him to meet me at the hospital? It's not looking good, and I can't seem to get through to his cell number."

"Of course. Do you want me to come with you?"

"No time—the ambulance is pulling in now. Just get in touch with the boy for me." With that, the line goes dead.

Manu dials Ari's number first, as she's always quicker to answer his calls than Natua. Voicemail. "Ari, you and Natua need to get on the first flight or ferry you can catch to Ra'iatea. It's his mother."

He hangs up and punches out the next number, only to hear a message saying the phone has been disconnected. *That's odd. Must not have dialed right.* He double checks the numbers before redialing, but the message is the same.

He heads into his bedroom to find the bag he keeps packed for work trips. If he hurries, he can catch the last flight of the evening to Bora Bora and track down Natua and Ari the old-fashioned way. He grabs his keys and tosses his half-finished speech and the recorder in the bag. He's on the phone with the airport when he dashes out the door.

Once he's settled on the plane, Manu starts dialing hotels. If he can determine which one the kids have checked into, he might be able to get a hold of them before he lands and they can meet him at the ferry.

He tries all of the main players outside of the over-priced resorts every Ma'ohi instinctively avoids. The 20-minute flight is nearly over, and he still doesn't know where he's going when he gets off the plane.

As a last resort, he dials Ari's old friend Ettie. He thanks his lucky stars that he'd insisted on trading contact information with her closest friends after the myeloma diagnosis. He's hoping Ari said something to her that can point him in the right direction.

"Hello?"

"Hey Ettie, it's Ari's dad, Mr. Fonua. Can I ask you something?"

"Sure."

"Did Ari happen to mention where her and Natua are staying on this little trip they took?"

She clears her throat. "Uh, not really. Why, is something wrong?"

"I need to talk to Natua and neither of the kids are answering their phones."

"Oh. I'm sure they're fine—you know they can both be pretty forgetful. Maybe they forgot to bring chargers with them and their phones are dead."

Manu sighs. "Yes, Ettie, that's quite possible, which is why I need the number for their hotel. Do you know where they're staying?"

"I haven't heard from them since they left, and Ari didn't mention it. Can't you just give them a few minutes and call back?" Her tone says, *Chill the fuck out, Mr. Fonua.*

"No. I need that number. There's been a family emergency."

"Oh god, I hope everyone's okay," she replies.

"I think it will be, but I need to get a hold of Natua."

Manu waits as Ettie sighs. There's the sound of papers rustling on the other end of the line. Manu starts to wonder if the kids are hiding something—if they've run off to elope or something. But he brushes the thought aside when Ettie finally speaks.

"I think Irene helped them with the details," she says. "I'll bet she'll be able to tell you where they're staying."

"Of course. Thanks, Ettie." He hangs up and calls Irene's cell. "Hey, how are you?"

"I'm doing quite well," Irene says. "In fact, I just sat down to dinner. Can I call you back?"

"No, it's an emergency." Manu talks fast, knowing Irene hates having her dinner interrupted even more than she hates work calls at home. "Listen, I can't seem to track down Ari and Natua—they're in Bora Bora for that basketball game on Saturday. Did you happen to help them with their hotel arrangements?"

"I'm sure they're fine," she says placidly. "No need to panic just because they can't be bothered to answer their phones."

Manu sighs. The woman always knows how to pry the good gossip out of people. "It's not the kids I'm worried about. Natua's mother is in the hospital, and things aren't looking good."

"Oh!" Before she can continue, the connection cuts out.

Manu curses at the dial tone, drawing looks from a few of the flower-laden tourists sharing economy cabin with him. The plane is about to land, and a flashing sign reminds passengers to turn off all electronic devices. And Manu still has no idea if he's going to get Natua to his mother in time.

. . .

The moment Manu clears the gangway, he dials Irene. "Just point me in a direction. I'm at the airport."

"Then you'd better get back on the plane. They're not in Bora Bora."

"What?" he yells into the phone. "You didn't think you should tell me that when you sent them off? My daughter has cancer for God's sake! Where are they?"

"They swore me to secrecy, and I'm not about to violate that. But I can give you the number for their hotel. Reservation's in Ari's name." She rattles off the number, and Manu swears under his breath when he recognizes the code for Paris.

"Can you give it to me one more time?" He checks that he has the right number and then hangs up with barely a goodbye. *What the hell are they doing over there?*

He's standing awkwardly in the center of the Motu Mute airport. Wandering towards the ticket counters, he calls the number Irene gave him.

"Hello, can you put me through to Arietta Fonua's room?" he asks when the cheery receptionist answers.

"It's quite early—I'm not supposed to put calls through before 8AM without the express permission of the room's occupant." Manu does the math—it's 6:30 Friday morning in Paris. For a split second, he prays to God they're in separate beds and then breathes a sigh of relief that at least they should both be in the room—as long as this clerk puts him through.

"This is Ms. Fonua's father." Manu grits his teeth. "There's been an emergency." *These people always think they know best.*

"In that case, of course. No problem."

The phone rings once. Twice. Three times. After what feels like an eternity, he hangs up and tries Ari's cell number again. No answer there either. Manu hopes the time difference is the only reason he can't get in touch with them. He calls the hotel again and leaves a brief message with the clerk.

He might not be able to reach them, but he can still get to Angela. The poor woman doesn't deserve to die alone. He shoots off an email to Natua, hoping the boy will at least have the sense to check *something* in the next few hours. After hitting send, he turns around and heads to the ticket counter.

"I need a seat on the next flight to Ra'iatea. The sooner the better."

. . .

By morning, Natua's collected himself and decides to give Ari a call from the payphone in the lobby. He wants to make sure she doesn't blow off her doctor's appointment later that afternoon from anxiety, and he wants to distract himself until his sister comes to meet him for lunch.

He gets her voicemail and wonders if she's avoiding his calls. Even though she said she wanted him to go,

Natua feels like he's abandoned her. *I'm not about to let her mess up this opportunity.* He gives the hotel a call, glad that Irene had insisted they each carry the number in their wallets.

"Hello, this is Natua Raina from room 319. Can you put me through to my room? I need to talk with Ari Fonua."

The man is about to put him through when he hesitates. "Wait, you are the young man staying with her? Is this about the emergency?"

"What? What emergency?"

"I have a message for your room. Someone's in the hospital." The man rustles through some papers and Natua's heart drops into his belly. "Yes, here it is—Ms. Fonua's father called. The message says only that Natua's mother is in the hospital and he needs to come home."

"What?! When was this?"

"About two hours ago."

"Shit, shit, shit."

Hearing the panic in his voice, the receptionist says, "I'm truly sorry, sir. By the way, I don't believe Ms. Fonua is in the room at the moment. Shall I put you through to the room or do you want me to leave a message for her?"

"Are you sure? Was she there last night?"

"I can send someone up to the room to check if you'd like."

"Could you? She's very sick."

The man puts Natua on hold, and the violin piece that plays does nothing to calm his nerves.

"Housekeeping said she wasn't there and the bed was already made."

"Oh god. Uh," he stammers, trying to figure out what he can do next when he doesn't even have a callback number to give the man. "If she comes in, just tell her I called. Thanks." Natua hangs up and his mind is racing. He drops in a few 1-euro coins and dials

Manu's cell, but the payphone doesn't support calls outside the EU. He's worried about his mother, but he's even more concerned by what the receptionist said about Ari. She promised to take it easy until her doctor's appointment—there's no way she'd bother making a bed when her leg is twice its normal size. *If she didn't go back to the hotel last night, where is she?*

· · ·

Ari is vaguely aware that she's in motion, but she struggles to open her eyes. "Where am I going?" she mumbles.

A strong female voice breaks through her mental fog. "Just relax, okay? We're taking you to the hospital. You need medical attention."

Her eyelids are so heavy. Are those sirens she hears?

A moment later, she turns onto her side and cracks her eyes open. She's alone, and there are IVs sticking out of her left elbow and wrist. She's not moving anymore. "What the..."

Speaking is exhausting and simply not worth the effort. She drifts off again, dreaming of her backpack. It's still in the restaurant, and it holds her ID, medical records for her doctor's appointment tomorrow, and all of her clean clothes. What will she wear if she's lost it?

The next time she comes to, a nurse is scratching notes on a chart. "Hello?"

The woman rushes over to her side and presses the call button next to her bed.

"Hi there. Can you tell me your name?"

"Yeah. Why am I here?"

"Your blood sugar crashed. We're giving you sugar and fluids—" she gestures at the IV bags. "But we're going to have you eat some solid foods to get you the carbs you need before you can leave."

"Backpack." Her throat is dry and gummy and it's painful to speak.

"What's that?"

"Backpack."

Seeing that Ari is getting agitated, the nurse tries to placate her. "The medics brought your backpack in with you, honey. It's right over there in a chair. Can you tell me your name?"

Ari coughs. "My name is Arietta Fonua. There are medical records—" she swallows hard. "In my backpack."

A second nurse walks in. A man, maybe in his thirties. "Is everything okay?"

"Yeah, my voice badge hasn't been working right since I dealt with that combative guy in 4. I thought the doctor would want to know that she's awake and talking. She says there's medical records in her backpack."

The man takes in Ari's eyes rolling in the back of her head. He shakes his head as if to say *yeah right*. He activates the device hanging from his neck and informs the doctor that the "patient in 612 is showing signs of consciousness." To his co-worker, he replies, "You have to realize she's not coherent, Camille."

"You don't know that."

"She's not even conscious anymore."

"The girl gave me her name," Camille counters.

"Good. Enter it in the system."

"I'm going to check her bag first. Should have some form of ID, at least."

"Now that she's stabilized, yeah, check on it if you've got the time. Probably should've had one of the techs do that hours ago, when she first came in."

"Well, it's been one hell of a night," Camille responds. "Lucky we've got time to do it now."

She unzips the main compartment and copies of records from a hospital in far-away Ra'iatea are sitting on top, though they're crumpled from days spent in the bag. Camille waves the papers in her co-worker's direction. "Incoherent, huh?"

When the doctor arrives, he scans the papers and Camille updates him on Ari's vitals. "I'm glad her sugar is bouncing back, but why is she still tachycardic?"

"We're not sure," she replies. "The patient is also febrile, and her blood pressure is still far too low."

The doctor shakes his head and takes in Ari's unconscious form. "I don't like this—there are other complications in her history, so keep a close eye on her. She's much worse off than we thought."

Chapter 14

Mariana arrives at the hotel a bit earlier than they'd agreed upon the night before. She'd hoped she would have enough time to find a restroom after a rushed morning in the law office she clerks for. Instead, she finds that Natua is already waiting for her. Through the glass, she watches him pacing up and down the poorly lit lobby, hands in his hair. *After all this time, I wouldn't have any patience left either.* She pushes the glass revolving door and calls out to him.

"You ready to go?" She has to consciously try to keep herself from smiling in this somber moment. The shock of the day before has mostly worn off. After a lifetime of believing she was an only child and months without a father, she's delighted to find out about her new sibling—even if she's hell-bent on keeping him away from her mourning mother.

"Absolutely not." Now that she's closer, Mariana notices the desperation, the agitation in his stance. It catches her off-guard but she decides to play it cool.

"Not quite ready to face dear old Dad?"

"That's not it at all," Natua replies. "My mother's in the hospital back home, Ari's missing, and I can't even call home because my cell was stolen and the stupid payphone won't handle calls outside the EU."

At the mention of someone being missing, Mariana is taken back to Armando's passing—the days of agonizing waiting, then the sickening certainty that followed. She collapses heavily onto the dingey brown couch in the lobby and her face pales.

"Mariana!" Natua taps his sister's shoulder. "Can you help me?"

"Help you? What do you need?" She shakes her head in an attempt to bring herself back to the present moment. "And who's Ari?"

"Remember how I said I was in Paris with a friend? Well, that friend is my adopted sister with cancer, and she never went back to her hotel last night. I need to call around to some hospitals, but I don't have internet access without my cell phone. Can't exactly start calling hospitals without knowing which ones to call or what their number is."

"Sure, sure, of course." She smooths her knee-length skirt, as if trying to bring order to quell the chaos within.

Natua interrupts her deep breathing exercise with a tap on her shoulder. "Your phone?"

"Right, right. Sorry. This whole thing is just giving me flashbacks to Dad's accident."

Now it's Natua's turn to do some deep breathing. "Let's not go there. Not yet." She plops the cell in his hand and he pulls up the internet browser. "Just breathe, just breathe." He's not sure if he's telling himself or Mariana as he dials the first Parisian hospital on the list.

He gets through three phone calls before Mariana's collected herself enough to ask questions, though she doesn't move from her spot on the couch. "Natua, did you talk to anyone from home about your mother?"

"No, no, I wish I had." His fingers clutch his sister's cell a little tighter. "It was a message left for us at the hotel we were staying at in Paris. But Ari never got the message because she isn't in the room, and I don't think she slept there. That's how I knew something was wrong."

"Right. Why don't you give someone from back home a call?"

"I would've, but the payphone doesn't do calls outside the EU."

She gestures towards her cell. "That will."

"But that'll be such an expensive call..."

"We're family, right? Families look out for each other. I'll take the payphone and call the next hospital on your list."

"Are you sure?"

"Yes, of course I'm sure! Just be quick—there's a lot of hospitals in Paris, so it'll go faster if we're both calling. We should probably get the police involved if we can't find her soon, too."

"Oh, that's a good idea. And thank you." He's already dialing Manu's number when Mariana interrupts him.

"What's your friend's last name?"

"It's Fonua. Arietta Fonua." He spells it for her.

She scratches it out on the back of a receipt pulled from her purse and then jots down the number for the hospital Natua wants her to call. "Got it."

. . .

He doesn't reach Manu at home, but when Natua tries his cell phone, the man picks up on the first ring. "Hello?" Natua is paralyzed by the sound of Manu's voice. "Hello?"

"Uncle." Natua finally manages to speak. "Is Mama okay?"

"I just got to the hospital—she's in the ICU. Afaitu found her in the pension in a pile of broken dishes. We're not sure what happened."

"Is she going to be okay?"

"She's stabilized for now, but she's still unconscious and she's not getting enough oxygen on her own. You two need to come home now."

Natua takes a deep breath.

"Natua? What's wrong? And where are you calling me from, anyway?"

"My phone got stolen, but don't worry about that."

"Look, don't feel guilty that something happened while you were gone. You and Ari just need to come home. It's time."

"Mr. Fonua..."

"What is it?" Manu's tone turns suspicious. Natua never calls him Mr. Fonua unless he's in serious trouble.

"I... I don't exactly know where Ari is."

"Come again?" Manu asks in disbelief.

"I came to Spain to find my dead father, and now Ari's gone!" he yells into the phone. The man working the front counter raises his eyebrows at the commotion.

There's a long silence in the phone. "You still there?" Natua says.

"You find my daughter, understand me? Find her!" Manu's voice trembles.

"Ye- yessir."

"And then get the first flight home. Both of you."

He hangs up the phone and sits on the couch. "This is all my fault," he wails. "I never should've left her."

Mariana walks over and stands in front of him. "I know this is tough, but we'll find her. Just have to work as a team. Can I see my phone for a second?"

He looks up and puts the device in her outstretched hand. She writes down a few more numbers and hands the phone back to him. "You're in charge of calling the police in Paris. We've got work to do."

He wipes his nose with his sleeve. "You aren't kidding." He fishes a few coins out of his pocket and holds them out to her. "For the long-distance call on your phone."

She holds up a hand in refusal.

"Use them for the payphone." He pushes the coins into her palm.

"Fine." She heads back to the phone booth.

Natua's hands are trembling when he punches out the number for the police department in Paris.

"How can I help you?" asks a friendly-sounding female voice.

"Hi, I'd like to report a missing person." He goes over the details as quickly and as thoroughly as he can. "I know she hasn't been out of touch very long, but in these circumstances..." he trails off, nervous fingers tapping his leg. "I would never forgive myself if something happened to her."

"We can certainly send someone by the hotel to check things out. Can you give me a physical description of the person in question?"

Before Natua can answer, Mariana rushes over to the couch and tells him to cancel the police report in hushed tones. He repeats her message to the police officer then hangs up in a hurry. "Did you find her? What's going on?" His grip on the phone tightens as he prepares himself for his sister's news.

"Ari's in that hospital near where you were staying," she says.

"Oh, thank god we found her! Did you talk to her?"

Mariana looks down. "No, they wouldn't put me through. We have to go, now. They wouldn't give me details, but I don't think she's doing well."

"But my mother..." Natua's unfinished sentence hangs in the air.

"That's not a decision I can make for you, little brother." She pulls him in close and Natua lets his sister bring him in for a quick embrace.

After they break apart, he asks, "Would it be okay with you if I texted Ari's father, to let him know she's in the hospital?"

"Just call the poor man back. I can't imagine what he's going through right now."

Natua shakes his head. "I can't bear hearing his voice again. This is all my fault."

"Don't take that on yourself." His sister gazes at him seriously, as if she's sizing him up. "It won't help anyone, and after all, we found her. Not like you would've been able to stop whatever health issues landed her in the hospital."

"No, but she wouldn't have had to go through it alone." Guilt settles like a cloud over his eyes.

"Natua, I'm serious. Let that go! Now tell the guy what's going on with his daughter."

. . .

When Manu receives a text from an unusual number, he ignores it at first. Angela's finally awake and they've been talking about this foolish secret trip the kids have undertaken to distract Manu from the fact that his daughter is MIA in a strange city with no family for thousands of kilometers.

"I should have—should have known he would go—eventually," Angela says. The words come slowly between labored breaths. "Every boy—wants to know his father."

"He's talked about it ever since he was a child. You know, that's why he's always called me 'uncle.' He informed me he already had a father."

"Oh, yes. That's a—a conversation we had—many times."

"He mentioned on the phone though that the man is dead. Seems he'll never get to meet him, but at least he'll have some closure."

Angela nods and the muscles in her face relax.

Manu doesn't want to pry, but he can't stop himself from asking. "Were you afraid Natua would stay in Spain if he found him?"

She shakes her head slightly. "No, it's not that."

Manu tilts his head, but politeness keeps him from pressing further.

Angela asks for a sip of water, and Manu helps her with the glass next to the bed. After she motions it away, Angela clears her throat. "I've been keeping a secret—from my son, from you, from nearly everyone. Armando may not have—ever come back. But we..."

Her face changes again. Manu thinks that maybe it's guilt he sees. "We wrote letters, here and there. He always sent—something for Ignacio's birthday. Something for Christmas."

She pauses, weighing her words. "But there was nothing this Christmas. He was either dead or done with the boy."

Manu tries to look passive and avoid seeming judgmental about this secret, but he can't hide his shock.

"He didn't want the boy in his life. He—he made that clear. He made me promise—to keep Ignacio away from his..."

An eternity passes before Angela finishes her sentence. "His 'real' family." Manu isn't sure if it's the light or if her eyes are misting over. "But he never forgot the holidays, at least."

"I'm sorry, Angela." Manu's words are genuine. It's clear, despite the years and the abandonment, that she truly loved the man.

She waves off his concern. "Much as it stung, I always held out hope... that it would change. That he'd come around, at least to meet our son." She grunts. "Guess I was wrong."

Manu takes her hand. "You deserved better than that. The boy did too."

She manages a slight shrug. "The fish cannot change the ways of the shark."

He reaches for his phone so he has something to do with his hands in the awkward silence that follows. That's when he realizes the text he'd gotten earlier was from the same number Natua used to call him. *Ari's in the hospital in Paris. Think it's pretty serious. I'm not coming home without her.*

"Oh God."

"What?"

"Angela—we've got a problem."

She takes as deep a breath as her damaged lungs will allow. "It's the kids, isn't it?"

"Mmhmm." He swallows hard. It's not until he reads the blurry text aloud to her that he realizes he's crying. "My little girl's all alone over there."

"No, she's not." She pushes herself up in the bed. "At least, she won't be for long."

"But Natua has to come home—you're all the family he has left. I'll have to go."

"Stop that nonsense." Her face is set, and she does her best to look commanding. "What if you don't get there in time? We—we may be a bit odd, but we're a family, and sounds like he knows that. Send him to Arietta. She doesn't—doesn't deserve to be alone. If you must go too, then go. But this way she'll have family by her side—as soon as possible."

Manu nods his assent. Not trusting himself to speak, he types out a message to Natua and tries to release the tension spreading throughout his body.

Chapter 15

"Hey Michel, room 612 is yours, right?" asks a nurse coming on shift.

"Yeah, Camille handed it off to me five minutes ago. Morning chart says you're in charge of 614 and 615." He quickens his step towards the nurse's station.

"Don't worry about *my* assignments. Call button's going off for 612. I was going to take care of it, but if you're right here and it's your room..."

"Guess I'll get it then." He turns and heads into the room, only to discover the patient is passed out and her vitals are tanking. He turns on his voice badge. "Doctor Laurent, you better get down here as soon as you can. Not sure what's happening since I only clocked in a few minutes ago, but the patient is unconscious, heart rate is skyrocketing, and blood pressure is dangerously low."

The doctor rushes in to find his patient crashing. "Charge the AED. If we can't get her stabilized, her heart's going to give out. How long has she been like this?"

"She was pushing her call button right before I came in, so safe to say she's been out less than 60 seconds," he says over his shoulder as he charges the defibrillator.

The doctor gestures towards the machine with his jaw. "No time to waste." He tugs on Ari's loose gown so the nurse can position the pads on her chest.

"Clear!"

Michel discharges the AED. Both men sigh in relief as her heart rate moves into a more normal—albeit still elevated—rhythm.

"Can you grab me her most recent blood work?" the doctor asks. "She came in with low blood sugar, but something else must be going on."

"It's right here," Michel replies. "Looks like her numbers were done real quick last night, and they were all over the place."

"Let's run them again and see if we can't figure out what's going on."

"Sure thing," Michel replies. He heads out to file the request, only to be greeted with two new patients who arrive in critical condition, one of whom codes in the hallway. He moves from emergency to emergency, blood work for the stabilized patient in room 612 pushed to the bottom of the priority list.

• • •

"Sorry Mom, I won't be able to make dinner tomorrow," Mariana says into her cell phone. She's standing near the door of Natua's hostel, trying to figure out how to get out of the party she'd organized herself to get her mother's mind off of her father.

Natua is still reeling from the morning's developments, and Mariana doesn't think he's registered why she's cancelling her plans. "No, it's not Francisco—something came up, and I can't make it." Mariana huffs. "I'm going out of town... It was a last-minute thing... No, Mom, nothing's wrong. Look, forget I said anything, okay? I'm sorry. I can't make it."

Mrs. da Costa isn't about to let something as strange as this go. "What is it?" she presses. "Is it work—is it that creep Marco trying to get you alone again?"

"Huh? Mom, that doesn't even make any sense."

"Well, is it work?"

"No, Mom, it's not work. Look, I'll talk to you about it some other time, okay? I've—I've really gotta go." She hangs up, feeling guilty for ditching her mother on *this* weekend, of all weekends, but her father isn't here to help his son, and he needs help.

Mariana glances over at Natua, twitching his leg and picking at his nails on the couch. His mannerisms remind her of her own, when she's trying not to fall to pieces. She has to be in France by Tuesday anyway for a client meeting. Might as well get there a bit early and do this with her little brother.

"All right, let's go." She heads over to the couch and holds out her hand.

"What?"

"You'd better go check out of your room. I called the airport, and we leave in four hours. That should give us enough time to stop by the cemetery and see Dad before we head off."

He looks up at her without really seeing her, a dazed look in his eyes. She waves her hand in front of his face. "Come on, we need to move!"

"You're right, you're right." He leads his sister up to the bare room, slings the bag he never bothered to unpack over his shoulder, and turns in his key at the front desk. They're on their way to the cemetery before things click in his head. "Wait, are you coming with me?" he asks as they walk briskly through sleepy city streets.

"No offense, but given the state you're in, I'm not sure you can do this alone."

"It's my problem. I need to take responsibility for it."

"You came all the way over here to find your family, right?"

"Yes, but—"

"Well, you found me. Wouldn't be fair of me to desert you now." She crosses the street and points in the distance, as though the matter is settled. "Over there—see that clump of trees?"

"Yeah."

"That's the cemetery."

. . .

Natua gulps. Inside, his stomach lurches. He's not sure he's ready to face this, but it's now or never.

"Are you all right?" his sister asks with a hint of concern.

"I'm fine." But he doesn't believe it and, based on the intensity of Mariana's stare, neither does she.

She stops walking and taps his arm. "Natua." He stops. "Do you need some more time?"

His eyes mist over, and he heads to an empty bench in silence. He sits, puts his head in his hands, and takes a few deep breaths before trusting himself to speak. "I just... this is not how I imagined it would be." He raises his head to look at his sister. "I'm here, I've tracked down my father, and met new family I didn't know existed. I should be able to feel at peace with this whole part of my life, but I can't even think straight because of what's going on with my mom, with Ari... I feel like I've let everyone in my life down all at once, you know?"

"Would you rather skip it?"

"No!" he bursts out. Quietly, he adds, "It's not that."

"Okay." Instead of pressing him, she takes a seat on the bench and puts a reassuring hand on his knee. "Take your time. You've had a long few days."

They sit together for several minutes while Natua collects himself, watching the traffic and people passing by. When he stands, he turns to face the graveyard. He doesn't meet his sister's eyes when he asks, "You said it's down there?" He waves a hand in the direction of the trees.

"Yeah." She stands and then draw in a deep breath. "Are you sure you're ready for this?"

"No, but there's no more time to waste. And if I don't do this, I'll need to add myself to the list of people I've disappointed this week."

"Okay."

They make their way carefully towards the cemetery. This isn't a moment to be rushed.

"Which way?" Natua asks. The place surrounds the road, and there are several entrances to choose from.

Mariana doesn't respond as she heads down one of the sandy paths leading towards the graves. She points out an impressive statue of a bullfighter here, a flamenco dancer there, as they make their way through the orderly rows.

Natua is awed by the sheer scale of the graveyard, which is empty of visitors aside from the occasional tourist grasping a brochure. "You know," he says, "we don't really have cemeteries in the islands."

She turns to face him as she walks. "What?"

"Most people would rather be buried in their yards. Return to the land you come from."

"A beautiful concept," she comments, "but impossible in a place like this. Too many asphalt roads and overstuffed apartment buildings."

"This is nice in its own way though. Puts life into a different perspective."

"I suppose," Mariana replies. In her distraction, she bumps into an older woman dressed all in black.

"Oh, sorry!" She quickly positions herself between Natua and the woman.

"Mariana? What are you doing here?"

"Thought I'd stop in to say goodbye to Dad before I leave town, that's all."

"Here, I'll go back with you." The woman shifts and catches sight of Natua's hoodie. "Who's your friend?" She peers past Mariana to get a look at his face. "Oh my God!" she cries and loses her balance. Mariana catches her arm before the woman reaches the ground.

"Mom, are you okay?"

Natua stiffens up as he realizes *this* is the grieving widow the ring was intended for. "I'm sorry, ma'am," he says in accented Spanish, as though he's at fault for existing.

"Who—who are you? And where the hell did you come from?" Mrs. da Costa has recovered her balance but not enough self-control to be polite, though she does make the switch to French.

He pulls the ring out of his pocket. "My name is Ignacio, and this belonged to my father Armando. I've been trying to find him."

"No, no, this can't be." She pushes the jewelry away. "That's not his ring, that's nothing like his ring. His ring was lost at sea." Her words increase in volume and speed as she talks. "It can't be—and you, you don't look anything like him. You've got the wrong man, you understand me? The wrong man!"

Mariana steps between them again. "Mom, this is my fault for not telling you what was going on—don't take it out on him. I didn't want to upset you, especially this week. Breathe."

Mrs. da Costa dutifully takes a few quick, shallow breaths. She's bordering on hysterics. "Do you realize what tomorrow is?" she yells over Mariana's shoulder at Natua. "Tomorrow is my 25th wedding anniversary, and YOU—you just killed my husband all over again!"

His sister's voice is stern as she says, "Mom, keep it together." She looks over her shoulder and mouths *I'm so sorry* to Natua. "It's not his fault."

"You're right. Of course you're right." Mrs. da Costa's breath is still ragged. "I need to sit down." She heads to the end of the aisle and takes a seat on a solid stone bench. "You knew about this?" she screeches at Mariana, gesturing wildly with her hands. "And you didn't tell me?"

"I only found out who he really was yesterday," Mariana says defensively. "I certainly didn't want to tell you *now*."

"When exactly were you going to tell me?" her mother counters.

"I—I don't know," she stammers. "Not like there's a handbook out there for this kind of thing."

"You should have told me."

"Sorry."

Their conversation stalls, and the two women look at Natua expectantly. "What do you want me to say?" he asks. He slides the ring on and off his index finger nervously. "I didn't know that coming here was going to be like this." He clears his throat. "If I'd known Armando was dead, I wouldn't have come."

His sister's hand flies to her mouth. "Natua, don't say that! I'm glad to have a chance to know you're out there, to know you."

"All I've done is dishonor the memory of our father."

"No, that's not true." Mariana puts a hand on her hip. "He did that himself. This is a blessing for me—I've never had a sibling before, and yet here you are."

"Yes, here you are," Mrs. da Costa echoes, sounding far less impressed. "You haven't done anything wrong though. Just exposed my husband's sins." The wrinkles on her face seem to multiply as she lets out her breath. "If only I'd been prepared for that."

He looks down at his scuffed sneakers. "Sorry—I didn't mean to add to your grief."

She shakes her head. "I can't imagine how you feel, knowing this whole time you've been chasing a ghost."

Natua shrugs. "Not the whole time."

"You've waited long enough," Mrs. da Costa replies. "Mariana, take him to see Armando." The widow can't even look at him, and he wonders briefly if she's being nice or just trying to get him out of her sight as quickly as possible as he and Mariana make their way to the family's above-ground niche.

They stop beneath the twisted branches of an ancient almond tree. Natua puts a hand on the crypt and is surprised at how chilled the smooth stone is.

"Hi Father," he whispers, his words swept up by the wind. "Sorry I'm late."

Mariana puts a hand on his back. "I feel bad you didn't get to meet him. He would've loved you. For all his faults, he really was a family man." After an awkward silence, Mariana retreats back to the bench to check on her mother.

His family has been cobbled together so haphazardly. Natua lets his mind wander to Ari, alone in a hospital bed with god knows what going wrong. Much as he wants to linger here and learn more about his father from this new part of his family, he has to go.

Reluctantly, he bids goodbye to Armando's resting place and walks over to the bench, where Mrs. da Costa is dabbing at tears with a wrinkled tissue.

"That was fast—everything okay?" Mariana asks.

"Yeah." He shuffles closer. "But it's time for me to stop worrying about the dead and gone. Ari needs me, and my mother needs me, and I'm not doing either of them any good standing in a graveyard crying over a crypt."

"Not to be too nosy, but who's Ari?" Mrs. da Costa asks.

"My adopted sister. I left her alone in Paris and we found out this morning she's in the hospital. Apparently, it doesn't look good."

"How awful! I'll pray for her," she says before looking to Mariana. "Is that why you're ditching me this weekend?"

"Yeah. Seemed like something Dad should've helped him through and, well... Dad's not here." She shrugs.

"When do you leave?"

Mariana checks her cell for the time. "Plane takes off in three hours."

"Then you'd better get over there. Give yourself time to get through security and find your gate."

"Thanks for understanding, Mom."

"I raised you to help your family—it'd be stupid of me to be upset with you for actually doing it. Now go." Mrs. da Costa shoos them away with her hands. "I need some more time here. There's a conversation I need to have with your father."

With that, the pair make their way back to the street. Mariana hails a cab, and once the cemetery is out of sight, Natua realizes he might be shedding many more graveside tears in the near future. He must have let out a little noise, because his sister's voice is soothing when she says, "We're almost to the airport. Don't worry—we'll be with her in no time."

"But what if we aren't fast enough," he mutters. He keeps his eyes fixed on the world outside the taxi cab window. *If Ari dies alone...* He doesn't let himself finish the thought. *Please hang in there. I'm on my way.* He vows to himself that once he and Ari are reunited, he'll stay by her side forever. He only hopes he isn't too late... again.

. . .

Although Manu doesn't want to think about anything except getting to his daughter, he knows he has to make arrangements for the bill before he leaves the islands. After all, getting this legislation passed will help thousands of other families with stories like his and stories much worse than his too. He can't risk losing the opportunity to right such massive wrongs.

He rummages through his bag for a charger and plugs in his laptop. Thank goodness his work bag is always ready to go and he can handle this from Angela's bedside as she rests. It's one thing to leave her alone in the hospital to take care of his child, and quite another to leave for the sake of red tape.

"Hey Robert," he types to his colleague, "looks like I'm going to need you to do my speaking for me after all. My daughter took a trip to the *métropole* without telling me and now she's in the hospital with some trouble from the blood disease. Kids, am I right?" He wraps up the email with a promise to send his finished remarks over by the end of the day and hits send.

He digs through his bag again until he finds the crumpled paper he'd written his introduction on. It's time for him to finish that speech.

A few hours later, he breathes a sigh of relief. It's done. He opens his email to send the remarks to Robert, only to find a new message from Diane.

Thought you should see this.

"See what?" he mumbles to himself. There's nothing more to the message than an attachment labeled *Fonua Bill APF 128.09.* "What's so important about that? I know what my bill says, Diane."

It's not until he opens the document that he realizes something is wrong. First of all, the title page his poor aide had to reformat three different times has been replaced with a few sloppy-looking screenshots. Manu squints, unable to read the tiny text without zooming in. It's from an email trail Robert started with the entire Assembly except for Manu. At first, he thinks it's simply an announcement of the speaker for the bill changing, but Robert also said something about last minute changes to the legislation itself.

Manu skips the rest of the screenshots and scrolls through the meat of the document. "Dammit!" Robert has gotten rid of all mention of nuclear waste disposal timelines. He scrolls further, and the section about declassifying relevant military records is also missing. If he lets Robert go to the Assembly with this bill, nothing will change. The Ma'ohi families counting on Manu—including his own family—will all suffer. *What a weasel.*

He takes a deep breath to calm himself. He has to fix this, but how? He can't exactly leave his daughter hanging in a French hospital. As relieved as he is that Natua is on his way, the boy doesn't understand how the *métropole* works. How Ari will get second-rate care because islanders have always been second-class citizens of France. No, he has to go himself and stand up for his daughter's rights and make sure she gets the attention she needs. And yet this bill...

Grabbing his cell phone, Manu makes his way through bleach-scented hallways until he's standing on the steps outside the hospital. After glancing around to make sure no one is listening in, he punches in Diane's number.

"Hey—thanks for sending me that. I have to leave the islands for a family emergency, so I really can't make it to the session... I know, I know... I guess what I'm asking is, what are we going to do?"

Chapter 16

The tension has settled in Natua's shoulders by the time their three-hour flight takes to the air. But there's still one thing on his mind besides Ari.

"How did you manage to get us on a flight so fast?" he asks. "I had to scrounge to get a ticket to Seville last minute. Something about the time of year." He looks at his sister as if she has magic powers.

Mariana scoffs. "Please. We have better places to go than Paris. Good thing she's not in Rome."

"Yeah, lucky us." His expression darkens.

"Hey, it's going to be fine, okay?" Mariana's deep brown eyes search her younger brother's as if to make sure he's holding himself together.

"You don't know that." He wishes he had a window seat so he could distract himself with something more interesting than rows upon rows of plain gray seats filled with snoozing vacationers.

"You're right, I don't. But worrying isn't going to change anything."

"Fair enough."

Mariana tries to fill the silence that follows, chatting aimlessly about the papers she pushes at the law firm and why she thinks they matter. She stops after Natua replies with *mhm* for the fourth time in a row.

"Look, I know it's still early, but I'm going to get some shut-eye. Probably gonna be a long night."

"Good idea." Natua closes his eyes too, but his efforts are in vain. Mariana is snoring lightly when the plane finally begins its descent into Paris, and he has to nudge her awake.

They navigate away from the airport and slog through metro lines crowded with rush hour traffic.

"Are you okay?" Mariana asks as she grips a fingerprint-streaked pole in the back of their crowded car for balance. Natua's face has taken on an impassive look, like granite or maybe ice.

He shakes his head a few times, as if breaking himself out of a trance. "Don't worry about me. I just really hate the metro."

"Why's that?"

He glances around the car and sniffs the air pointedly, eyebrows raised. "Why wouldn't I?"

She lets go of the pole and rubs her palms against her jeans. "Would you rather head aboveground and grab a taxi?"

"No, we're already here. I don't want to waste any more time or money."

"You sure? I can pay for it."

"Forget I said anything. It's fine." He stares off into the middle distance for a few more stops, then turns to his sister. "Do you know what time visiting hours end?"

"What? We're family—that shouldn't matter." She sighs. "Then again, we *are* in France."

"Why does everyone have such an issue with France?" he snaps. "I'm French. Does that make *me* a bad person?"

"Of course not. Besides, your blood is Spanish," Mariana huffs. "Anyway, I wouldn't worry about visiting hours. She's your sister."

"*Adopted* sister," Natua says. "And it wasn't a very official thing."

"What does that—oh, this is our stop."

He follows her out of the station, inhaling deeply once they spill out onto street level. "Going underground is for the dead," he says. "It's revolting that people travel down there."

Mariana fiddles with her scarf as they wait to cross the street. "Hey, what did you mean back there, before we got off the train?"

"About what?"

"You said the adoption wasn't official. I don't understand what that means."

"It was informal, you know? We had a party and my mom put some stuff in her will about who will take care of me if something happens to her. They didn't bother with the official paperwork—said it wasn't worth the hassle."

"Huh. I don't think that's a thing here, so let's not mention the 'unofficial' part at the hospital. Deal?"

"Wait, really? That sucks."

Her hand waves dismissively. "I mean, it makes sense. What if someone isn't fit to be a parent and they take on a child? Or what if something happens to the adopted parents too and the kid's left in legal limbo? That can't be good."

"I guess. At home, everybody knows everybody, so that's not really a problem."

Mariana slaps her brother's shoulder good-naturedly and says, "Welcome to life outside of the Pacific."

"Yeah. It's nothing but rainbows and sunshine up here."

The crosswalk signal turns green, and she pokes her brother. "Hurry up. We're almost there."

. . .

"There's got to be some kind of misunderstanding." Natua is trying his best to keep his voice calm. "We called just this morning and they told us she was here and that we should get down here as soon as possible."

The receptionist furrows her brows and clicks around on her computer screen. "Are you sure it was this hospital?"

Natua glances at his sister, and she pipes up, "Of course we're sure! We came all the way from Seville on the first flight we could book. Maybe you spelled her name wrong?"

Natua spells out Ari's name for the woman, and she types it in again.

"I'm sorry, it looks like she's not in this hospital anymore."

"Where the hell is she then? I'm worried sick about her, and our father is stuck in Polynesia because my mother's in the hospital. Please..." he ignores his pride and pleads with the woman. "I need to find her. Do your records tell you where she went? Was she discharged?"

The woman shakes her head. "She wasn't discharged. It looks like she was transferred to a research hospital." She gives them the name of the facility, and then adds, "It's fairly late already—you won't be able to get there before their visiting hours end at 20:00 hours."

"But we're her family," Natua says, as if the receptionist has the power to grant him an exception.

"You'll have to take that up with her current facility. My suggestion would be to call them now and tell them what's going on. Keep in mind, though, if she's in a fragile condition, they'll want her to get as much rest as possible."

"She'll rest easier knowing she's not alone."

The woman sighs. "Look, this isn't a decision I can make. If you plan on going there tonight, it would be best if you get on your way and contact the folks at that hospital as soon as you can."

"Thank you for your help," Mariana says before pulling her brother away. "Look, we might be able to make it there faster if we take a cab. I'll go flag one down if you want to call the hospital." She digs her cell out of her coat pocket and offers it to him.

"I'm on it. Let's move."

. . .

"Are you going to be all right on your own, Angela?" Manu asks. He's finished making arrangements for the bill, and Irene is working on a flight to Paris. So far, though, he can't get on a plane until Monday morning. He's holding out hope Irene will be able to work some last-minute magic to get him on his way sooner.

Angela murmurs incoherently underneath the oxygen mask in response to Manu's question. At his puzzled look, she pulls the mask aside. "It doesn't matter. You have to go, so go."

He's reluctant to leave his friend alone, but it's impossible for him to stay. "Afaitu will be here in a couple of hours, but I can't stick around that long. There are some things I need to take care of in the office before my aide heads home for the weekend. Did you want me to contact Alain for you before I head out?"

She waves her hand dismissively. "No, no, Afaitu can handle that if need be. I'm not sure I'm up to seeing him anyway."

"But—but he's your brother," Manu spits out before he can stop himself.

"You have been more of a brother to me all these years. Alain and I... we took different paths in life. And that's okay." She replaces the oxygen mask over her face, breathing hard from the exertion of talking.

Standing in the doorway, bag over his shoulder, Manu hesitates.

"Now go," she says beneath the rhythmic whirr of the oxygen. She closes her eyes as if dismissing him. He hopes she'll be able to get some rest, but as he heads down a hallway clogged with gurneys and overworked nurses, he doubts it.

A daze comes over him, and he's sitting on the ferry heading to Huahine when Manu realizes he doesn't know how he got there. His only thought is reaching his daughter and helping her pull through this.

. . .

The hospital has granted them fifteen minutes with Ari. "I wish I could allow you to stay longer today," the woman explained politely over the phone, "but her condition is very fragile and we don't want her to overexert herself for the sake of any visitors. It's all about what's best for the patient. Surely you understand that."

Natua had begrudgingly agreed, and now he pauses, standing in front of her room's closed door.

"Do you want me to go in first?" Mariana asks. "This could be quite the shock for you."

He shakes his head. "She doesn't even know you. Just give me a minute alone with her first, okay?"

"Of course."

At his light knock, a frail voice Natua barely recognizes as Ari's tells him to come in. He takes a deep breath and opens the door.

It takes everything in his power to follow the nurse's instructions and control his surprise. IV bags are strung up like out-of-season Christmas decorations all around the bed, and her face has an unnatural reddish tint to it.

"I got worried," he says. "You weren't at the hotel, and then I couldn't reach you…"

"Sorry."

"No, no, don't apologize. I'm the one that should be sorry—I never should have left you alone in the first place. I'm glad you're okay."

"Well, sort of anyway." Ari raises her arms to gesture around the room, but the motion pulls on the lines in her elbows. She winces.

"Hey, relax. It's going to be fine. Do you know what happened?"

"Passed out late last night on my way back to the hotel. Apparently my knee didn't heal the way it was supposed to, and now it's infected."

"At least they're treating it, right? That's good."

"Yeah." Her uneasy smile doesn't quite reach her eyes. "But I'm not healthy enough to get the pills I came here for."

"Oh. Not so good."

"No, not so good." A light bulb seems to turn on in her head. "Hey, did you find your dad?"

"Yeah," he says softly. There's no need to tell her the rest. "Mariana tagged along with me. She's outside—do you want to meet her?"

"Sure, but don't expect much outta me. I'm more exhausted than I've ever felt in my life."

"Don't worry about that, silly. She obviously knows you're sick." He moves to the door and beckons his sister inside. "Mariana, this is my friend Ari. Ari, this is my sister Mariana."

Ari gives the woman a small wave and focuses on greeting this familiar-looking stranger with Natua's wavy hair framing her perfectly smooth face and his same dark eyes looking back at her.

"Nice to meet you," Ari says.

"The pleasure is all mine." Mariana had folded Ari's hands into her own as she spoke, but now she lets go and retreats into a far corner of the room. "But please, don't let me interrupt your reunion."

"Lots of reunions lately," Ari says. "About time."

The conversation stalls as Natua silently tries to come to terms with Ari's condition. All of the IV lines and beeping monitors are freaking him out.

"You're still really swollen. What's up with that?" he asks.

"Kidneys aren't working. Can't treat it until the infection goes away."

"I'm so sorry you had to deal with this stuff alone. I should've been here for you." Guilt weaves worry lines across his forehead.

"Stop apologizing to me." The monitor measuring her heart rate records a small jump.

"Sorry."

They both chuckle.

"I'm just glad you're here now."

"I never want to leave your side again," he says softly.

"Ditto." She manages a half-smile as she struggles to keep her eyes open.

He sits in the chair next to the bed and takes her right hand in his.

"You still have the ring. You didn't give it back to your dad?"

"We both know poor Mama will have my hide if I come home without that ring." *If Mama's still around when I get home.* He tries to swallow the lump in his throat, but it refuses to go away.

"You okay?" Ari asks.

"Yeah, uh." He starts, then stops. "Yeah."

"Okay."

"Okay." Ari doesn't sound convinced. Natua's thankful that she's too tired to dig the rest out of him.

A nurse knocks on the door. "I'm sorry to interrupt, but Miss Fonua is going to need to get some rest now. You can return tomorrow after lunchtime."

"Not first thing in the morning?" Natua asks.

"The doctors will be assessing her progress and possibly scheduling dialysis in the morning. It's hospital policy that visitors wait until at least noon so any planned treatments can be taken care of."

His eyes widen at the mention of dialysis, and it's a struggle to take this, too, in stride. He turns back to Ari. "I guess I'll see you after lunch, then."

"I'll be waiting."

"So will I. Good night," he says. Mariana is in the hallway talking to the nurse while she waits for him, but Natua isn't ready to leave quite yet. He leans over the bed and kisses Ari's forehead.

"Night," Ari says. "And Natua?" She pauses. "Thanks for coming back."

"Of course. I'll always come back for you."

Out in the hallway, on the other side of her room's closed door, Natua's carefully constructed demeanor crumples and his eyes fill with tears. He leans against the wall and lets the air out of his lungs.

"Wow."

"You okay little brother?"

"I don't know... she's so much worse than I thought. She can't even get treated for the cancer, and that's the whole reason she made this trip."

"I'm sorry."

"Me too." He wipes his eyes on the sleeve of his hoodie and clears his throat.

"Hey, let's go get some dinner, all right?" Mariana says. "You have to be starving."

"What I could really use is a drink."

"Either way, we've gotta get out of here." She takes his arm and gently leads him outside into the brisk March air.

They wander into a quiet restaurant a few blocks from the hospital. The place is tiny, yet welcoming, and Natua sinks into the plush red booth the waiter indicates. The pair stick to light chitchat until the wine glasses have been filled and emptied several times.

"This salmon is delicious. You want to try some?" Mariana holds out her loaded fork.

"Are you kidding? We're way too far inland for decent fish." Natua's tipsy grin fades as he thinks back to Ari's dissatisfaction with her own seafood just a few days ago.

"What's wrong?"

"It's nothing—just thinking about Ari."

"You really love her, don't you?"

"Of course I do. We've been friends since we were old enough to talk."

"I'm not talking about the kind of love friends share." She pauses and takes a sip of water.

Natua's cheeks warm at the suggestion. He tries to tell himself it's the wine, but even as he thinks it, he knows that's not it at all. Instead of answering, he takes another bite of bread. Mariana's gaze is intense as she waits for him to respond.

"Look, it's not the right time for that," he says. "She's so sick, and my mother hasn't been healthy in years, and—"

"This might be your last chance to tell her. Would you regret it if you let it slip away?"

"I know you're my sister, but we don't know each other well enough to be having this conversation."

"Don't mean to be pushy. I'd just hate to see important things go unsaid, you know? Like they did with Dad." Her eyes drop, and she cradles her wineglass in her hands.

"That's not on me. My mother must have known how to get in touch with him—he stayed at the pension for god's sake. She could've talked to him, and then maybe he would've come back. Sent me letters, or something. Instead, he died without even knowing I exist." He puts down his glass and rubs his hands together. *It's always so freezing in this damn city.* "Why are we even talking about this?" he asks sharply.

"I... I guess I don't know," his sister confesses. "I don't wanna see you holding back, waiting for a better time that might never come. Think about it for me, will you?"

"Nothing to think about," he replies. "She needs to work on getting better, and that's it."

Her French is a bit slurred when she says, "*You could be the reason she focuses on getting better.*"

"It's just a distraction. It'll only upset her."

"I saw the way she looked at you, baby brother." Her eyes glint with mischief.

"Forget it."

"Have it your way, then. It's forgotten." But the twinkle doesn't leave her eyes.

A few hours later, they take another taxi—this time to the hotel Natua last left with Ari by his side. They stumble in well after midnight, and it takes Natua two full minutes to find and then extract the room keycard from his wallet.

"Would you hurry it up?" his sister asks with a laugh. "The hallway's going to start charging us rent."

He inserts the keycard upside down, then tries again and finally throws the flimsy door open. "Home sweet home," he says. "At least, for a few more days."

Ari's backpack is gone, but her phone charger is still plugged into the outlet next to the bed and the Walkman is still in the locker. Natua tosses the cord on the table between the beds so Mariana can plug in her own charger. He's trying to figure out how he's going to tell Manu about all of this when his sister's phone rings.

"Hello?" she says. "Oh, hey Francisco... wait, what? ... Slow down, baby..."

Natua's ears perk up, but her slurred Spanish quickly becomes impossible for him to follow. What he does understand is that his sister is getting more and more agitated by the second. Her free hand scrunches and pulls at her hair, and she paces in a tight circle at the foot of the bed. The phone call goes on for several minutes, and the only word Natua is sure he recognizes is *aeropuerto*. After she hangs up, he stays quiet. It takes her a moment to remember that he's in the room.

"Do you think you can make it back to the hospital on your own?" she asks.

"What? Why? I thought that was your boyfriend—is Ari okay?"

"That wasn't about Ari. Just answer me. Do you think you can make it there again alone?"

"Yeah, I think so," he says. "Why? What happened?"

"Someone broke into our apartment and ransacked the place."

"Oh my god!" His hand flies to his mouth.

"It gets better. I had some confidential papers in the apartment from the law firm, and he wouldn't know the first thing about whether any of those are missing. I... I have to go home and figure out if anything's been stolen. If any of those files disappear, I could be in huge trouble." She takes a few shaky breaths to calm herself down. "I have to go back, first thing in the morning. I'm so sorry, Natua."

He closes the distance between them and puts his hands on her shoulders. "Hey, hey, it's fine. I'll be fine. Why don't you just drink some water and breathe for a minute?"

Mariana sits heavily onto the bed. "At least I'll be able to make Mom's party." The still-tipsy siblings catch each other's eyes and dissolve into a fit of nervous laughter.

Chapter 17

On Sunday morning, Natua jumps out of bed and reaches for the room phone. He punches out the numbers to Manu's cell phone, fingers shaking with dread after a horrible dream about Mama.

"Hello, Uncle? It's Natua."

Immediately, the man peppers him with questions. "How is she, Natua? It's still early there, isn't it? Did something happen overnight?"

"Sorry Uncle, I didn't call about Ari. I haven't seen her since we talked last night." He fiddles with a loose thread on his pants. "Listen, are you still with Mama by any chance? How..." he trails off, afraid of the answer.

"I left a few hours ago. The doctors are concerned that the emphysema has done too much damage for her to go off the oxygen. Your mother is a fighter, but she's very tired. Afaitu is staying overnight with her. The doctors... they're not sure she's going to make it this time."

"Wha—what?"

"When are you coming back?"

"My flight is supposed to leave tomorrow, but I promised Ari we'd fly back together, and she's still in the hospital—there's no way she can travel. I don't know if I can stomach the thought of leaving her alone again, but our flight was non-refundable and I can't afford another ticket. Are you going to get here by then?" His fingers tap a nervous beat on the wooden bedside table.

"I'm working on it," Manu says, "but Irene isn't having much luck. Looks like I won't get there until Tuesday afternoon Paris time."

From his spot on the hotel bed, Natua's shoulders slouch in defeat. "Her condition could change a lot in 24 hours."

He isn't sure if it's intercontinental static or if Manu sighs into the phone's receiver. "Look, I don't want her left alone either, but you kids have made quite the mess. There's no money for another return flight for both of you, and from the sounds of it, Ari's never going to manage that flight on Monday. I'll do what I can to get there earlier. Just make sure you come home."

"I'm sorry, Uncle. I should've tried harder to talk her out of this whole thing. The trip made me uncomfortable, but she was so insistent—"

"We all walk our own path, Natua. And Ari is determined enough that she would've walked hers with or without your help."

"Yeah, I know," he says. "Listen, can you give me the number for Mama's room at the hospital? Mariana and her phone left town, so I can't look it up if I need it."

"You should be able to contact her through me or Afaitu until your flight leaves, but in case you can't reach us, here's the number."

He scribbles the information on his arm with a pen. "Thanks, Uncle. Let me know if anything changes, please."

"You do the same. You're the only one over there with my daughter."

"I know. I'll be there as soon as they'll let me in."

He hangs up the phone and sinks back into bed, covering his head with his hands and trying to still his racing heart. When he moves, he goes for the phone again.

This time, there's no answer to the dull ringing on the other end of the line. He leaves a message, wondering if she's able to hear it.

"I love you, Mama," he says quietly before hanging up.

. . .

At the hospital, Natua tries to cheer Ari up by singing a few traditional songs. His singing voice is awful, but that only serves to make her smile all the wider. He continues until she drifts off to sleep, her Walkman tucked in protectively next to her.

The thought of leaving her alone tomorrow plagues him, but he can't exactly have a conversation with her while she's comatose and she needs the rest anyway. The dull beeping of her monitors eventually lulls him to sleep.

He dreams an enormous tupa crab is chasing him. His mother used to tell him stories about how the crabs were tools of the gods. Right now, those gods are all angry at him. No matter how hard he runs, he can't escape the crab. Its large claws close around his arm. "Aah!"

He knocks it away, only to realize Ari was shaking him awake. Head still foggy from the dream, he gasps. "Oh my god, are you okay? I didn't hurt you, did I?" He scoots his chair closer to the head of the bed, as if trying to quell his sudden panic with motion.

"No, no, nothing like that," she says. "Can we talk for a minute?"

"Of course. What's on your mind?"

"Is tomorrow Monday?"

"Yeah." His face falls. As much as Natua knows this is a conversation they have to have, he's been dreading it ever since he found out Manu wouldn't make it to Paris on time. He hasn't even told Ari that the man is coming, that their little ruse is over.

"Our flight..." she trails off.

"I know."

"Are you going to go?"

He clears his throat. There's one more thing he hasn't told Ari yet. He hates to dump it all on her now, but there's no time left for dancing around the situation. "I have to," he says. "Mama's been in the hospital since Thursday, and they're not sure she's going to make it."

"Oh no, Natua!"

"I'm so sorry—I know I promised we would go back together."

"What's going to happen now? You can't exactly show up without me."

"Ari, for a while there I thought you were a goner—I talked to your dad. He's on his way."

She sucks in her breath. "He what? Was he mad?"

Natua shakes his head. "Not at you, but I think I'm a different story. You know how Uncle is. He's too busy worrying to be angry with you."

"Sounds about right," she comments. Her fingers fiddle nervously with the bedsheets. "When will he get here?"

"I'm not sure if he was able to get a different flight or not, but last I knew he was leaving the island Monday morning."

"And that's when you're leaving Paris."

"I wish it wasn't like this," he says. "I hate that I have to leave you, but you know I can't afford a full-price ticket home—especially since I already owe Irene the rest of the money for this trip."

"I know, I know," she replies. "Stop blaming yourself, okay? If I wasn't having such a terrible time from that stupid infection, I'd be right there with you." She pats his hand. "And that's exactly where I want to be."

"Couldn't agree more." He lays his other hand on top of hers. He's only trying to be comforting, but he can't keep his eyes from showing what he's too afraid to say out loud.

Ari breaks the silence that falls between them. "Look... I don't know what's going to happen to me. But if I make it through this—"

"You mean when," he interrupts, surprising himself with the force of his emotions.

"No," she counters. "I mean if."

"You have to make it through this," he replies, staring at the Walkman Ari moved to the bedside table so he doesn't have to meet her gaze. "I don't want to live in a world that doesn't have you in it."

She squeezes his hand gently. "I understand. I don't want to live without you either, Natua." Her eyes are glistening in the light when he finally looks up to meet them.

"Is this about me leaving? Because you're only going to be a couple of days behind me."

"No, it's not about that. I'm saying what we should have said years ago." She presses on. "I love you, Natua. I always have. And I always will."

Butterflies erupt in Natua's stomach when Ari says the words out loud. He wants to say them back, but he doesn't trust himself to speak. Instead, he leans over until his lips meet hers. He slides his fingers through the hair framing her face, careful not to get tangled in the IV lines dangling around her. When they finally break apart, the fear has left her eyes.

"I love you too," he says. "I'm sorry I have to leave."

"Don't worry about that," she replies. "I'll see you at home."

"And then?"

She doesn't say a word, just takes his hand. It's the only answer he needs.

• • •

Natua calls Manu one more time from the hotel's room phone the following morning. The news is grim, and Manu makes the boy promise to get in touch during his layover in LAX. "I don't want you out of the loop for 24 hours," he says. "Your mother is on a ventilator. There's still hope, but if there's any sort of emergency, we need to be able to contact you."

"Of course—I'll do what I can to stay in touch," Natua promises. "But won't you be in the air yourself by then?"

"Actually, I'm at the airport now for an overnight flight. According to Irene, I'll be at LAX when you get there if our flights are both on time. Find a payphone and call my cell if you don't see me at your gate. We'll have lunch together."

"Uh, okay," Natua replies. He's still not sure he's ready to face Uncle. While the man's been nothing but comforting to Natua, he's also interrupted their conversation three times already to yell at the people in the airport about safety protocols.

But Natua knows that if the updates about Mama continue to get worse, it'd be best if he's not alone when he hears them. He writes Manu's flight number on his arm just in case and then it's time to go.

"See you in LA."

Onboard the plane, it's hard for Natua to stop staring at the empty seat beside him. He tries to distract himself with the in-flight movie, but he quickly tires of the fast-paced English he can't quite keep up with. The French subtitles are cut off at the bottom of the screen, so he turns the film off.

To keep himself occupied, he alternately stares out the window at the endless expanse of the Atlantic and examines the flight's progress. The tiny monitor mounted to the seat in front of him has replaced the movie with an interactive map. The plane ticks along slowly on-screen at a thousand kilometers per hour, moving from one continent he will never call home to another.

An elderly woman across the aisle is working on a crossword puzzle, gray hair in a loose up-do. From her self-assured, relaxed posture he guesses that she is going home, and that wherever she went was kind to her. She glances affectionately to her right every now and then at the balding man snoring in the seat next to her. Contentment radiates from within her, as though this plane ride is the culmination of everything good in life.

She's a stark contrast to Natua, who is conspicuously alone. His leg jiggles of its own accord from nerves too tightly fraught to stay still. It's only after his knee hits the folded-up tray table for a third time that he consciously notices the movement.

His restlessness worsens once the airbus leaves the Atlantic behind. He gets up and tosses his backpack into Ari's empty seat. *There. At least I can be the first person off this damned plane. Not that that'll help me get to Mama any faster.* To calm himself, he softly hums an old traditional tune. They're nearly to their destination before he remembers that it's the song he and Ari had learned to dance to all those years ago, right before her diagnosis. He hopes they will be able to dance together again someday.

"Please remember to check the overhead bins and under your seats for personal belongings before disembarking. Thank you for flying with us, and enjoy your stay in Los Angeles."

Upon hearing the warm female voice over the loudspeakers repeat the announcement in French, Natua takes a deep breath and exhales slowly. It's time for him to face Manu and whatever news the man is bringing of home.

He slings his tattered pack over one shoulder and makes his way down the cramped aisle and through the gangway, which is shaking from the weight of the Americans' over-packed rolling luggage.

He pauses at the gate to look for a payphone, but he quickly gets bumped in the back by a hurried businessman. "Stand in the middle of the aisle, why don't you?" the man grouses as he rushes by.

"Sorry," Natua says, but the suit is already gone. He shuffles to one side, wishing he still had his phone so he would know what to do. His stomach rumbles, but he doesn't want to move yet if Uncle's on his way.

The other passengers filter out, and then the flight attendants and finally the pilots disembark, waving breezily to each other as they head off in different directions. The area has emptied out before he realizes they don't let non-passengers so close to the gate in this country.

A little laugh escapes him as he makes his way out of the lounge and down a set of escalators to a food court area. Manu waves at him from a table near the McDonald's.

The first thing Natua notices, even from a distance, is how tired Uncle looks. *Is that gray in his hair?* It's as though he's aged 10 years since Natua and Ari left the islands last week.

The man rises to greet him, putting his hands on the boy's shoulders and tapping cheeks in a quick *bisou*.

"I'm so sorry about everything," Natua says when they separate. "This wasn't supposed to happen."

"Shh, I know," Manu replies. "*Les petits poissons grandissent.*" *Little fish get bigger.*

"I should've convinced her to stay." Natua stares at his dirty sneaks as he shifts his weight from foot to foot.

"We both know that wouldn't have worked. Come on, let's grab something to eat. I've had buckets of coffee to stay awake, but what I really need is a decent meal." Uncle holds out his hands and they tremble in the air.

"I assume that means you didn't sleep on the flight over?"

Manu shakes his head. "I may not panic in the air like Ari, but flying is never easy for me." He sighs. "Which is too bad because I had an overnight flight and a quiet cabin, but oh well. Coffee it is."

Natua's wanted to ask about Mama since the moment he spotted Manu from the escalator, but he's terrified of the answer. Instead of bringing it up now, he asks, "So, where do you want to eat?"

They quickly polish off a lunch of chicken sandwiches and fries, keeping to small talk during their meal. Manu seems to understand that Natua isn't quite ready, even if he's desperate for news, so he waits until their meal is over before mentioning he'd heard from Afaitu that morning. Natua snaps to attention and nearly drops his soft drink in the process.

"How is she?" he blurts out.

The somber look on Manu's face is accentuated by the deep bags under his gentle brown eyes. "Afaitu is staying with your mother night and day until you can get home," he says. "He's afraid of letting her die alone."

"What? No, no, no, she'll recover. She always does."

"Eventually we all have to go, Natua. Of course I'm hoping and praying for her to get better, but right now, your mother is hanging by a thread."

Natua puts his head into his hands to hide the fact that he's about to lose his shit in a foreign airport. "I never should have left her for so long," he mumbles through his fingers. "All that extra stress—this is my fault."

"No, it's not. Just go home and be with her, okay? You're a good son." Manu pries the boy's hands away from his face and takes them in his own. "And you're wonderful to Ari. Angela doesn't blame you for running off with her, or for going to look for your father. It's okay."

Instead of replying, Natua yanks one of his hands away to wipe at his eyes. "Thanks for lunch, Uncle. Can I uh, can I use your phone to call the hospital? I want to talk to her myself."

Manu digs his cell out of his pocket. "Don't forget to dial 689—we're not in Polynesia anymore."

Natua resists the temptation to remind Uncle that he's been doing that for days now. Instead, he takes the phone with a simple thank you and dials the number for Angela's room. He stands and starts pacing a few meters away from the table. "Can you put Mama on the phone?"

"Natua, I really wish I could," Afaitu responds, his voice cracking. "Your mother is off on the journey we all must take alone."

Natua crumples to the floor, all worries about losing his shit in an airport forgotten.

.   .   .

Uncle rushes over and kneels down next to him, retrieving his phone off the floor in the process. Vaguely, Natua hears Uncle and Afaitu talking, but it doesn't matter. None of it matters.

He can't stop shaking. *How did Ari deal with so much death when we were kids?* He reminds himself it's probably easier when it's not your fault, and that's when he realizes Manu is off the phone, trying to comfort him.

"I'm sorry, my son. I'm so sorry."

"I'm too late," he squeaks. "I was too late for my dad, and now I'm too late for Mama too."

Uncle hugs him a little closer. "You did the best you could. You're a good son. And they both know that."

"I didn't—all that stress, it's my fault, I—"

Uncle cuts him off before he loses himself to hysterics. "You can't blame yourself for that. Your mom has been on borrowed time for years now. You have to let go of the blame."

"Okay, but what do I even do now?" The words tumble out in a rush, and he knows he's blubbering but he can't help it. "Mama's all I've got."

"You are going to go home and help put your mother to rest. I'm sure Afaitu will be there to help, and your Uncle Alain."

"And you?"

"I'll be home with Ari as soon as she's well enough to travel. But no matter what, I'm never more than a phone call away." He pats Natua's cheek. "Do you think we can stand up now?"

He murmurs in assent.

"I love you, son. We will get through this together, you hear me?"

Natua stands and brushes off the dirt that's collected on his pants. "I hope so."

Uncle gets up and puts a hand on his shoulder. "No matter what, you're not alone."

"I know—I shouldn't have said that Mama's all I've got. Love you, Uncle."

The pair settle back into their seats, and Manu calls Afaitu back. He fills Manu and Natua in on the details and takes some extra time to reassure Natua that she was at peace. Once the dust has settled, Manu checks in with the hospital in Paris and they discover that Ari's been cleared to receive dialysis, but she's still too sick for cancer treatments.

"Yes, I'm on my way—I'll get there tomorrow afternoon. Please, just take care of my little girl."

After he hangs up, Natua raises his eyes to meet Manu's. He doesn't know what to say.

"The sea never rests," Manu says grimly.

An hour later they have to part ways, but neither one is ready to go on alone.

Chapter 18

When Natua arrives in Pape'ete, the sun has long since disappeared for the night, and he's grateful the flight's arrival time forced Irene to book a stay in the airport motel. He's relieved to be spared the emptiness that awaits him at the pension, even for just one more night.

Although he is completely spent, sleep refuses to come. His eyes wander over every tiny shadow cast by the bumps in the popcorn ceiling and linger on the flowery artwork on the wall—no doubt painted by some European artist that tourists recognize with delight.

In Paris, it's already midmorning on Tuesday, and he wonders if anyone's checked on Ari today. Manu had a layover in London, but Natua doesn't have the presence of mind to remember what time he was supposed to land or what time that would translate to in the islands. Thinking about Ari helps keep his mind off the guilt he feels for hearing of Mama's death secondhand. For not being by her side as she sailed off into the unknown.

Eventually, his thoughts drift to tomorrow and how exhausted he's going to be boarding his 06:45 flight. As he's wondering what funeral arrangements Mama would've wanted, he drifts off to a deep, dreamless sleep.

The fierce Pacific sun awakens him at quarter to 6, and he groans. Even just a week in Europe has conditioned him to leave the room curtains open, and the early morning glare is giving him a headache.

"Ugh, why did they leave those open?" he grumbles as he rolls over, away from the floor-length window. "Why did *I* leave those open?" He hides his head under the covers, but despite the fatigue pulsing behind his eyes, there's not enough time to go back to sleep.

Feet slap the floor. Might as well start the day by nabbing some free grub from downstairs. His body might be confused about what time it is, but his stomach doesn't care. He's starving.

After demolishing the abysmal breakfast buffet, Natua checks out of the motel. He speed-walks down the hill towards the bustling airport and passes a few tourists struggling with overloaded luggage on the steep incline. His own worn bag is feeling heavier and heavier the closer he gets to home.

. . .

Manu is utterly exhausted by the time he leaves airports and runways behind. It may be the middle of the afternoon, but back on Huahine, sunrise is still hours away. His eyes itch to close, so he snags a cup of coffee before heading out of the airport.

"I'm coming, baby girl." Manu heads towards the line of cabbies waiting outside. "Hang in there."

Just over half an hour later, he rushes in the front doors of the institute, startling the young clerk watching a sitcom behind the check-in desk.

"Tell me what room my daughter is in," he orders. The desperation in his voice dares to be trifled with.

"What's the last name?" The clerk diligently types Ari's information into his computer. "I need to see some form of ID so I can print you a family visitor's pass."

"Of course." Manu hands over his passport and waits an eternity for the blurry name tag to print.

Finally, he's winding his way through a series of identical-looking hallways, counting the turns and checking room numbers carefully. The last thing he wants to do is get lost from rushing and leave Ari on her own even a second longer than necessary.

The door to her room has been left open, and for a moment, he swears he's in the wrong place. But behind the tubes going every which way, dressed in an ill-fitting gown and looking emaciated, he recognizes his daughter's sleeping face.

"I'm here Riri, I'm here." He speaks in a low whisper to reassure himself, and then he touches her hand gingerly so as not to wake her. It relieves him to feel the warmth of her body. His eyes burn as it hits him. He'd been preparing in case she was gone.

He can't sleep, so instead he spends the empty hours learning the rhythms of her monitors and watching the rise and fall of her chest. He times his own breaths with hers, an exercise that helps keep him alert and focused.

A nurse comes in to check Ari's vitals, her clinical expression softening at the sight of Manu. "The cafeteria will open in an hour—would you like me to have something sent to the room for you?"

"No, that's quite all right. Can you just tell me how she's doing? What's going on with all of this?"

She consults her clipboard. "She came to us Friday afternoon after one of the hospitals up north couldn't manage to treat her for a simple infection. According to the paperwork, she came in for hypoglycemia and then they couldn't get her vitals stabilized." The woman sighs. "And because she has cancer, they decided to ship her here."

"Are you going to be able to treat her cancer?"

"That's not a priority right now." She looks up from Ari's chart. Manu has been caught off-guard by his daughter's condition. His grip on the armrest tightens until he's in danger of breaking a nail. Seeing the tears pooling in his eyes, she adds, "I'm sorry, this must be such a shock. I can't imagine seeing my own child like this."

Instead of speaking, Manu lets go of the chair and waves for her to continue. His throat feels thick with emotions he refuses to give into right now.

"We've been able to get the infection under control, but recovery has been complicated by the fact that her kidneys aren't working. The situation isn't critical, but we're keeping a very careful eye on it. Now that she's had a round of successful dialysis, our next goal is to see some signs of kidney function return."

"And the myeloma?"

"We're holding off on any direct treatments a little longer because the last thing we want to do is start a new medication while she's in such a delicate state. The patient is receiving a magnesium supplement to regulate the calcium in her bloodstream. As soon as those levels are under control, kidneys should bounce back. *Then* she'll be healthy enough to talk about treatment options."

"Oh." Manu's heart sinks at the realization that, even though she's improved, his daughter is still in an incredibly fragile condition.

"I have to move on," the nurse says apologetically, "but someone should come check on her vitals again in around two hours. If you have any questions in the meantime, the nurses' station is down the hall and to the right."

"Thank you," he says stiffly. His stomach is churning, and he wonders briefly if he's going to vomit. *Just breathe. She needs you, and you're here. You're here. That's what matters.*

He's trying to stifle a sob when Ari squeezes his hand.

"Hi Papa." She swallows hard. "I missed you."

"Oh honey, I was so worried about you," he says. He resists the urge to envelope her in his arms, instead returning her slight pressure and blinking to keep the tears from falling. "But we're together now. Everything's going to be okay."

Ari lets her head relax against the pillow, and her eyes close. "Love you."

"I love you too."

. . .

It's not even 8 o'clock when the plane touches down at Huahine, and Natua's hoping it's still too early for Irene. The last thing he wants to do is explain why he came back alone. But when he trudges off the tarmac, she's there waiting for him.

"Mr. Fonua told me what happened," she says. Her bangles and her eyes glisten in the sunlight spilling in through the windows. "How was she when you left her?"

Natua just shakes his head. "Not great, but she'll survive. You know how stubborn she is. She's not about to give up."

"That's true," Irene agrees. "Though sometimes it'd do her good to go with the flow a little more."

"I don't know 'bout that—current's not taking her anywhere I'd wanna go." The woman considers this for a minute, but before she can come up with a reply, Natua says, "Listen, I have to head out. I'm about ready to fall asleep standing up. If you hear from Manu before I do, would you please let me know?"

"Um, sure," she says, sounding confused. Natua's already heading towards the lone cab waiting outside when she asks, "But why wouldn't he just call you?"

"Lost my phone!" he calls back, voice echoing around the empty airport.

When he gets into the cab, the first place he heads is downtown Fare to grab a new cell. None of the stores will open for another hour yet, but he's a little intimidated by the thought of the empty pension. So, he wanders the quiet streets instead.

"Natua!" a familiar voice calls.

He looks up to find Wan, waving as he unlocks the grocery.

"Hey Wan," he replies. "Thought you didn't open until 9."

"We don't. But if you need something, then come on in." He motions Natua over.

"Thanks man," he says. Wan holds the door open for him as Natua steps inside.

"What's got you in town so early?" he asks. "Haven't you been on vacation?"

A sarcastic chuckle flies from Natua's lips. "Something like that. Just got back this morning." He pauses. "Wait, how did you know that?"

"Temata's been delivering my bread himself. And giving me comments on my early morning Mandarin."

"What? He doesn't speak Mandarin."

"Not those kind of comments. He thinks I'm crazy."

"Well..." Natua shrugs. "Not too many people get up at the crack of dawn to work on personal projects like that."

"What can I say? I'm a morning person."

"Must be," Natua replies. He turns from Wan to browse the orderly shelves. "Where do you keep the cell phones in this place?"

"Aah, we had to move them behind the counter. Too many kids with sticky fingers. What happened to your old phone?"

"Turns out kids with sticky fingers are a pretty universal problem."

"Where'd you end up going, anyway?" Wan asks as he notes Natua's purchase down on receipt paper.

"Spain." Because he doesn't want to talk about Paris, he leaves that part out.

"Isn't your dad from there?"

"Yeah, he is." His voice takes on a twinge of regret. "He doesn't live there anymore though."

"Too bad. It's still cool that you got to go there, see where you're from. I'd love to take my parents to

Nanjing, but it'd be next to impossible to close up the shop for that long."

"I had to settle for a really short trip, but I know what you mean." He stops to consider whether the trip was "worth it" or "authentic" or any of those other hollow phrases the tourism board always used to market the pension. He doesn't have an answer. "I hope you're able to make your trip someday."

"We'll see," Wan responds as he fiddles with the cash register. "Looks like our system isn't online yet—mind paying in cash?"

"That's fine." He pulls out his wallet and quickly counts out a few bills.

"Hey, that's not a franc," Wan says when he finds a 10-euro note.

"Oh, oops." Natua stuffs the creased currency back into his wallet and tosses Wan the thousand franc note he'd meant to give him. As he does, Natua wonders just how much his European trip cost him. "Anyway, I guess I should let you get back to work. Thanks, Wan."

"Anytime. See you around."

"See you."

Despite taking the long way on purpose, Natua's feet find their way home all too quickly. The cobblestones in the courtyard seem to echo more loudly than normal. He fishes his keys out of his bag and their jangling fills the morning air.

The wooden door groans open. The first thing he notices after he steps inside are greasy wheel tracks running through the front hallway. It takes him a second to connect the grime with the gurney that carried Mama out of her home for the last time.

He squats down. His bag slips off his shoulder and slaps the brown tiles. When he picks it back up, the bottom is coated in a thick layer of dirt. *What a mess! Mama's going to be furious.* He thinks the words automatically, and it's when he remembers Mama isn't coming home that his breath catches in his throat.

. . .

The doctors come in and out with more regularity than Manu had taught himself to expect, and when he questions them later that evening, he's pleased with the care they're giving his daughter. He thanks his lucky stars that she was transferred to such a high-quality facility—the hospital she was originally admitted to only confirmed his worst fears about the status of islanders in the *métropole*. Despite feeling assured Ari is getting adequate care *now*, Manu still worries about leaving her alone even for a moment.

He pulls a copy of his printed remarks out of his bag. In order to prevent Robert's sabotage of his legislation, Manu will have to fight his jet lag and video conference the entire Assembly from Ari's hospital room at 2 in the morning. He's scratching a few notes in the margins of his speech and finalizing what he's going to say when Ari starts to stir.

"Hey honey, can I get you anything?"

She opens her eyes a crack and shakes her head slightly. But she's flexing her hands into fists and shifting in bed. Manu slips the papers onto the floor and puts a hand on her arm.

"What's wrong?"

She shakes her head again, and a few tears escape out of the eyes she's pinched closed.

"Do you need me to get the nurse?" Seeing her so agitated is making Manu nervous, and he talks to fill the silence. "Are you in pain?"

"It's not that," she mumbles.

"Here, let me get you some water."

"No. It's not that." Her voice is clearer and more insistent this time.

"Then what is it?" he asks. He's surprised at how terrified he sounds. "Are you okay?"

"I have to tell you something," she says.

"Anything, honey."

Ari struggles to sit up.
"Just relax, okay? What is it?"
"It's about Henri."

PART IV: HOME

Chapter 19

Ari gulps. She's heard the doctors talking, and she knows things aren't looking good. For one thing, nobody has talked about myeloma in days and for another, her kidneys still aren't working. If this is the end, then her father deserves to know the truth.

"What about Henri?" he asks.

She hates herself for how much he trusts her, how badly she's betrayed their family. The words are slow in coming, but she forces them out. "The day of..." The words lodge in her throat, but her father gently squeezes her hand in understanding. Some things are better left unsaid. "I went to the airport."

"I know, baby, I know."

"You do?"

"Oriata told me he sent you away. And I'm so grateful that he did."

"You don't understand."

"What is there to understand?"

"The—the crash. I know what happened."

"What happened is in the past, Ari, and that's where it should stay. Why are you worrying about this now?"

She turns away from her father, unable to face what she's about to do to him.

"Have you been having nightmares again?"

"It's not... it's not about the nightmares. It's about why I have them." Manu studies his daughter's profile, her pain reflected in his eyes. She continues, "I deserve to have them. Papa, I... I was in the plane that day."

The heart monitor's beeping speeds up, and he tenderly tucks a few loose strands of hair behind her ear. "You've got to let that go," he says. "It wasn't your time."

"It wasn't Henri's either!" Ari's voice shakes as she continues. "I was playing around up there, running through the—the pre-flight check list. Sometimes, when I rode with him, he'd let me do it, and I always forgot to test the radio. I wanted to get it right that time." Her next words catch on a sob. "But I tripped on a loose wire when I crawled under the instrument panel, and I... I didn't tell anyone. I was so scared of getting into trouble, and then Ori kicked me out and—"

Before she dissolves into hysterics, Manu stands and pulls her head close to his chest. "Breathe for me," he says.

"It's my fault," she sobs. "It's my fault that he's dead."

"No, darling, it's not, I promise." He strokes her hair and tries to sound soothing.

"If it wasn't for me tripping on that wire, nothing would have sparked. He would've had a chance to cut his seatbelt and get out."

"Shhhh." His reassurances don't stop Ari's heart from doing double time, and the monitor's insistent beeping punctuates his next words. "You were just a child, a blameless child. It's time you know the truth that I've run from for so long—the real blame lies with me."

"What do you mean?" She looks up and absently wipes a tear from her cheek.

"Honey, nobody knew those planes better than I did. I was one of the only full-time pilots for years. You might have tripped on the loose wire, but I already knew it was there. The fussy seat belt, too."

Her eyes widen.

"In fact, I meant to tell Henri about both of those issues, but I kept forgetting. The maintenance slip for that plane was way overdue because I didn't take the time to fill out paperwork before rushing home every day." He takes a deep breath to calm his trembling body. "Your mom had already been gone a few years, but being a single parent never gets any easier. And there wasn't anyone there to stop me from cutting corners when it came to the cargo planes. I wish to God there had been." He draws his daughter in a little tighter. "It wasn't your fault at all. His blood is on my hands. Only mine."

"I'm still so sorry, Papa."

"Me too, Riri. Me too." He backs up a step and turns her face towards his. "I just wish you'd talked to me about this before instead of carrying that burden around all these years."

"And how could I have said anything? You got so mad at everyone you possibly could over what happened—the safety officials, people at the airport, the entire country of France... I was terrified of what you'd think of me."

"Oh, honey, no." He wraps his arms around her again, cautious of the lines entering her elbows. "I didn't mean to hurt you too."

• • •

At first, Natua doesn't register the noise as a ringing phone... at least, as a ringing phone *he* needs to answer. Mama had always insisted on keeping a landline in the pension, but he hasn't used it since he started working at the bakery and paying for a cell back in high school. He'd brought one of the handsets into his cluttered room before dozing off, but it takes three rings before he remembers that no one's around to answer but him.

On the fourth ring, he picks up and manages a bleary, "Hello?"

"Natua? It's Afaitu. How are you holding up?"

"Okay, I guess." He sits up and clears the sleep from his throat. "Jetlagged."

"That's right—when did you get in?"

He glances at the bedside clock. "Couple of hours ago."

"Ouch. Listen, I don't want to bombard you with details right now, but there is one thing I wanted to talk to you about right away."

"What's that?"

Afaitu's voice is gentle. "Your mother never ended up reaching out to your uncle. And now..." He sighs into the receiver. "I think this is news that should come from family."

"No, you're right. You've done so much for us. For Mama. You're just as much a part of the family as Uncle Alain, if not more so. But you're right. I should be the one to call him. I'll reach out today."

"Good. Now, I don't like the idea of you staying over there all alone—"

"Don't be silly, I'm not some irresponsible kid."

"That's not what I mean," Afaitu replies. "If you don't have any plans later, come over for dinner. We're eating at 21:00 hours, and Veroa is making *i'a ota*. It's just the thing to strengthen you after your long journey."

"Thanks, Afaitu. Yeah, it'd be nice to be in the company of friends tonight."

"We will see you then, my boy. Now get some rest."

"Okay. See you later."

Natua hits the end button and drops the handset onto the floor. The jarring *clunk* when it hits the worn wooden planks echoes in the empty pension, reminding him of how alone he truly is.

. . .

Ari is in a deep sleep when the doctor comes in to do her evening rounds. Manu takes this chance to ask the questions he's afraid to have answered.

In hushed tones, he asks, "Is my daughter going to be able to have her cancer treated any time soon?"

"It's looking good for her on that front, yes." The doctor gestures towards the empty tube on her tray. "Just need to confirm that with another round of bloodwork and a scan of her body to see what condition the cancer itself is in. But since the patient is sleeping now, I'll send a nurse down to take care of that in a few hours. She needs to get as much rest as she can, and I'd rather give her a little more time to improve before making my decision."

"And you'll make sure to send someone along to notify us of the results?"

The doctor scratches a note on her clipboard. "Soon as we have them."

"Thank you." He draws in a breath before continuing. "What happens if she can't get the treatments?" His voice quavers just a little when he asks, "Is my daughter in trouble?"

"Based on the information in her medical records, we have no reason to believe the cancer is life-threatening at this point. A few more days isn't going to hurt anything." The doctor moves towards the door and puts a reassuring hand on Manu's shoulder, her dark eyes gentle and serious. "We are doing everything we can to help her through this."

"I appreciate the level of care Ari's receiving here. I truly do."

"Of course, sir. I have to go check on my next patient now. If your daughter wakes up before the nurse comes in, just hit the call button and someone will come right down to get her taken care of."

"Okay."

The doctor closes the door softly behind her, and Manu glances at the clock. It will be hours before the Assembly is ready for him. He doesn't trust himself to wake up if he naps, so he pulls out his remarks and goes over them for what he thinks will be the final time.

Maybe it's the jetlag or his emotional state or Ari's revelation, but his speech seems all wrong. It takes two or three read-throughs before his exhausted brain can figure out why. *Bitterness.* It's the common thread throughout his speech, but he realizes the feeling reaches far beyond that—it's the source of his disdain for the French, the vengeance he wants to exact on the *métropole,* the way he's lashed out about safety regulations instead of facing his own culpability...

And look where it's gotten me, he thinks. He's isolated his only surviving child, causing her years of guilt that should've been his burden alone. Over the years, his resentment has also strained many of his friendships—most notably with Angela, who relied on good relations with the *métropole* back when the pension was still in business.

Anger won't bring Henri back to life. Or Amy, or Oscar, or any of the other friends and family he's lost. Yes, his actions have done a lot of good... but they have also hurt many of the ones he loves the most. His current speech just won't do.

He fishes around in his bag for a few clean sheets of paper and starts fresh. The bill is still important—more important than ever—but it's not about him. It was never about him.

. . .

Natua's sleep is troubled by dreams of a young tourist couple who had somehow booked a room at the pension. "You can't stay here. We've been closed for six years," he had explained, but the man—barely older than Natua himself—insisted on checking in anyway. They'd rolled their oversized luggage right into Mama's room and refused to leave. Locking the door behind them, the couple then proceeded to throw his mother's things out the window, where they landed in jumbled mounds on the dewy back lawn.

When he awakens, he can't shake the feeling that something is amiss in Mama's room. He pads down the empty hallway, silent as a cat in his socked feet. But when he's standing in front of Mama's closed bedroom door, he stops.

His mother had always been a particularly private woman. Years of being surrounded by tourists taught her the value of boundaries. Even though he knows she's gone, he can't help but feel he's about to commit an act of sacrilege by spying around in her bedroom.

Deep breaths. It was just a dream. He wants to walk away, but something in his gut won't let him.

"I'm just going to make sure everything's okay, Mama." In the hush, he doesn't speak much above a whisper and yet his voice still booms in his ears.

He takes another deep breath and turns the knob, wincing as the wooden door creaks in the muggy afternoon. Instead of tripping through the room to open the curtains or switch on one of Mama's many lamps, Natua stands in the doorway until his eyes adjust to the dark. There's a long pause before he dares cross the threshold.

Surveying the room, everything looks essentially the way he left it after fishing Armando's ring out of her jewelry dish just last week.

"You can have it back now, Mama," he says out loud. He fumbles for the ring in his pocket. "Just needed to borrow it for a little while." His hand trembles as he plops the tarnished piece of jewelry back into the tangled pile of bracelets it's called home for the last two decades.

As he turns to go, a cardboard box jutting out of the closet with the lid askew catches his attention. "You meant to put that back, right?" he asks the air. "So, let me take care of it for you." He leans down and tries to slide the lid back into place. One of the sides is bent, so he lifts it up to fix it.

As he does, his eyes fall on an envelope with a return address in Seville. The lid slips out of his hands. *What has she been hiding?*

"Sorry Mama, but this concerns me too," he mutters as he drags the box into the hallway. At first, he only intends to check that one envelope, but soon all of the contents of the box are spread out around him.

Letters from his father. Dozens of them, some as short as packing slips—"You mentioned that Ignacio is really into football, so I picked up a FIFA jersey in Spain's colors for his birthday."—while others are extended letters, pages long, and filled with discussions about *him*.

"What the hell?" Natua runs fingers through messy hair. "What the actual hell?" When he stands, the letters piled on his lap flutter to the ground. *And she acted like he didn't even know I existed!*

"How could you do this to me?"

The silence in the house is overpowering, so he runs out to the yard, under the coconut trees where Mama will soon be put to rest. There, at least the crying koleas attempt to fill the gaping hole in his heart.

. . .

Manu's bleary eyes are trained on the clock hands, but the numbers are no longer registering. He's too strung out on exhaustion to calculate the time difference, but thankfully, Diane's got his back. Ten minutes before he's due to come on, his email dings. *You're up next. Be ready to test your connection in five.*

He sits up and drinks the last few sips of his hours-old coffee. It's hard to resist the urge to spit the bitter tasting brew out, but he's in danger of falling asleep without some sort of caffeine jolt. A splash of freezing water on his face from the bathroom sink and a few slaps on his cheeks serve to push back on the jet lag. "You got this, you got this," he mumbles to himself.

The connection is weak, his video feed skipping all through the introductions. When the president of the Assembly finally turns it over to him, Manu's afraid that his words will be lost, so he takes care to speak slowly and enunciate each word.

"I wish I could be there with you all today in person. Unfortunately, my daughter is in critical condition in a hospital here in Paris. She's in this position because of a disease linked to radiation exposure, an issue still affecting Ma'ohi families to this day. We cannot fully understand how much of an impact this has on our families until the French military declassifies all documents related to our public health." Manu pauses to clear his throat and wipe his eyes. "That same radiation exposure also damaged my wife's arteries, later playing a part in her miscarriage and untimely death. We need to take action *now* to protect future generations from reliving these tragedies. In order to act, we need to have all the resources we possibly can at our disposal. That is why this proposal is so, so critical. The *métropole* needs to take responsibility for what happened, but most importantly, they need to help us understand the scope of the mess and effectively clean it up so that no more lives are cut short."

He continues on, speaking with more energy as he elaborates on the disposal timeline, funding, and other details required to bring his proposal to life. His eyes glisten in the pale light from the laptop screen, and, halfway across the world, his compatriots can clearly see how close Manu holds this bill to his heart. He notices a few misty-eyed Assemblymembers as he wraps up.

"Any questions?" he asks, feeling drained already.

Robert raises his hand, and the president of the Assembly motions for him to go ahead. "As co-sponsor of this proposal, I just want to say that this is truly an ambitious legislative effort. Manu here has put so much time and so much of his own experiences into how he has crafted this proposal, and I couldn't be happier that we will be able to vote on this matter during the current session."

After Robert's remarks, several hands go up. The president nods to a senior politician named Philip.

"Isn't this piece trying to do too much?" the man asks, scratching his beard. "I mean, France already has a compensation program in place for people to claim damages for cancers caused by the testing."

"The compensation program is a start, but it doesn't do anything to protect our people—our children—from legacy radiation in the first place. The defense ministry has said in the past that parts of Mururoa Atoll are at risk of caving in, which would mean the nuclear waste enclosed in rock there is at risk of seeping into our ocean. We need to act before a new tragedy unfolds in our waters.

"It would also be a mistake to suggest that the compensation program functions properly. The process is unnecessarily convoluted, and the number of applicants that have received any form of compensation was, the last time I checked, less than 3%."

The next Assemblymember to speak is a hard-hitter named Colette. "I'm sorry to hear of your personal losses in connection to the nuclear testing sites," she begins. "Is this particular issue too personal for you, though? Will this legislation truly benefit all French Polynesians, or simply the ones closest to you?"

Manu coughs a bit; the question has caught him by surprise. "Well, I can certainly understand your concerns. That is why I worked with my dear colleague Robert on this proposal, and I had my office comb through the programs that are already in place to identify critical gaps. I think it's quite fair to say the entire territory will benefit from identifying, understanding, and taking care of any and all legacy radiation in the islands."

"But where would the waste go?"

"Somewhere safer than an atoll at risk of collapse," he snaps. "But I think the answer to that question should be determined by the experts, not a public servant like me."

A dozen more hands are in the air after he finishes replying to Colette. When he finally cuts the connection with the Assembly, he slumps back in his chair in defeat. The vote won't happen for another couple of weeks, but after the grilling he received, he doubts anyone will back the legislation without massive alterations.

He shuts down the laptop, his face drawn tightly together. His eyes are already closing when Ari lays a hand on his arm.

"You did great," she says, turning to catch his eye. Her hair is spread out around her face like a wild halo.

"I didn't wake you, did I? I'm so sorry, I should've moved to a lounge or something—"

"Papa, relax. I'm glad I got to hear your speech. It was good."

"Thanks, honey," he replies. "I feel like I blew it with the questions though."

"They've all gotta pretend to play hardball."

Manu shakes his head. "I don't think they were pretending."

"Still. I'd vote for your bill."

He smooths out a strand of her hair. "You should get some sleep if you can, dear. It's late, and the doctor said you might be getting treated for the myeloma in the morning if your bloodwork comes back good."

"I think I have something else I'd rather do first." She squeezes his hand.

"And what's that?"

"I'd like to go home."

Manu smiles. "We'll talk to the doctors about it in the morning."

Ari smiles. "Sounds like a plan. In the meantime, you look like you could sleep for a week." She holds out an extra pillow she's been using to prop herself up with. "Here. I don't need it when I'm sleeping."

"Thanks." Manu marvels at how, even from a hospital bed, Ari manages to find ways to take care of him. "Good night, Riri. I love you."

She snuggles under the blankets, a weary smile briefly crossing her face. "Love you too. G'night, Papa."

Chapter 20

The sun has long since bid the island goodnight by the time Natua walks the familiar path between the pension and the two-room hut where the Teni'irais live. A few solar-powered lanterns mark the curves in the worn track, but Natua hardly needs them. He knows every bump and twist in the half-kilometer trail as surely as he knows his own name.

While Natua's always announced himself before entering Manu's house, here he simply opens the rickety screen door and walks in. Afaitu is sitting at the table, hands crossed over his big, comfortable belly. The tangy scents of lime and fish hang heavy in the air.

"My boy," Afaitu says heartily by way of greeting before standing and approaching him. The older man grips Natua's shoulders with enormous, calloused hands. "Your mother may no longer be physically with us, but her spirit will wander between our homes forever. She will always be welcomed here."

Natua reaches up and covers one of Afaitu's hands with his own. "You have always been a true friend to us. Thank you."

"Of course," he replies. Over his shoulder, he calls, "Ey, Veroa! We've got our world traveler back in one piece!"

His wife turns away from the counter where she's finishing up coconut sauce for the fish. "Natua! Good thing dinner's almost ready. You need the strength only *i'a ota* can impart."

"Here, sit down." Afaitu waves towards the table, which is surrounded by simple, sturdy chairs.

After Natua obeys, Veroa sits next to him and takes his hands in hers. "We are so sorry for everything that's happened. But I want you to know, your mother didn't fault you for leaving. None of us did."

Veroa gazes into his eyes. A spark of anger is hiding there, behind the defeat evident in his slouched shoulders and haggard face. She stays still and waits for him to speak.

"It didn't have to come to this." Natua's words are laced with the conflicting emotions. "But Mama made sure of that herself. Did you know what she was hiding? The letters in the closet?"

Afaitu, who has been standing behind his wife, leans to one side and they exchange a meaningful look. Before either one can speak, Natua asks softly, "Did everyone know except for me?"

"No, honey, not at all," Veroa says. She tries to keep her voice as reassuring as possible. "Your father..." she trails off, searching for the right words.

"My father didn't just know I was here—he wanted to be involved! And instead of letting him, Mama passed off his gifts to me as her own and kept the mail under lock and key so I'd never find out!" His voice cracks as he continues. "She stole my only chance at having a relationship with my dad."

Afaitu shakes his head. "While it's true she hid the letters from you, Angela wasn't the one who wanted all that secrecy."

"What?"

"Your mother sent him word when you were born, and his first reply back was—"

"Rude," Veroa interjects. "He gave her an alternate place to send mail to avoid causing problems with who he referred to as his 'real' family."

"He did promise to send her whatever she needed for you, but on the condition that you were kept in the dark," Afaitu adds.

"But, but," Natua sputters. Mariana and Mrs. da Costa had talked about how much of a family man Armando was—and Natua is indisputably a member of the man's family.

"He was worried you'd come find him if you knew where to look," Veroa replies. She squeezes his fingers gently. "And he made it very clear that he didn't want that."

"I'm sorry you had to find out like this." Afaitu's eyes are kind, sympathetic. "It wasn't that he didn't care for you—he was just unwilling to own up to his mistakes and disrupt the status quo with the rest of his family."

"Oh." Blood drains from his face as the thought forms in his head. *Armando never cared about me.*

Their dinner afterwards is a quiet affair.

• • •

The next morning, a gray-haired doctor with oversized glasses talks father and daughter through Ari's latest test results. "It seems the infection is clearing, but I'd like to keep you on IV antibiotics for another three days or so to be sure you are stable before we start treating the cancer."

Ari turns to her father, whose hair is crumpled from sleeping in the generic blue armchair he's still sitting in. "Actually, I wanted to talk to you about my plan of care. I would like to go home before beginning the cancer treatments."

The doctor heaves a sigh. "I understand that completely, but aren't you from Polynesia?"

"What does that have to do with anything?" Manu asks with a huff.

The doctor turns to Manu, white coat swishing with the movement. "That is a very long journey to make. It could weaken your daughter and further delay her treatment."

Satisfied, Manu squeezes Ari's hand. "What do you think?"

She smiles sadly. "It might be tough, but the islands will give me strength. Let's fill that prescription and go home."

Chapter 21

Natua lets Afaitu take care of the arrangements for Mama, signing paperwork and only speaking up about where in the backyard she'll be interred. None of the rest matters to him.

The day Manu and Ari are scheduled to fly into Huahine, Natua drives Uncle's ancient green jalopy up to the airport and waits in the lobby with Irene. He tries to shoo her back to work, but she refuses to leave his side until a middle-aged surfer wanders in asking which island he should book a flight to next.

With Irene out of his hair, he wanders over to the row of chairs he'd occupied with Ari barely two weeks ago. He closes his eyes and focuses on breathing, remembering how Ari's hands trembled when she'd handed him her boarding pass.

He picks at the dead skin on his thumbs, trying not to overthink what it will be like to see her again. Their few phone calls since his arrival home have been awkward, Manu casually interjecting into their conversations like nothing has changed. Natua's not sure what Ari has told her father, or if her feelings have changed now that her health has started to stabilize.

On the overhead speakers, an indistinct voice announces the arrival of a flight from Tahiti. Shortly after, Manu wheels Ari off the tarmac. Her smile blooms like the *tiare* bushes outside when her eyes find Natua, and his doubts disappear.

"How are you feeling? You must be exhausted." He rushes over to give both of them a *bisou* and then takes Ari's hand, her fingers warm to the touch.

"I'm done with planes, that's for sure," she replies, giving his fingers a light squeeze. "I'm so, so sorry about your mom."

"Yes, how are you holding up?" Manu asks.

"I've missed you both so much," Natua replies. "Thank god you're back."

"Yes, thank god," Ari agrees. "You should stay with us for dinner tonight." She gestures towards the exit with her free hand.

Natua lets go of her hand to wave off the invitation. "You must be exhausted, surely you don't want to bother to entertain."

"Nonsense," Manu replies firmly. "You're family—not a bother." He strides towards the exit and calls over his shoulder, "Besides, you're in charge of helping Ari into the house."

"Uh, okay," he calls. He motions towards Manu's retreating back and asks Ari, "Did you...?"

"I didn't need to say anything, actually."

Natua wonders if she's blushing a bit. "Oh, okay. And he's...?"

"He's fine. Delighted, really. He already loves you like a son."

"Yeah, I know." Natua doesn't know what to do next. He stares at his sneakers, feeling his neck heat up.

"Um, so, should we go?" Ari's words are stilted, and somehow it relieves him to know that she's feeling as awkward as he is.

"Yeah, let's go." He wheels her towards the car, a smile peeking through. A familiar jangling sound reaches his ears as they approach the exit. "Irene, you mind taking the wheelchair back to the terminal for me once Ari's in the car?"

"Anything you need, of course." She huffs a bit as she catches up to them and then says to Ari, "How on earth are you holding up? You gave us all one hell of a scare!"

"Just glad to be back, thanks." Ari pats the bag sitting in her lap. "And I got the treatments I needed. You're a literal lifesaver."

"Oh, now, just trying to do my part." The woman's eyes mist over. "You're just so young, and, and..."

"And thank you," Ari replies.

After Natua finishes cleaning up dinner that evening, Manu disappears into his bedroom with a casual, "Knock if you need anything."

It's the first time he and Ari have been alone since everything between them changed. She pats the couch next to her. He sits stiffly next to her, which makes her giggle. He dares to put a hand on her thigh and turns his body towards hers. "Hi."

"Hi." The fading sunlight comes to life again as it dances in her bright brown eyes.

Just before their lips touch, Natua pulls back a fraction of an inch. "I love you too."

"Too?" she questions. He can feel her forehead wrinkling in confusion.

He speaks quickly, before the joke he can see her formulating ruins the moment. "I never said it back before. In the hospital room. And, I mean, it didn't seem like something you say for the first time over the phone."

She reaches up and caresses a lock of hair by his ear. "Right. Still, you told me in your own way. Tell me again?"

. . .

Angela's funeral takes place that weekend, and Natua's surprised at how many people show up. It seems everyone on the island has a story or two about the caring heart she kept hidden underneath that tough exterior. Even Uncle Alain manages a few words.

Afaitu has arranged for the local pastor to conduct a simple, tasteful service in Mama's church. She was always too reserved to enjoy the limelight, and Natua is relieved Afaitu knew better than to organize any of the more elaborate ceremonies favored by some islanders. Plus, the simpler ceremony is short enough for Ari to attend, even though Manu demands she go home to rest instead of coming to the burial.

It's late in the afternoon before the mourners—and casket—arrive at the pension. Natua had marked out her burial place the night before and now there's a neat hole waiting for her below her bedroom window. Hidden nearby under a plain white tarp lies the corresponding pile of dirt that will blanket his mother forever.

Once everyone is in place, the minister leads them in prayer and intones a blessing on the dead. The casket has been opened for one last look, and Mama's hands are folded neatly over the dark floral print dress Veroa made for the occasion. Natua lets his gaze rest on his mother's fingers, worn from years of keeping up with the demands of the pension and its guests.

The minister concludes his blessing with a somber "amen." He's motioning for the men to close the casket when Natua holds up a hand.

"Wait!" Dozens of eyes stare and for a moment, he is frozen in place.

"It's okay," Manu murmurs from his place just behind the boy. "You have to let her go."

"I know," he replies, the spell broken. "But there's something she needs to take with her."

He steps towards the coffin, his red pareo brushing against his knees. Angela's cold hand isn't stiff like he'd expected, and the ring he'd stolen away from her in her last days slides easily onto her shrunken thumb.

He leans over and kisses her hair. "This belongs to you. Didn't seem right for me to keep it." His duty done, he melts back into the group.

Natua is lost in his thoughts, his grief. Out of the corner of his eye, he sees Afaitu nod towards the men. It's time to proceed with the burial.

Even the birds seem to understand the solemnity of the moment. The lawn is consumed by a great quiet that's marred only by the gentle *thump* of dirt clods as they hit the casket.

. . .

The weeks slip by. While the cancer treatments exhaust her and the doctors are noncommittal about how well it's working, Ari still makes showing up at the pension a priority. The silence is too heavy there. Natua tries to shield her from it, but she can see the grief and regret weighing heavily on his bony shoulders.

"Come on," she goads him one afternoon, pointing at a stained wall in the pension's private dining room. "That water damage has been there since we were kids. Why don't you just fix it?"

"I'm not a handyman." He throws his hands up in the air. "And I can barely manage the bills on the place without spending extra on projects. If it's been there this long, it can wait a little longer."

"I thought you'd say that," she replies. "Which is why I brought you some supplies! Papa left instructions, too. Said it was super easy."

He groans. "Can't we just... have lunch and relax?"

"No offense, but nothing about your cooking is relaxing. Now come on, the stuff is in the entryway."

"Fiiiiineee." She listens to the sound of his footsteps as he pads away. "Hey, this is a long list of instructions!" he yells.

"Good thing we've got nothing else to do today, right?" she calls back.

"Yeah, yeah, yeah." He walks back in and rolls his eyes. "First thing's easy enough, anyway. Just need to break the old stuff off." He pulls on a sneaker and gives the wall a swift kick. "Ouch!"

"Your mom was right—you really are dramatic."

"Don't take Mama's side," he says with a laugh. "She would've loved that way too much."

"Well, it's true." She shrugs.

"No, this really hurt. Messed up sheetrock shouldn't be that hard. Your dad made it sound easy." He bends down and pulls some of the broken pieces away.

She keeps chatting, glad she was able to work Angela into the conversation while keeping things light. But after a minute, she realizes Natua's stopped listening.

"What's going on down there? Did you break a toe or something?"

"No, there's something back here."

"You mean, like, an animal?" She pulls her feet up instinctively.

"No, no, it's—it's a box?" He pulls out a small briefcase. It must have an inch or more of dust on it.

"How long has that been in there?"

"Don't know," he mutters, grabbing his stained cloth napkin from the table. "Wonder what's in it though. Probly something that belonged to my grandparents."

Ari sits in silence as he painstakingly cleans the top and the handles from his spot on the floor.

"Shit."

"What?"

"It's locked."

"Well..." Ari gestures towards the box of supplies. "Pretty sure there's a hammer in there. I doubt that lock is all too sturdy."

"Hold on. I might have the key." He darts off, leaving Ari alone once more.

She breathes deeply, hoping that there weren't, in fact, any snakes or rats in those walls keeping Natua's mystery box company. There weren't any tracks on the briefcase, so she takes that as a good sign.

When Natua returns, he's carrying a silver chain hung with a simple black key. "Look at that! It fits!"

The lid creaks open. Ari can't see the contents, but she can see Natua's face. He's in shock.

"Weeellll," she intones impatiently. "What's in there?"

Wordlessly, he swivels the briefcase around. The case twinkles in the soft fluorescent lighting. It's full of black pearls, diamonds, and vintage gold jewelry. "God, that stuff must be worth a fortune! Why didn't your mom break into that instead of closing the pension?"

"I don't think she knew about it," he replies. "This necklace was my Nona's. Mama was always too proud to admit to her that we were having trouble, and anyway, Nona passed away the year before we had to close down."

"Damn. Guess she should've said something."

Natua shrugs. "She left a riddle, remember? But nobody could make any sense of it. Too late now. But it's not too late for me to take my girl out for a nice dinner."

She gestures towards the plates on the table with a grin. "Or maybe a nice lunch?"

. . .

The jeweler Natua visits in Pape'ete does his best to act nonchalant over the vintage settings and the precious stones, but the gleam in the old man's eyes gives him away. Natua sells him most of the items from the briefcase for what he feels is a hefty sum. Hefty enough that, on the ferry ride home, a plan begins forming in his head.

He stuffs the cash into a beat-up shoe box and slides it as far under his bed as he can reach, then pulls out the piece he'd had the jeweler re-set for him and slips it into his pocket. To Ari, he texts, *We still on for tonight?*

• • •

The doctor Ari's seeing today has kind eyes that remind her of her mom. The woman leans forward and gently pats Ari's hands, which are folded neatly in her lap, before she speaks. At this point, Ari's been through enough doctor's appointments to know how bad of a sign this is. "Are you waiting for anyone to join you?"

The exam room feels a bit colder already, and a shiver raises the hair on her arms. She takes a shaky breath before whispering, "No." *Of course,* this *is the doctor's appointment I decide to handle alone.* Both Papa and Natua wanted to come today, but she had pushed them away—a decision she's instantly regretting as the doctor purses her lips and sighs.

"There's no easy way to say this. Unfortunately, the scans show that the cancer has metastasized throughout your body. Treatment is slowing it down, but you are too weak right now to handle another round. You're in kidney failure, and your white blood cell counts are some of the lowest I've ever seen." The doctor goes on, detailing other symptoms of her failing body, but Ari stops listening. There's silence, and Ari realizes she's waiting for a reply.

She swallows hard. "What are you saying?" Papa may only be at some political meeting down the street, but he might as well be in the *métropole.* Natua hated the idea of her going alone, but Ari's not ready for him to see how quickly the disease is progressing, how poorly she's really feeling. She doesn't want him to suffer the same panic that's been building in her belly for weeks as her joints ache and her pee darkens.

The doctor clears her throat and sets her chart down on the counter behind her. "I'm so, so sorry. Any treatments we try at this point would kill you—there's nothing we can do. I'll send you home with some pain medications to help keep you comfortable."

"Oh," she squeaks. "Ooh." Her eyes fill, and she stammers, "Well—well—how long do I have?"

The doctor's eyes are wet as well. "Not long enough. A few weeks, maybe a month or two if you schedule dialysis. I'm truly so sorry. I wish I had other news, other options."

A single tear escapes down Ari's cheek. "Me too." She pulls out her cell phone, not sure if she's intending to call Natua or Papa. There's a text from Natua—she'd forgotten that they'd planned a date night. *Too exhausted to go out, but I need you. Come over for dinner?*

"I'm just gonna—gonna call my dad," she says out loud. "Can you stay with me until he gets here? I... I don't want to be alone."

"Of course."

. . .

The meeting is moving slower than a turtle out of water, and Manu's been itching to leave since his first sip of coffee. He still can't believe he let Ari head to that appointment alone—her symptoms are getting harder for her to hide, and her smile harder to find.

But, if Ari needed him to play along and pretend things were normal, that's what he would do. The worry that has been building in his gut would just have to stay there.

His cell finally rings. Manu's halfway out of the door by the time Ari speaks. The way she says "Papa" tells him everything he needs to know. He takes off down the street, sandals flapping against the sticky pavement.

. . .

The mood at dinner is somber, and Natua's afraid to ask about Ari's appointment. So, instead, he rambles about the jewelry he sold and how he's planning to reopen the pension with the cash. "Mama would have wanted that, you know? My Nona and Pop, too. It'll be a lot of work to get the place back into tiptop—heck, even decent—shape, but I need to do something. I hate seeing how empty it is."

Ari pats his hand, but he can see that her thoughts are far away. He pulls her hand into his and squeezes her fingers.

"Come on, Ari. Let's head to the veranda for a bit. We can watch the sunset together." When she glances up at him, his cheeks flush with warmth.

She takes her place in Uncle's rocking chair and motions for Natua to take the seat to her left.

"Before I do, there's something else I wanted to talk to you about." He shifts awkwardly from foot to foot. Part of him wishes he'd just sat in the chair, that he'd picked a better night. But he's already wasted so many days and so many nights. Time to just get on with it.

"Well, what is it?" She attempts a smile, but it dies on her pallid lips.

"I, uh, I didn't sell all of the jewelry." He clears his throat. "Um. Actually, I sold all of it except for one piece. One very important piece."

She looks up at him expectantly, a sparkle in her beautiful dark eyes. It gives him the courage to go on.

"Look, it does break my heart to see the pension empty. But it's going to take more than just some silly, self-absorbed tourists to make it feel like home again." He fumbles with his pocket and pulls out the ring he'd had made especially for Ari's finger, its polished jade perfectly balanced against the inset diamonds and the yellow gold band. Getting down on one knee, he holds the ring out with a shaking hand. "And that's because you are my home now, Arietta. Will you marry me?"

She leans forward and takes him in her arms. "Oh Natua," she whispers. "You don't know what you're asking."

"But I do," he murmurs. He slips the ring over his pinky and uses his free hand to caress her cheek, already damp with tears. "I don't care how sick you are. Cancer can't change my love for you—you know that, right?"

"I know, and I love you too. It's just..."

"Shh. Whatever it is, it doesn't matter. All that matters is you and me, for however long we have left together." He takes her face in his hands, touches his forehead against hers. "So I'm going to ask you again. Will you marry me?"

Ari nods silently, and her tears fall freely. "Yes."

Knowing their time is short, the pair organize a small beachside ceremony for the weekend. Nona Alii and Pop Tama busy themselves preparing a feast, with plans to make seemingly enough coconut cream to feed the entire island.

"Ugh, what am I going to wear?" Ari murmurs as she flips through her wardrobe the night before the ceremony. The men have worked with family and friends to handle nearly all of the planning after a short conversation about what she wants the most. Natua, in particular, was concerned about making sure she's well-rested for the big day. But in the chaos of menu planning and finding a *Tahua* to officiate, then organizing guest lists and flower deliveries and musicians, choosing her wedding dress has fallen by the wayside.

Already out of breath, she steps back and sits on the bed. *Should've asked Moehara to video chat me on her last flight to Pape'ete.* Her old friend has always had impeccable taste and an uncanny knack for estimating people's sizes. She would've picked out something incredible. No time for that now though.

A knock on the doorframe startles her out of her thoughts. It's Papa. "I have something for you," he says.

"You didn't have to," she says. "What is it?"

He hesitates, then holds up a traditional white pareo. "This was what your mother wore to our wedding. I know it's trendy to wear Western dresses now, so maybe this is a little old-fashioned, and you don't—"

"No, I'd be honored to have a piece of her, of our family's history, with me."

Papa's eyes mist over. "Her spirit is so happy, I can feel it. She wouldn't miss this for the world."

"Thank you, Papa." Her finger draws circles on her bedspread. "I still miss her, you know."

He comes in and lays the pareo over a chair before sitting next to his daughter. "Me too, honey. Grief like that never disappears—it simply ebbs and flows like the tide."

Ari leans into her father's shoulder, taking in his fresh, soapy scent. They sit like that for a long time listening to the quiet of the house—the whirring of the refrigerator in the next room, the cricket songs and pitter pattering of rain from the open window. Finally, Papa breaks the spell that's fallen over them and heads to bed.

. . .

The bustle of planning and maintaining Ari's faltering health has kept Natua's emotions at bay. But when Ari steps out of the canoe and onto the beach, the hem of her pareo dotted with sea spray, he's reminded of what this is all about. Joy mists over his eyes, and he smiles so wide that his face feels like it's going to split. His eyes flutter as he breathes in the sweet, heady scent of the bougainvillea arch.

At the edge of the rows of chairs, Afaitu blows the conch shell. The long, haunting call of the *pu* summons the gods and the elements to witness the ceremony. Ari completes the short walk down the aisle as its last echo fades.

The *Tahua*, in his rich red and yellow robes, loosely ties their wrists together with Auti leaves and pours ocean water over the knot to strengthen their bond. Natua leans forward and places his forehead against Ari's.

He repeats after the priest the vows he'd pulled from the internet the morning before, then adds a line of his own at the end. "I promise to hold you in my arms for as long as we both shall live, and in my heart forever."

Ari's eyes are brimming with happy tears as she repeats the vows back to him.

"Mihiau and Hauata Raina," the *Tahua* proclaims, giving them their Tahitian names, "I now pronounce you husband and wife. You may seal your bond with a kiss."

The crowd erupts into whoops and cheers when their lips touch, and they don't quiet until the pair has made their way to the edge of the beach, where Ari's aunts have arranged their wedding feast. Nona is waiting for them, with a handmade Tifaifai quilt in her arms.

She gently wraps the couple in it. "Your two souls are now united into one." She gives each one a peck on the cheek. "And I love you dearly."

They sway through their first dance, but Ari's energy is flagging by the song's end. They enjoy the feast before Afaitu drives them back to the pension, leaving their family and friends to celebrate as long as their hearts desire.

. . .

The Monday after the wedding is Ari's first scheduled dialysis treatment, and the process is grueling. The boat ride on the first day alone fractures her brittle bones in two different places.

After the third treatment and yet another cracked rib, Ari decides she can't do it anymore. She and Natua spend their afternoons cuddled up in the pension, and their evenings relaxing on the beach where they'd celebrated their wedding.

Two weeks after her last dialysis treatment, Ari suggested they spend the evening at Manu's house instead. She doesn't want to admit it to Natua, but the walk to the beach is too much for her exhausted body. After dinner, Ari hobbles out to the veranda and sinks into her dad's rocking chair. Natua follows her out, poised to catch her if she stumbles.

"Hey, it's getting a bit late—did you want to head home?"

Ari heaves a sigh. "It's so far, Natua. Can't we just... stay here a little while longer?"

He pulls over an ottoman and sets it in front of her, then gently places her feet in his lap. "Whatever you need, Ari. I'm not going anywhere unless you say the word."

Manu pads out in his bare feet and sits next to Ari, in the chair furthest from the door. "You didn't seem to have much of an appetite today, Riri. Would you like something to drink?" He offers her a glass of water.

"Thanks, but I'm okay." She pushes it away, then notices movement by the stairs. "Oh, I didn't realize you were having company tonight."

"Is somebody here?" Manu asks. But Ari's no longer listening. The person who appears at the top of the stairs is Mama, and she has baby Oscar on her hip.

"Mama? How...? You can't possibly..."

Mama stops next to Natua, who looks like he's about to cry. She leans forward, grips Ari's toes and gives them a little shake. "A mother is always there for her children," she says simply, her words smooth and melodic.

"It feels good to hear your voice," Ari replies. "I've missed you so much."

"I know, my dear one. You've made me so proud all these years—you've kept your father from falling apart more times than you know."

Ari takes her eyes off of Mama long enough to glance at Papa. The glass of water is shaking in his trembling hand, droplets spilling onto the cool wooden floor.

"But I've made so many mistakes. And brought so much shame on our family."

Mama shakes her head. Her earrings reflect the starlight as she moves. "You and your father have already gone over this, Arietta."

There's a noise inside the house, and Ari gasps when Henri walks in. "Mom, she's got to hear it from me."

Ari shrinks in her chair, afraid of the judgment she's passed on herself a thousand times coming from her brother's lips. Instead, he laughs lightly and strides over to the rocker.

"Our time will come whether we're ready for it or not, kiddo. Don't worry about what happened anymore, okay?"

"But I—but Henri, I—"

"Shhh." His gaze flickers between her and Papa. "You've both held onto what happened that day far too long. You've gotta forgive yourselves."

"But what happened is—" Her eyes fill with tears and she finds herself unable to finish the sentence.

"I've forgiven you. You should too." He bends over and hugs his sister. In her ear, he whispers, "But it was never your fault."

"I'm still so sorry," she whispers.

"You've gotta let it go, kiddo."

"As long as you tell me it's okay." Ari closes her eyes.

His voice comes again. "It's okay."

Ari exhales. "Thank you." A sense of peace falls over her like a warm blanket.

. . .

Natua barely breathes as Ari's talking to the spirits. He and Manu trade nervous glances after she closes her eyes. Just when Natua thinks she's gone, her chest rises and falls again. He takes a shaky breath, a tear trailing down his cheek.

Manu sets a hand on his knee. Before he speaks, he watches for her labored breath to come again. "I don't think you're going anywhere tonight," he says softly, then gestures towards the half-empty glass. "I'm taking this back inside—is she cold? Should I grab her a blanket?"

Natua nods. "Actually, our Tifaifai is in the car."

"Good idea." Manu bustles about until the glass and the quilt have been sorted. "This pattern is beautiful," he remarks as he drapes it over his daughter.

"Veroa's an incredible craftswoman," Natua responds. He's about to go on, but he waits until Ari's chest rises and falls once more. It's an uncomfortably long wait. "Anyway, Nona Alii asked her to make our Tifaifai the minute she found out we were dating."

"She mentioned that," Manu says. "I'm glad it was ready in time for the ceremony." Now he's the one watching for Ari's next breath. Several minutes pass before they realize it isn't coming.

By sunrise, exhaustion pulls on Natua's eyes. He hasn't slept yet, despite how comfortable Manu's couch is. Ari's body is wrapped in their Tifaifai in her old room, positioned on the bed as though she's merely sleeping. Nothing could have prepared him for this moment, but at least the clinks of Manu's seemingly bottomless coffee cup have kept Natua company in the darkness.

The two men's eyes meet in the morning light. "What do we do now?" Natua asks.

Manu shakes his head. "I don't know. I might never know."

. . .

Several days pass before Manu dares to go into Ari's room again. When Sunday comes, he decides to sit for a moment before going to church. But the blankets still smell like his daughter and a few of her tee shirts are in a pile on the chest under the window. Before he realizes it, the entire morning is gone.

He stands and goes to her closet. There's an overwhelming number of decisions he should be making about arrangements, so many he can hardly think. Instead of worrying about whether Ari would want religious services or not, or if there's enough room in the side yard for another grave beside his or whether she should be buried at the pension with her husband of a few weeks, he browses through the dresses in her closet as though he's shopping in a boutique.

He flips through the clothes slowly, pausing to remember the last time she wore each item. There's a bright orange halter dress she hasn't worn since high school graduation, and a number of floral getups that she liked to wear to work. In the back he finds a dress with sea turtles outlined in white against a dark green background.

The dress doesn't strike Manu as familiar—in fact, he can't say if he's ever seen it before. He lifts the hanger and sets the item carefully across her rumpled bed. The tag is still attached under the armpit, and he whistles when he sees the price. *She must have planned on wearing this somewhere special. But where?*

He decides she will wear it to the grave, and then the tears arrive.

. . .

Natua wakes up early. The last thing he wants to do is spend his entire day in the pension, which is once again too empty for comfort. But he doesn't want to bother Uncle—who will probably be at church anyway—so he forces himself to wait until noon before making the short walk over to his house.

Manu's coughing drowns out the slap of the screen door, and Natua follows the sound into Ari's bedroom.

There, he finds the older man wiping his sloppy face with his sleeve, and Natua takes a seat next to him on the bed.

"Don't sit there!" Manu cries.

Natua bolts back up in alarm, only to find he'd sat on some of Ari's clothes. "Sorry," he apologizes. "Do you need me to get you a tissue or maybe a drink?"

Manu shakes his head. "No, my son, thank you."

Being careful to move the clothes, Natua sits and puts a hand on Manu's shoulder and waits for the man to speak again.

"It's just so hard being alone," Manu says finally, voice hardly more than a whisper. "Even when I lost Amy, when I lost Henri, it wasn't like this—I had kids to be strong for. But now? There's no one left."

"This is going to be hard on both of us," Natua replies. "But you're not alone, Papa. You've got me."

"Did you..." Manu is too spent from grief to even formulate the question. "But you..."

"Armando was never a father to me. He had that choice, and he chose to stay away. He never wanted me; never bothered to come meet me or send any letters for me to read or respond to." He swallows hard. "But you've always been there, even when you didn't have to be. You really are my dad, and I've never taken the time to thank you for that. So thank you."

Manu leans over and kisses the boy on each cheek. "Thank you," he breathes. "We need to stick together to get through this."

Natua murmurs in agreement.

"Now." Manu clears his throat and grabs a turtle print dress. "What do you think of this for Ari's burial? I have a feeling she wanted it for a special event—she spent a near fortune on it—but she never ended up wearing it."

The question catches Natua by surprise. "Hey, I know that dress."

"What?"

"She sent me a picture of it after she bought it. You remember, a year or two back, when we were going to head to Tahiti for the *Heiva* with Ettie, but we missed the ferry over?"

"Oh, I remember. You couldn't even get her to think about boarding a plane, and all of the other ferries were booked solid because of the festival." Manu's lost in thought as he considers how much things have changed since then.

"Anyway," Natua says, interrupting Manu's reverie, "she was going to wear that dress to some conservation dance she was dragging me to. It was hosted by one of the clubs. I think they were raising money for Take 3 or something like that. You know, the clean beach people."

"Sounds about right. Ari loved the ocean. And you."

Natua averts his eyes. "I just wish we'd had more time together."

"Me too, my son," Manu says gently. He pats the boy's hand.

Natua nods towards the dress, which Manu has laid back on the bed. "Anyway, to answer your question, I think that dress is perfect."

. . .

The next weekend, Nona Alii leads Ari's burial services in the side yard of the pension. A light scarf is wrapped like a euphemism around the girl's neck, hiding a newly fractured collarbone and a dislocated shoulder.

With the summer season coming to a close, the heat is relentless until a rainstorm rolls in. Nona struggles to make her thin voice heard above the downpour.

Manu doesn't bother trying to hear his mother-in-law. His thoughts overwhelm him until he's swaying in the wind like a shallow-rooted flower, unable to support his own weight. Natua's hand reaches up to help steady him.

Nona's speech ends, but the downpour continues.

Manu's thankful he'd thought to set up a small canopy over the casket. Much as Ari loved the water, he didn't want the rain to muss the carefully done makeup and the scarf. He'd opted for an open casket, but the last thing he wants is to traumatize her youthful friends, still so inexperienced when it comes to the bleak realities of death and dying.

Nona steps away from Ari's side, making room for Manu to walk over and say his last goodbyes. His hands have been kept busy rubbing a shell necklace he'd found on Ari's dresser—one of the sort traditionally used as a parting gift before long goodbyes. He untangles it from his fingers now and gently wraps it around Ari's wrists.

"Oh Riri," he whispers. "If only there was a way for me to take your place. You deserved more than this. I'm so sorry, my dear." He brushes her cheek with his fingertips. A few of his tears land on Ari's face until it looks like she's crying too. He wipes them away gingerly, then notices Natua's hand once again, this time on his shoulder.

"Don't blame yourself, Papa," Natua says, voice too low for anyone else to hear.

"The radiation exposure was my fault," Manu says, his voice cracking. "Even Ari's mom wasn't sure about heading down to the test sites. She didn't think it would be safe but I pushed. That decision hurt Ari. And the exposure also weakened several of Amy's arteries—we probably wouldn't have lost her, Oscar, or Ari if we had just stayed home. Maybe even Henri would've been spared."

"Ships might be safe at shore but that's not why we build them," Natua replies. "You did the right thing."

"And yet I was still wrong."

"Hey," Natua says, shifting until he's standing by Manu's side. "She wouldn't want you to blame yourself. You have to let that go."

Manu blows his nose into a tissue. "Easier said than done, but you're right, my son." He takes one last, long look at his daughter and then places Natua's hands on his wife's jewelry-wrapped wrists. "I'll leave you to your own goodbyes."

. . .

After Papa vanishes from his side, Natua's legs feel weak. "Ari, I don't know how to do this," he murmurs, "but I don't have a choice, do I?" He presses his lips together, thankful for the privacy the pounding rain provides. "I would give anything for another day with you. For things to have turned out differently." He grabs the sides of the casket to steady himself. "You'll always have a place in my heart. I'm so sorry this has to be goodbye."

He wipes at the tears—*the rain*, he tells himself—trailing down his cheeks and steps back out into the storm.

The next morning, he runs his bread route half-asleep. He'd stayed awake most of the night. Every time he managed to drift off, he was haunted by dreams of the dead.

When he drops his knapsack back off at the bakery, the sun is just peeking above the edges of the ocean. Instead of heading home, he hikes outside of town, up an overgrown trail he used to know like the back of his hand. It takes much longer than he remembers, but eventually his eyes are greeted by a shadowy clearing. The space is dominated by a single banyan tree swaying from its spot on top of a small rise.

The tree is remarkably easy to climb. Natua jumps onto a low-hanging branch and looks out, past the clearing and the forest to the billowy pink clouds taking up residence in the sky.

"This always was the best place to be alone with your thoughts," he says to himself. "Best place to be alone, anyway."

Images of Ari circle like a whirlpool in his brain, the grief threatening to drown him. His feet kick nervously at the air, and he doesn't pay any mind to the beauty of the soft morning light as it spills onto his scuffed sneakers.

"I miss you," he whispers into the breeze. "Both you and Mama deserved better. But the world just failed you. Over and over and over again. And there's nothing I could do to fix it. I'm so sorry."

He leans back against the trunk of Ari's old thinking tree, remembering that rainy night long ago when she needed him most—the night when it all began. He's asleep before the morning dew evaporates.

. . .

Robert had wanted to vote on Manu's bill as scheduled, but at Manu's insistence, the Assembly has tabled the vote until their next session. Despite knowing it's best to let the bill wait until he can give it his full attention, Manu wishes he had the bustle of political life to fill all the hours he doesn't know what to do with. The crying lasts for a full month after the funeral, and then his grief quiets—though he knows it will never stray far from the surface.

Midmorning light falls softly across Ari's bed. It's Sunday and, once again, he's missing the church service he's sure he needs. Instead, his eyes wander around his daughter's room and note the scattered ephemerae of her life. Rubber bracelets. Ticket stubs. A worn pamphlet about oceanography courses at UPF.

Just like that, he needs to move. Not bothering with shoes, he makes his way to the island's edge and sits on a boulder. Ocean spray mists his face and waves lick at his feet.

The endless, rolling waves don't comfort him like he'd hoped. A discarded cup clinks against the rocky shore. Somewhere nearby a plastic bag crinkles in the wind.

Before Manu even processes what he's doing, he's back on his feet. *Dammit. Should've grabbed some flip flops.* Pebbles bite at his heels, but he ignores them as he roots around the beach.

Finally, he lays eyes on the cursed plastic bag and snatches it up before the wind can carry it off.

"Might as well take two more things while I'm at it," he mutters, bending to grab an abandoned straw. Soon, he's filled the plastic bag and begins stuffing detritus in his pockets too. "Good Lord, this ocean needs help," he mumbles. He's picked up all the garbage he can carry, but as he walks away, he notices an empty condom wrapper wedged under a rock. "Damn teenagers."

After reaching home and upending his pockets into the kitchen bin, his heart feels a little less empty. It's not much, but it's a start.

Chapter 22

Weeks bleed into months, and opening the pension begins to replace grief as Natua's primary preoccupation. His job at the bakery keeps him just busy enough that the run-down dining area and neglected guest rooms seem to get worse instead of better, but he's afraid to give up steady income for the unknown.

Half-finished projects in nearly every room pile up until he spends his weekends hiding in his bedroom, shades closed to shut out the weedy garden and the pile of tools he left by the coconut trees.

Ding. The screen on his phone lights up with a new email from Mariana. They've become fairly close since they parted ways in Paris, though he prefers to keep their conversations light.

Hey baby brother! Found some things of Dad's that belong to you, but they're too important to send off in the mail. I'm going to escort them to Huahine myself— I can be there in around a month. Think you've got a spare room for me?

"Guess I'm going to have to wrap up some of these damn projects." He sighs. To his sister, he writes back, *Definitely got plenty of empty rooms, and you're welcome anytime! Just tell me when your flight comes in and I'll pick you up. You said Armando had things that belong to me—what kind of things?*

His sister's reply is vague, and Natua doesn't get a satisfying answer until the day she arrives.

Thanks to plenty of help from Afaitu, there is, indeed, a completely revamped spare room in the pension. His fishing skills and the reliable vegetable garden—which is thoroughly weeded the day ahead of Mariana's arrival—have kept the fridge filled with the fresh foods he knows his sister will appreciate, even if Natua still hasn't gotten the hang of cooking.

"Baby brother!" she calls, waving enthusiastically when she spots him in the airport.

"Hey!" He gives her a quick set of *bisous* and adds, "Let me grab that for you," while motioning to her wheeled suitcase. "Taxi's ready and waiting."

"Thank goodness." She looks outside at the harsh sun. She's barely even moved since leaving the plane, and already there's a line of sweat forming on her brow. "Please tell me they have AC."

"Don't worry, it's a short drive. Come on!"

Once in the pension's cool front hallway, Natua releases his grip on her overstuffed luggage. "Whooh, that was the hottest taxi I've ever ridden in!"

Mariana wipes her face with the back of her sweaty hand, still breathing hard. "So much for a nice ocean breeze!"

"Here, let me grab something to drink. Iced tea?"

"Please!"

After Natua returns with a pitcher and a couple of glasses, the siblings head to the dining room.

"So," he says as he pours, "think now you can tell me what things Armando could've possibly had of mine?"

Instead of responding, Mariana pulls a metal box out of her duffle bag and sets it on the table.

"That's not mine," Natua says instinctively.

"Look inside," his sister replies gently.

He cracks the lid and a few sloppily folded papers flop out. *Me, Mama, and Papa* reads the faded red crayon scrawled across the top of one sheet. Stick figures populate the page. "How... where did you find these?" he finally asks, voice husky. He's careful not to touch them, as if the papers might burn him.

"Remember how I told you Dad died in a boat wreck?"

He nods.

"Well, the guy who runs the boat rental called us last week. Found some stuff Dad put in one of the lockers before heading out on his final trip." Her eyes rest on the loose papers. "But there's more than just drawings in there."

"What?" His hands are still poised above the box. Paralyzed.

"Look for yourself."

Papers rustle. There are maybe half a dozen or so of Natua's childhood drawings in the small tin. But there's also a sheet of neat, glossy paper poking out from the bottom of the pile. Natua sets aside the pictures he'd longed for years to recreate and gasps when he realizes what it is.

A boarding pass. Several of them, in fact. Granada to Madrid. Madrid to San Francisco. San Francisco to Pape'ete. And, on the very bottom of the pile, Pape'ete to Huahine.

He glances at the dates and chokes on a sob. "He would've been here for my twentieth birthday."

"His boating trip was only supposed to last an afternoon according to the owner of the rental shop, but he'd told us he was spending a month at sea."

"My god." Instead of sorting through the confused mess of emotions he's feeling, he coughs and his voice hardens. "But he didn't have to wait so many years. He could've sent me a letter for any of my birthdays—even just a photo would've meant so much. Or letting Mama tell me where my birthday gifts came from." Natua stares hard at the slips. All of Armando's actions suggested he hadn't cared, hadn't wanted anything to do with him. He refuses to be impressed by overdue grandstanding. Or the implications of crayon drawings the man had saved for over a decade. "Can a boarding pass really make up for all of the opportunities he made sure he missed?"

"He had his flaws," Mariana concedes, "but he did care about you."

Natua changes the subject rather than respond. "Wait, you said the boat guy only called you last week—you were coming here anyway. Why?"

She digs through her purse this time.

"Seriously, Ana, can you tell me what is actually going on?"

She fishes out a thick envelope and slides it across the table. Natua's Spanish has improved considerably since his trip to Spain, but he still struggles with the document's overly formal language. The logo stamped in the upper left-hand corner offers no clues either. After several minutes, he gives up trying to decipher the letter's contents. "I'm not sure I understand. What is this?"

"I don't know what laws you have here, but in Spain, everyone is entitled to an equal portion of their parents' inheritance after they pass away. Now, we had no idea you existed when Dad died to divvy things up the right way... But Dad did." She tucks a lock of hair behind her ear. "About a month ago, Mama and I found records of a lock box in Dad's name at a bank my mother had never used. It contained all the information you need to redeem a life insurance policy on Dad—it's your half of the inheritance."

Natua scans the papers again and spots a number at the bottom. He lets out a low whistle, then points at it. "Is this...?"

"Yeah."

"Holy shit."

"You can see why I wouldn't trust it to the mail."

Natua's too stunned to say anything for a long minute. The amount is enormous, more money than he's touched in all his life.

"He may not have been in your life," Mariana says diplomatically, "but Dad wanted you to be taken care of. And he did what he could to make sure you were."

"I don't need his money," Natua replies. He's struggling not to get overwhelmed by all of this in front of his sister, and an easy way to rein in his feelings is to stay angry at Armando. "What I needed was a father and he wasn't there."

"I can't fix his mistakes, but at least, in his own way, he did try."

"No use dwelling in the past anyway," he says, a little too dismissively. "So, how about we head into town for some dinner?" Anger still dominates the typhoon of emotions swirling in his gut, but he doesn't want to argue with his sister about Armando. "My treat."

"Lead the way, baby brother."

. . .

It's still early for dinner, so Chez Maitai is empty. The server walks the siblings over to a tiny table. But before they have a chance to sit, a familiar voice calls over, "Natua! Why don't you join us?"

He looks up to see Manu waving him and Mariana over from the corner booth. Manu is sitting with his aide, Peter, and there are papers scattered all over the table.

"We wouldn't want to interrupt if you're on business," Natua replies politely.

"Nonsense. Come on!"

Natua shrugs. Mariana and the server follow him to the table, where Natua makes quick introductions.

The two men slide closer together to make room for the siblings, and Peter orders a round of drinks for the table.

"What are you working on?" Mariana asks. "I clerk in a law office back home, so please forgive my curiosity."

"Not a problem at all," Manu replies. "I don't know what Natua's told you about my work, but I've been drafting a bill to address nuclear waste problems here in the islands."

"Didn't they vote on that today?" Natua asks. He'd been so busy trying to get ready for his sister coming to town that he'd forgotten to ask how the vote went.

"Yesterday," Manu corrects. "It didn't pass—"

"But only by a 3-vote margin," Peter interrupts. "For a brand-new Assemblymember, that's pretty impressive."

"Anyway, we're regrouping and looking at what we can do next."

"I'm sorry to hear it didn't pass," Natua replies. "What in the world could anyone find wrong with that bill?"

"It's not a matter of what was wrong, but what was missing," Manu explains. "There hasn't been any reliable research done about the nuclear tests and legacy radiation in French Polynesia."

"So even though everyone knows it's true, it's hard to quantify the scope of the problem," Peter adds. "Even harder to say how much it will cost to rectify it."

"What about the military documents you wanted to declassify? There has to be plenty of information in those."

"More than likely... but legislating based on documents you can't even read is quite the gamble. And there's no guarantee that the *métropole* would cooperate and declassify them just because we voted on it."

"Too bad more politicians don't have guts like you do."

"Even so, no amount of money can replace what we've lost." Manu looks down at his water glass. "But we owe it to all the Polynesians who have suffered to fight for justice."

"We owe it to Ari," Natua says quietly.

"Yes, we owe it to Ari," Manu echoes.

After a somber lull, Natua turns to his sister. "You told me when we were on our way to France that your law firm works with a bunch of research companies, right? You think one of them would help us get a study off the ground?"

"You were listening to that?"

Natua feels like his sister's eyes are going to bug right out of her head. "Of course I was. Just wasn't in much of a mood to chat."

"If you're willing to loop me in on an introductory email, I can take it from there," Peter chimes in. "I can also draft up some sample language for you to use to talk about the nuclear testing."

"Nuclear testing... of course! The execs at this one organization we work with have invested quite the stack of cash over the decades campaigning against nuclear weapons proliferation. They might even be able to conduct the study, rather than just do a consultation."

"I'd rather not turn the entire project over to European hands," Manu says. "No offense, but mainlanders are the ones who made this mess."

"None taken," Mariana replies.

He continues, "Our people here are very knowledgeable on the impacts, where foreign companies wouldn't even know what questions need to be asked. It would be nice to have a European firm involved to get the *métropole's* attention, but I want an indigenous research team. If you can convince a firm to simply rubber stamp the result, maybe provide a portion of the funding, that would be best."

"I think we can make that work. After all, this is the kind of international work that will do wonders for my law firm's reputation, and our clients too." She turns to Peter and offers him a business card pulled from her wallet. "I'll have to run it by my bosses, but once I get approval, I can work with you on the project over email."

"Only one more hurdle," Manu says. "Where are we going to get funding for something like this? It's not like we have a spare nine million francs hanging around in our budget for a scientific study. Even with help, that's a huge sum when we can barely keep hospitals running in certain areas."

Before Peter can respond, Natua says, "I'll pay the balance."

"You'll regret it if you use the money you've set aside for the pension," Manu declares in his most serious dad voice. "We will find another way."

"I'm not going to," Natua says matter-of-factly. "Armando left me a life insurance policy. A big one. I'd love to spend some of it on something so important to our people. To you."

Manu's eyes open wide. "When were you going to tell me about this?"

He motions towards his sister. "I only found out about it today."

Mariana adds, "I didn't want to mention anything to Natua until I could deliver all the paperwork in person. And help baby brother decipher the Spanish legalese."

"What great news," Manu says. "You two are both generous, honorable, thoughtful... The family resemblance goes well beyond your faces." He raises his wineglass. "This calls for a toast—to family." He glances at Peter and tips his glass in the aide's direction. "Including found family."

"To family," the others repeat. The clinking of their glasses fills the otherwise empty dining room.

. . .

With his legislation defeated and Peter working with Mariana on next steps for the research study, Manu is once again left with idle hands that betray the void in his heart. But this time, he's better prepared for it.

Instead of sitting in Ari's room and trying to drown his grief by surrounding himself with his daughter's stuff, he calls up a woman named Esmée and asks if he can drop by her shop.

"My afternoon is wide open today, and I'd love to have you," she replies.

Two hours later, he's laying back in a chair wrapped with plastic wrap and wincing as the slender French woman tattoos the outline of what will become a pink sea anemone just above his heart.

"Remind me, what made you decide on this little guy?" she asks lightly as she dips the machine and its tightly bunched needles into the waiting ink cup. "Most people who want sea life get turtles, though of course I've done the odd octopus and shark too."

"My daughter—" he starts. The needles touch his skin again, and he inhales deeply.

"You all right?"

"Ye-yeah. Sure."

"This is one of the worst spots to get a tattoo, yanno. Just remember—it's not the kind of pain that's going to kill you, though it is awfully unpleasant. So, why don't you tell me a little more about Ari? How'd she help you decide on the tattoo?" Huahine is a small island, so Manu's sure Esmée already knows the answers to her questions. But he engages in the conversation anyway to help distract him from the pain.

"She loved the water. Diving, snorkeling, surfing; all of it. It was always her dream to study the ocean, clean up the Garbage Patch." Manu sighs with relief when Esmée once again turns to reload the needles. "I'm sure you know that sea anemones can be fierce predators—"

"Aren't the little buggers related to jellyfish?"

"Yeah. But they're also really sensitive to plastic pollution." Just then, she starts shading part of the outline and Manu sucks in his breath. Esmée doesn't speak—partly because she's focused on her work and partly because she's waiting for Manu to go on.

Closing his eyes, Manu pictures Ari. In his mind, she's healthy, free. Her hair is slick with salty ocean water, and she's smiling. In spite of the agony in his chest, the image gives him peace.

Pain under control, he continues. "The sea anemone is a reminder of how delicately life is balanced for all of us. And that even when the odds seem overwhelming, we can always do something to make a difference."

Manu doesn't think Esmée is paying attention, but after a moment she mutters under her breath, "Most optimistic shit I've heard all day."

The sun is setting on the ocean when he emerges from the shop. The dying day casts pink light on columns of clouds and throws the waves below into dark contrast.

"You will always be with me," he whispers into the wind. For the first time since Ari's last night on the veranda, he can imagine feeling whole again someday.

. . .

After Mariana leaves town, Natua and Afaitu finish the rest of the updates in the pension, leaving Natua to focus on the process of reopening the business. The paperwork he has to muddle through before opening—and the tourism associations he has to register with and the website he has to get built and the cooking classes he must take and on and on—takes Natua far longer than he would have liked. But he's ready to accept reservations by the start of the next peak booking season.

The day his first guest is scheduled to arrive, he wakes up feeling jumpy. Cash stashed under the bed or not, he doesn't have enough going on to justify hiring anyone to help him. Anxiety has him doing circles around himself until the guest's estimated arrival at 14:00 hours.

Ten minutes ahead of time, he takes up his spot in the front hallway behind a makeshift check-in desk. It consists of a podium borrowed from his mother's old church and a 3-ring binder he emptied of high school biology homework just this morning. He sets the room key his solo guest will need on the podium, then picks it back up immediately to turn it over in his hands.

Each passing minute contains lifetimes, and he finds himself wondering how he's going to handle everything on his own. His mother's voice echoes in his head. *Quit being so melodramatic. You'll be fine.*

Finally, a cab pulls up. The rusted gate creaks open and he can hear the clatter of wheels rolling over the uneven stones in the courtyard.

When the door to the front hallway opens, a well-toned woman enters, her skin glowing golden brown in the sun. There's a duffle on her shoulder, a surfboard under her arm, and a rolling suitcase dragging behind her. High humidity has thrown her black curls into a frizzy mess, and for a moment Natua recalls how Ari used to struggle to contain her own wild hair on days like today.

"Hi there," she says when she spots him behind the podium. Her voice lilts musically, disrupting the pension's thick silence.

Struggling to keep the smile on his face and the sadness out of his eyes, he greets his very first guest. "Good afternoon, and welcome to The Winged Victory of Huahine." Even though he already knows the answer, he still makes it a point to ask, "Your name?"

"The paperwork's under Tapeta. Jo Tapeta," she replies. "But you can just call me Jo."

"You're in Room 4," he says. "Sign this for me."

After she scrawls her name on the indicated line, Natua grabs the room key. It's warm and sticky from all the nervous handling.

"Let's get you settled in." He wheels her luggage down the hall past Mama's bedroom and the dining room, towards the cluster of guest rooms in the back of the pension. As they walk, he rattles off a few housekeeping details.

"Thank you so much," she says after Natua unlocks the room and gestures for her to enter. She plops her duffle bag on the bed, and an old Walkman spills out.

"You're welcome," he says. Motioning towards the tape player, he adds with a laugh, "Now that's old school. What kind of music do you listen to?"

"Techno, but there's no music on the tapes I brought with me. Just a collection of old stories from my childhood. Helps me go to sleep."

"No kidding," he murmurs. When he finally tears his gaze off the scuffed-up device, they lock eyes. "I'm sorry, I didn't mean to pry."

"You're fine," she responds. Afternoon light is pooling in her alert brown eyes, and when she smiles, her whole face crinkles. "Everything okay?"

"You just remind me of someone," he says. "Anyway, you're welcome to join me for dinner at 20:00 hours in the dining room. I'll be serving *i'a ota* to give you strength after your trip over from Bora Bora."

"What a perfect touch! That'd be wonderful," she replies with a grateful smile.

His eyes stray once more to the Walkman on the bed, then out the window, where he can see the frangipani blooming over Ari's resting place. "I'll see you then."

Afterword

While the events of this novel are fictional, the nuclear testing done in the Polynesian islands was all too real. Over the course of three decades, nearly 200 bombs were detonated in the Mururoa and Fangataufa Atolls—41 of which were atmospheric. Everyday residents of the islands, politicians in the Territorial Assembly, and multiple countries and organizations across the globe were involved in various protests throughout the program's existence. A Greenpeace ship was sunk by the French military in 1985. After particularly fierce protests in Pape'ete at the end of 1995, the program was finally shuttered.

The French government had claimed for decades—both during and after the conclusion of the testing program—that the explosions were conducted safely and that the risk of health problems from nuclear fallout was minimal. However, recently declassified documents have allowed scientists to estimate that the fallout from just one of the atmospheric tests, code-named Centaur, exposed over 110,000 people living in the region to radiation 500 times the maximum accepted levels.

The government's official estimations of exposure have been consistently lower than scientists' by a factor of two to 10 times. This has complicated the process of citizens receiving compensation for related health conditions—mostly cancer. Of the many tens of thousands of people who have been affected over the years, only 63 Polynesian citizens had been compensated by the French government as of 2021.

The military documents related to these tests weren't declassified until the conclusion of a lengthy legal battle in the mid-2010s, and no studies that considered the documents in their totality were published until 2021. France continues to control all of the information about damage that the testing has caused to the atolls where underground tests were conducted. Concerns about nuclear waste leaching into the ocean and contaminating fishing stock or harming fragile, endangered coral ecosystems continue to be top of mind.

Ma'ohi people have, to this day, never received an official apology from Paris.

Acknowledgements

This novel would not have been possible without the support of so many amazing people who lent a hand along the way. First of all, I'd like to thank my husband, Gary, who fully accepts me as I am and who loves me unconditionally. Thank you for giving me the safety and clarity I need to be who I am, both as a writer and as a person. I love you.

My family and my husband's family have all been wonderful resources for talking out plot problems, determining how to move forward as an indie author, and providing moral support, whether in the islands or at the kitchen table.

To Catherine Burroughs, Bruce Bennett, and my parents, for helping me find my voice and pushing me to make the most of my writing.

To Devin DeMarco, an incredible editor, writer, teacher, and friend—this book has benefited immeasurably from your eye for detail and the great questions you pose.

To my sister, Abigail McKalsen, who designed an absolutely stunning cover and kept a level head no matter what curveballs I threw her way—you're a boss, girl, and don't you forget it.

I'd also like to thank Marsha Gomes-Mckie for providing incredibly detailed, honest feedback as this novel's sensitivity reader. Your comments were invaluable in shaping this book, particularly in its final chapters.

There are many others who have helped nudge this manuscript and my writing journey as a whole along and take it to the next level. I'm grateful to you all.

And finally, I'd like to thank you, dear reader. Your support means the world to me.

About the Author

Bekkah Frisch believes in the power of bravery and authenticity to make the world a better place. Her writing invites readers on a journey to discover radical empathy, compassion, and tragic optimism.

She holds a Bachelor of Arts in English from Wells College. Her non-fiction essay, "The Black Dog," has been published in *The Healing Muse*. She lives in Fulton, NY with her husband, daughter, and their two lovable, untrainable dogs.

The Great Quiet is her debut novel.

For updates, visit:

bekkahfrisch.com

Instagram / Facebook: @authorbekkah

A Note About Type

The text has been set in Museo Slab, a serif font designed by Dutch typeface designer Jos Buivenga. The font design invokes friendliness, while maintaining legibility and a modern aesthetic.

This font was chosen to enhance the accessibility of this work for people with dyslexia and other visual processing disorders.

9 798987 742105